I0761894

SKEPTIC IN SALEM:

AN EPISODE OF DEATH

(A Dubious Witch Cozy Mystery—Book Three)

FIONA GRACE

Fiona Grace

Fiona Grace is author of the LACEY DOYLE COZY MYSTERY series, comprising nine books; of the TUSCAN VINEYARD COZY MYSTERY series, comprising seven books; of the DUBIOUS WITCH COZY MYSTERY series, comprising three books; of the BEACHFRONT BAKERY COZY MYSTERY series, comprising six books; and of the CATS AND DOGS COZY MYSTERY series, comprising nine books.

Fiona would love to hear from you, so please visit www.fionagraceauthor.com to receive free ebooks, hear the latest news, and stay in touch.

ISBN: 978-1-0943-9084-0

BOOKS BY FIONA GRACE

LACEY DOYLE COZY MYSTERY
MURDER IN THE MANOR (Book#1)
DEATH AND A DOG (Book #2)
CRIME IN THE CAFE (Book #3)
VEXED ON A VISIT (Book #4)
KILLED WITH A KISS (Book #5)
PERISHED BY A PAINTING (Book #6)
SILENCED BY A SPELL (Book #7)
FRAMED BY A FORGERY (Book #8)
CATASTROPHE IN A CLOISTER (Book #9)

TUSCAN VINEYARD COZY MYSTERY
AGED FOR MURDER (Book #1)
AGED FOR DEATH (Book #2)
AGED FOR MAYHEM (Book #3)
AGED FOR SEDUCTION (Book #4)
AGED FOR VENGEANCE (Book #5)
AGED FOR ACRIMONY (Book #6)
AGED FOR MALICE (Book #7)

DUBIOUS WITCH COZY MYSTERY
SKEPTIC IN SALEM: AN EPISODE OF MURDER (Book #1)
SKEPTIC IN SALEM: AN EPISODE OF CRIME (Book #2)
SKEPTIC IN SALEM: AN EPISODE OF DEATH (Book #3)

BEACHFRONT BAKERY COZY MYSTERY
BEACHFRONT BAKERY: A KILLER CUPCAKE (Book #1)
BEACHFRONT BAKERY: A MURDEROUS MACARON (Book #2)
BEACHFRONT BAKERY: A PERILOUS CAKE POP (Book #3)
BEACHFRONT BAKERY: A DEADLY DANISH (Book #4)
BEACHFRONT BAKERY: A TREACHEROUS TART (Book #5)
BEACHFRONT BAKERY: A CALAMITOUS COOKIE (Book #6)

CATS AND DOGS COZY MYSTERY
A VILLA IN SICILY: OLIVE OIL AND MURDER (Book #1)

A VILLA IN SICILY: FIGS AND A CADAVER (Book #2)
A VILLA IN SICILY: VINO AND DEATH (Book #3)
A VILLA IN SICILY: CAPERS AND CALAMITY (Book #4)
A VILLA IN SICILY: ORANGE GROVES AND VENGEANCE (Book #5)
A VILLA IN SICILY: CANNOLI AND A CASUALTY (Book #6)
A VILLA IN SICILY: SPAGHETTI AND SUSPICION (Book #7)
A VILLA IN SICILY: LEMONS AND A PREDICAMENT (Book #8)
A VILLA IN SICILY: GELATO AND A VENDETTA

CHAPTER ONE

Mia Bold plastered a green tea mask on her face. She was *still* trying to get the grime out of her pores after yesterday's excursion, tramping through the Hockomock Swamp. Her Border collie mix, Tandy, and her white kitten, Rose, watched her curiously, not sure why their mistress had green goo all over her face.

"It's just a pore cleanse," Mia explained. "Ten minutes from now and I'll look normal again, I promise."

Tandy looked at her skeptically, not sure what the ritual meant exactly.

Yesterday, Mia and Tandy had gone location scouting for her podcast, possibly soon-to-be cable show, *Bell, Book, and Candle.* They drove an hour and a half south of Salem, Massachusetts, to tramp through the tangled area known as the "Devil's Swamp," part of the infamous Bridgewater Triangle and a hotbed of paranormal activity. A half dozen electromagnetic readings later, Mia and Tandy had headed home, covered in mud and bug bites and slightly sunburned even though the weather was cool. Even with all the discomfort, it had been a great day.

Now, Mia was back at her apartment on Essex Street wrapped up in a terry robe, skin flushed from a steamy shower, hair knotted on top of her head, and the green-tea mask tingling on her face. She imagined she could feel her pores tightening. Mia made her way to the kitchen, grabbed a coffee, and headed for her desk, stepping over files and weaving around the stacks of books peppered across the living room floor. This was research week and her usually tidy apartment looked like a hurricane had passed through. There was also the fact that she and Tandy had tracked muddy paw and boot prints everywhere after their day in the swamp. She'd finally given Tandy a bath while Rose watched from a safe distance, leisurely cleaning her pink kitten nose and white whiskers as Tandy was scrubbed down vigorously, leaving a ring of dirt and debris in the tub. But there was no time to clean the apartment. She had to finish her research before M-day turned her life upside down!

Mia looked at the calendar above her desk, where a giant "M" was scrawled in red marker. Tomorrow was the day her family, the Middletons, were due to arrive. Once that happened, they would undoubtedly distract her with a million questions and activities. Today was the last day she had to complete her research in time, since the production meeting to discuss the next show was also scheduled for tomorrow.

Thanks, guys! Great timing!

As soon as she had her research done and felt prepared for the meeting, she planned to dive into tidying the apartment. In its current state of chaos, the place would give her mom and stepdad a fit.

Mia sighed and looked over at her map of the Devil's Swamp, spread over the coffee table and covered in sticky notes. Each sticky marked sightings of Mothman, Bigfoot, an infamous red-eyed swamp beast, and various ghosts. But even though the swamp was a dream location, in the end she'd decided that the show would need more people and equipment to film that rugged area than *Bell, Book, and Candle* could afford. That was okay though; she had already come up with a great list of other sites.

In most cities and towns, haunted places were a rarity, but not in Salem. Ever since Mia moved to the small town with a spooky reputation, the sheer number of hauntings was astounding. It seemed like everyone in town had a story about a haunted encounter. She had been inundated with so many myths, stories, and ghost sightings, she could barely keep up. In fact, her inbox was so out of hand, she was going to have to ask Will the intern to help her answer mail soon.

She settled back at her desk and typed an email to her producers, Graham Stone and Ollie Cooper:

RE: Locations for next Episode

After visiting a dozen sites, I have narrowed my top 3 choices for our next episode to the following locations:

The Joshua Ward House in Salem

Dungeon Rock in Lynn

Fort Sewall in Marblehead

I also want to discuss as a possible future location should the series be picked up: Hockomock Swamp, Bridgewater Triangle.

Talk to you soon.

She pressed *Send* and smiled to herself. That should hold them off for a while. A little teaser before the big meeting. Even though she had decided against the Devil's Swamp for now, she hoped to do a show there in the future. Now, she just needed to prepare for the inevitable questions from her producers and crew about each location. She needed to review lighting, terrain, ghost sightings, the history of each place, and other random details. Maybe she was being overly cautious, but she hated being caught off guard. Another full day of research would make her feel calm and confident.

The fact that a cable network was interested in their show was so exciting! Mia thought. According to Graham, the network *loved* their last episode. And Ollie had said the cable network was considering a full run of episodes. Both producers were pushing everyone to turn out a great second episode of the show.

Mia had to admit, her career was going really well. Up until recently, *Bell, Book, and Candle* was just a podcast. Now, after filming a single episode, they were under consideration to be a cable show. Mia had never imagined she would host a TV show, but that was exactly what was happening. And though she was easily putting in twelve-hour days, she loved her job. And now she was even earning a salary. It wasn't much yet, but it was an upgrade from working for free!

Mia looked at the clock. Her best friend, Sylvie, who lived down the hall, would be waking up soon. She was the *Bell, Book, and Candle* sound engineer and editor. They always had a million things to discuss, from boyfriends to camera footage. Today, they were planning to head down to Café Noir, their favorite local restaurant, owned by Hugh Wolfe, the sexy, six-foot-tall chef Mia was dating. Well, *one date* so far. But they had both been dancing around the idea of a second date. The thought of handsome Hugh Wolfe gave her butterflies in her stomach. Maybe today he would ask her for a second date over some delicious French cuisine. All in all, this promised to be an excellent day!

Tandy put his paws on Mia's lap and tried to lick her mint-green face while Rose curled up in a growing patch of sunlight and purred. Mia had found the small abandoned kitten in the street. Now she was growing and fast becoming a silky cat with faint silver stripes under her white fur.

Mia made a note to herself to talk to Will about installing the cat run kit she'd ordered. Her landlord, Tom Hatter, had given the project a green light, even though he claimed white cats in Salem were bad luck. The box was tilted against the wall by the kitchen.

There was a loud knock at the door.

Finally! That would be Sylvie. Time to wash off the green goo and get ready for a delicious breakfast. And to see sexy Hugh Wolfe, of course.

"Come on in," Mia called out, stepping over a stack of papers.

As the door swung open, Tandy jumped up and barked loudly. *That's weird,* Mia thought. Tandy rarely barked and never at Sylvie. Then a horrible sinking feeling hit Mia. She realized what was happening, but it was too late.

"Oh no," Mia said as she saw who was standing at the door.

CHAPTER TWO

Mia clutched her robe tightly, staring at her surprise guests as the green tea mask cracked across her face like the Sahara Desert. She wanted to curl up and disappear. *How could this be happening?*

"I—I thought you were coming tomorrow," Mia managed to say. Standing in the hallway was Mia's entire family: her stepfather, Daniel Middleton, dressed in a soft tweed jacket, deerstalker hat, and travel pants; Mia's mother, Madison Monroe Middleton, who wore a stylish car coat and scarf tied around her frosted blonde updo; and her stepsister, Brynn, dressed in a plaid Chanel jacket, designer jeans, and kicky heels with brass buckles. Finally, Daniel had brought his assistant, Reynolds, who stood off to one side, dressed in a plaid shirt and khakis and wearing wire-rimmed glasses.

"Oh! Good gracious, Mimi!" Brynn said, covering her mouth to stifle a laugh. "Is that you?"

Mia nodded helplessly. Then it struck her that her apartment looked like a zoo, one where the animals had all escaped and gone on a rampage.

"Maybe I could meet you later—" Mia said, trying to block the view of her apartment.

"—Nonsense! We've come to take you to breakfast," Daniel said and barged through the door. Mia stepped back as the herd of Middletons marched inside. Brynn called Tandy over and patted him.

"Boo boo baby? How've you been, boy?" Tandy wagged his tail, happy to see her. Then she saw Rose. "Ohhhhhh! Who is this?" she said and scooped the small cat up in the crook of her arm. Rose reached her pink nose up to nuzzle Brynn.

"Rose," Mia said, overwhelmed. "My kitten."

"Well, she is adorable!" Brynn said and walked close to Mia. "I guess we took you by surprise," she whispered.

"A little heads-up would have been nice, Brynn," Mia whispered back, her throat tightening. "You could have texted." Underneath the green mask her face was bright red from embarrassment.

Reynolds, Daniel's assistant, looked down at his feet, mortified as he realized Mia had just been caught, not just by surprise, but in flagrante delicto.

"Sorry, Mia," Reynolds whispered anxiously.

Madison stepped inside the apartment and took in the mess as if she were the lady of the manor.

"Oh dear," she said imperiously. "Do you always keep your apartment like this?"

"Of course not, Mom!" Mia said. "I'm working on a project."

"What kind of project?" Daniel said. He walked over to the map on the coffee table and squinted at it curiously. "The Jersey Devil and Mothman?"

"I'm scouting locations," Mia said. "You know, sightings."

"I see, you're hunting things that don't actually exist? I'm not sure that's the best use of your time," Daniel said, scanning the living room with distaste, noting the muddy paw prints everywhere. "I certainly hope you aren't always this messy," he said. "Reynolds? Let's look into getting Mia some cleaning help."

"Yes sir," Reynolds said.

"I don't need help," Mia said lamely. "I'm just researching. I went to a swamp yesterday and I've been busy going through my findings."

"A swamp? That doesn't sound very ladylike," Madison said.

"The Devil's Swamp?" Daniel said, peering at the map. "Hmmmm."

"That's all right, dear," Madison said, slipping her arm through Mia's sleeve. "I can see you need a moment. I'll make some coffee while you get dressed."

Mia gazed at her maps covered with stickies and sighed wistfully. Her plans to do more research had just gone up in smoke.

Brynn raised her eyebrows and made a brushing sign to Mia to go get herself cleaned up and dressed.

"I *know*, Brynn," Mia said. "I'll be right back."

She disappeared into the bathroom and quickly splashed water on her face until the mask dissolved and the water ran green. As Mia pulled on some jeans and a T-shirt and brushed her long wavy dark hair, her mind was already in full freak-out mode. The Middleton clan was off to a rousing start. She couldn't believe how badly things were going. Daniel clearly disapproved of her job, her place was a mess, and now she was going to have to wing it at the production meeting. Could this situation get any worse? She walked back into the living room to shut down her computer. The whole family was in the kitchen. Mia ran around the room tidying up the piles and picking up stray glasses and cups. When she walked in the kitchen, she found all the Middletons jammed together. Reynolds leaned on the counter while Daniel sat stiffly in one of the kitchen chairs, like a king presiding over his court. Brynn was texting on her phone, while Madison had started doing dishes.

"Mom! Stop," Mia said.

"It'll just take a second, dear," she said and glanced down at the tile covered in paw prints before releasing a sigh.

"What are you doing here?" Mia said. "Weren't you supposed to arrive tomorrow afternoon?"

"Daniel got an opportunity to upgrade to first class," Madison said.

"I had Reynolds send you a copy of the itinerary," Daniel said.

"Last week?" Mia said.

"The *updated* itinerary. Yesterday afternoon." He pulled a piece of paper out of his pocket and unfolded it. Then he tapped the first slot on the section marked today. "Do you see here? Morning. Breakfast."

Mia stared at the itinerary and realized she was trapped. Once Daniel committed something to his itinerary it was set in stone. He must have changed everything while she and Tandy were wandering through the swamp. She'd been so exhausted when she got home, she fell asleep early without checking her email. So much for another day to finish up her research.

There was another knock at the door. *What now?* Mia thought. This time Tandy ran over and wagged his tail. Sylvie walked in wearing tartan trousers, a black top with crisscross straps, a cropped leather jacket, and Doc Marten boots painted with flying pigs.

"Ready? What the—" she said and stopped, taking in the fact that the entire Middleton clan was wedged into the tiny space.

"Um, surprise," Mia said and inclined her head in the direction of the kitchen. Sylvie's eyebrow went up in surprise, but she recovered on the fly and went into diplomacy mode.

"You must be—don't tell me," Sylvie said and extended her hand. "Brynn? I recognize you from your phone avatar. Mr. And Mrs. Middleton? Can I call you Daniel and Madison? Love the car coat, Maddy. And this must be Reynolds?" They all nodded, happy to be recognized.

Mia was amazed at the way Sylvie handled her family. She felt so grateful that she had such a wonderful best friend.

"You're Sylvie Payne?" Daniel said. "Mia's next-door neighbor?"

"And sidekick." She grinned and shook their hands. "I know a great little French cafe. Shall we?"

Mia shook her head, trying to dissuade Sylvie from taking her family to Café Noir. After Mia's first date with Hugh, she was trying to figure out his interest level and her own feelings. She wasn't sure she wanted to subject him to the entire Middleton clan! Not just yet, anyway. Sylvie saw the look on Mia's face and signaled back that everything would be fine.

Mia decided to trust her and pulled on a jacket. They all walked down the narrow steps and out front where Tom Hatter was sweeping. He was wearing a checkered shirt and a shop apron emblazoned with *Hatter's Emporium* across the front. His gray hair was tucked under a newsboy's cap.

"I see your people found you, Mia," Tom said and jangled his keys. "If you folks need any more maps or historic information, stop by the shop."

"I might take you up on that, Mr. Hatter," Daniel said. "Thank you for your time and the guidebook."

"My pleasure," Tom said.

"Er, thanks," Mia said. *So that was how they got upstairs!*

As they started down the street, Daniel turned to Mia and added, "Lovely man, knows his history."

The Essex Street mall was busy with tourists and street performers. The Middleton party passed a Wicked Witch of the East and a group of costumed time travelers congregating on the corner.

Mia tossed some coins in the hat as her stepfather sniffed in disdain.

"You shouldn't encourage the riffraff, Mia," Daniel said.

"You know how Daddy feels about street performers," Brynn said, rolling her eyes.

"Well, I think the town center is quite charming," Reynolds said, casting a sympathetic glance at Mia. If anyone knew what a handful Daniel Middleton could be, it was his long-suffering assistant.

"I certainly don't think a town with this kind of history should cheapen itself with such vulgar displays," Daniel said in a huff.

“It’s all in good fun, Dad,” Brynn said. “Anyway, you know Mimi loves this kind of stuff, don’t you? All the witches and ghouls and ghosts?”

Mia was about to open her mouth and explain that her real interest lay in exploring the truth behind paranormal phenomena. After all she had equipment that measured electromagnetic activity, EVP recorders, night vision cameras, and other technical gizmos to measure haunted places. She was about to explain all this, but Sylvie grabbed her arm.

“It’s not worth it,” she whispered in a low voice. “Just humor them.”

“So, how’s your hotel?” Mia said, trying to distract them.

Across the street was Charnel Tours, which would drum up some bad memories. The company had briefly shut down after the owner turned out to be a murderer, but had reopened with a new owner, former employee Albee Abernathy.

The local reporter Suzy Sharpe had badgered Mia’s family with phone calls and updates on the case. The last thing she needed was to open up that particular can of worms.

Albee Abernathy stood outside the storefront dressed in a Victorian waistcoat and tall hat. He spotted Mia and Sylvie and waved.

“Who’s that?” Daniel said.

“The local warlock,” Sylvie said. “Er, I mean tour guide.”

“I see,” Daniel said. “ Does everyone know you around here from your show?”

“Not really,” Mia said. “Up until a month ago, *Bell, Book, and Candle* was just podcast.”

“And now?” Daniel said.

Mia’s stomach twisted into a knot. She had avoided telling her mom and stepdad about the cable show. Daniel had made his feelings very clear about the acting profession, and while being a co-host of a televised program might not be considered acting, technically, it was still a no-no in her stepfather’s book.

“A cable network is interested in us,” Mia said.

“A television performer?” Daniel said, but before he could get too concerned, Madison interrupted him.

“Oh, Daniel!” Madison said. “Look at the soaps. They have flower petals inside.” Madison had stopped at a street vendor’s table. Daniel stepped up to gallantly pay for his wife’s packet of soaps. The vendor was a stout man, with tattoos and bowler cap on his head.

"Do you know my daughter here?" Daniel said, inclining his head toward Mia. For the second time in a day, Mia's cheeks blazed bright red. Were they going to embarrass her the whole time they were here? she wondered.

The storekeeper looked Mia up and down, his lip protruded.

"I can't say that I do." He swiped Daniel's credit card. "Should I?"

"Well, according to her she's the star of a cable show," Daniel said.

"*Bell, Book, and Candle*," Mia said, trying not to die of embarrassment.

"You mean the show with Johnny Astor?" the man said.

Of course, Mia thought. Everyone knew Johnny Astor, while she was chopped liver, apparently.

"That's the one," Sylvie said, trying to help. "There it is, our very own French café."

Mia shuddered at the thought of her family meeting Hugh Wolfe, the guy she was kind of, almost dating. She guessed that now would be a test of her budding new relationship. She closed her eyes and steeled herself as the group walked into Café Noir.

CHAPTER THREE

The café was busy that day with frantic servers bustling about. Mia was nervous as she searched for Hugh Wolfe. Then she saw him hard at work behind the back counter, supervising his employees.

Hugh Wolf was a handsome man. Tall and athletic, he had dark hair, pushed back behind one ear with a few locks falling over his deep brown eyes. He was tan, outdoorsy, with a strong jaw, toned body, and rugged features that were unequivocally handsome. He looked up and caught Mia's eye, noticing the crowd around her. She smiled as he tilted his head curiously, not sure why she had shown up with this group of people. Mia smiled back meekly and waved.

He took off his apron and hung it up before making his way across the crowded restaurant. In the meantime, Daniel and Madison looked around Café Noir with happy expressions on their faces. The beveled windows, original tile, elegant dining tables, and interior touches, dating back to the early twentieth century, all had captured their attention. This was what they had expected to encounter in Salem; charm, elegance, and history.

"This is more like it," Daniel said, looking around the café appreciatively.

"Very nice," Madison said.

Brynn smiled at Mia knowingly. They had both grown up in the same household and knew exactly what Daniel and Madison were like. They were good people but when it came to appearances, they were snobs.

At that moment Hugh arrived and gave Mia a warm hug, practically lifting her off her feet. Mia blushed from head to foot and glanced at her mom and stepdad, but they were busy pointing at the carved acoustic ceiling panels. The last thing she needed was for Daniel and Madison to pry into her personal relationships. Brynn, on the other hand, clocked the embrace and raised a curious eyebrow.

"Who are all these people?" Hugh whispered in Mia's ear. He let her down gently.

"Boy, are you in for it," she whispered back. Then she introduced her family. "Hugh, I want you to meet my parents, Daniel and Madison Middleton, my sister, Brynn, and our friend Reynolds, who works with Dad," she said. "This is the owner of Café Noir, Hugh Wolfe."

"A pleasure," Daniel said. There was a flurry of handshakes as Hugh met the Middletons.

"Well, well," Hugh said. "We are going to have to get you a table." He motioned to a couple of the busboys and they sprang into action, moving a few smaller tables until they formed one large table able to accommodate Mia, Sylvie, and Mia's unexpected guests. In a flash, the busboys set the table, stacking plates on chargers, then two forks, two teaspoons, a dessert fork and spoon above the setting, cups and saucers, bread plates, water and wine glasses, and to top it all off, napkins fanned like seashells.

Daniel puffed up with delight as he watched the careful construction of their dining experience.

"*Voilà,*" Hugh said and led them to the table.

"*Est-ce que tu parles français?*" Madison said to Hugh as he held out her chair.

"*Pourquoi bien sûr, madame,*" Hugh said and winked at Mia. "Now if you'll all excuse me I need to supervise the preparation of your *le petit-déjeuner*."

Hugh nodded gallantly and disappeared behind the counter, putting his apron back on before he disappeared into the kitchen.

"What exactly did he say, Mrs. M?" Sylvie said.

"Only that he spoke French and he was going to prepare us breakfast," Madison said and sighed. "He has an impeccable accent, by the way." Madison nodded toward Daniel with approval.

Sylvie looked at Mia and raised her eyebrows. She was certainly getting the full Middleton treatment. The next step in her assimilation would be one of their cosplay dinners, where they all had to wear historical outfits.

After a rocky morning, Hugh had managed to shift the energy with her family in just minutes. Mia was so relieved she started to relax a little bit. Hugh's niece Becca arrived with menus and passed them along the table before reciting the specials of the day. They all ordered and settled down to wait for their meals to arrive.

"Top-notch," Daniel said, flicking open his napkin and placing the cloth across his lap.

"Wait until you taste the food," Mia said and smiled. She could tell her stepfather was feeling happy from the way he surveyed his surroundings like a lord in his castle. Her mother took a deep breath of the fragrant aromas coming from the kitchen.

"Well, I must say that smells lovely," she said.

"Where are you all staying?" Mia asked.

"Reynolds has a friend in town who he's staying with so they can catch up. The rest of us are at a lovely little place called the Salem Inn. Right down the street from you, dear," Madison said.

"Built by Nathaniel West," Daniel said.

Mia knew the Salem Inn well. Each room had its own character and if you believed the local gossip, one of them had a ghost. "What rooms are you in?"

"Well, let's see, we're staying in the Derby room," Daniel said. "And your sister is staying in one of the smaller rooms."

"Which small room?" Mia said.

"Seventeen," Brynn said.

"Didn't they tell you it was haunted?" Sylvie said. "You might want to switch rooms. Katherine the ghost is kinda famous around town. You might be okay though, they say she hates men."

"They did tell me, but I didn't take it seriously," Brynn said. "Besides, they're all booked up. I couldn't move if I wanted to."

"Enough of this haunted nonsense," Daniel said and took his itinerary out of his pocket. He unfolded the paper and spread it onto the table.

"I have a full day planned," Daniel said. "We can start with the Ropes Mansion. After that, there are a number of historical residences I would like to see. Mia? Are you available to take us?"

"Well, the Ropes Mansion is within walking distance." Mia picked up the list and looked it over. Daniel had gone crazy; these houses were scattered all over town. "Wow, this is a lot."

"There's a lot of history to get through," Daniel said proudly. "But it's not just all fun and games. This is a working holiday, right, Reynolds?"

"Yes sir, Mr. Middleton." Reynolds grinned before exchanging a knowing look with Mia. Everyone who knew Daniel understood that he never stopped working. He was absolutely passionate about antiques. When Mia was a kid, family vacations were spent in auction halls and combing through country estate sales hunting for unique items. By the time Mia was in high school, Reynolds was working for Daniel. They both knew that once Daniel got going, he would barely have time for Mia. And since *Bell, Book, and Candle* was about to film, she hoped that fact would keep the entire family busy for the next few days at least.

"Why don't you start with the Ropes Mansion, the Jonathan Corwin house, and the Phillips house? Those are all in the Chestnut Street District," Mia said. It was all coming back to her. Daniel was so Type A, he did not have a spontaneous bone in his body. When it came to research, he would comb every inch of this city. After going through the historical residences, he would start looking for antiques. Then he and Reynolds would spend all their time cataloguing every possible antique they could find. Not just the ones that they planned to buy that day, but possible follow-up purchases too. Mia was exhausted just thinking about all the anxiety that would go into their walk-throughs of these seventeenth- and eighteenth-century homes and antique shops.

"That sounds like a good plan," Brynn said, her attention drifting off. That was Brynn's way of coping with her father. She tended to play dumb or just disconnect and follow her own whims.

The food arrived at the table in a flurry. Becca Wolfe carried a tray and had enlisted another server behind her to carry a second.

Brynn had ordered thick slices of French toast with wedges of creamy butter melting over the stack, sprinkled with powdered sugar. Balancing at the edge of the plate was her own small bottle of pure, golden maple syrup. Madison chose Pâté de Campagne with homemade French bread and Daniel had bucked the breakfast trend and ordered a Salade Niçoise with olives, green beans, hard boiled eggs, and anchovies. Reynolds had opted for crepes garnished with fresh lemon slices, powdered sugar, chocolate, and whipped cream. Mia and Sylvie stuck to less exotic French omelets. The pièce de résistance was when Hugh Wolfe arrived with complimentary cappuccinos, decorated with fleur-de-lis in the crema.

Daniel and Madison were beside themselves. The authentic cuisine and stylish presentation had won them over. Mia watched her mom's and stepdad's pleased expressions in awe. Hugh had managed to impress her parents so effortlessly. She shouldn't be surprised, really. She was just as taken by Hugh's European manners and easygoing confidence, not to mention his food.

"Mr. Middleton, when you're done with breakfast, would you like to see my collection of Salem photographs?" Hugh said.

Daniel looked at Hugh, then at the delicious meal in front of him, and history won out.

"Could we take a peek now?" Daniel said.

"Sure," Hugh said.

Mia hoped he wasn't insulted that her stepfather would postpone his meal to look at photos. But Hugh didn't seem to mind.

"Start without me. We'll just be a minute," Daniel said and was whisked away by Hugh to look at his excellent collection of street pictures of Salem's town center.

The moment Daniel and Hugh were out of earshot all eyes turned to Mia.

"Is that the man you're dating?" Brynn said.

"We've only been on one date," Mia said. "But yes, we plan to go on another."

"Impressive, isn't he?" Sylvie said.

"He certainly is," Reynolds said and smiled at Mia. Although Daniel had spent years of his life trying to get Mia and Reynolds together, they had an understanding. For one thing, Reynolds was gay, even though Daniel didn't seem to notice that obvious fact.

They all dug into their meals and Mia was pleased to hear oohs and aahs around the table as they each savored their selection.

Moments later Hugh brought Daniel back. Mia could see that her stepfather was thrilled by his little tour of the city of Salem. Seconds behind them Becca Wolfe arrived with a complimentary plate of croissants with chocolate swirls. Mia looked at Hugh, amazed. He was really pulling out all the stops. But if it kept her family happy, she was elated.

Suddenly her phone rang. Mia looked down to see that one of her producers was calling, Ollie Cooper.

"I have to take this," Mia said and stepped away from the table.

Usually, Daniel would've found that a profound infraction of etiquette, but he had just done the same thing. Besides, he was too busy with Hugh to notice Mia stepping out to the front patio.

"Mia Bold," she said.

"Mia? Oh good, I'm glad I caught you," Ollie Cooper said. "Listen, we have a new location that's just come up. But it's time sensitive, and we need to get over there today."

"Today?" Mia said, surprised. "But—"

"Let me put you on with Graham," Ollie said.

There was a shuffling as the phone switched hands, and then a blustery voice blasted into her ear. Graham Stone always spoke as if he were announcing something.

"Hey, Mia, Graham here. We got a line on a haunted house in Swampscott, you know where that is?"

"Isn't that the town just southeast of Salem?"

"That's it, only a few miles away. Thirty-minute drive tops. I'll text you the address. The crew's going to meet there at noon. Got it?"

Ordinarily, Mia would be annoyed to drop everything and rush off to see a location she'd never heard of before, especially after sending them top-notch, vetted locations that were perfectly suitable for their needs. But today the Middleton family was in town and she was the opposite of mad. She was thrilled. This was just the excuse she needed to ditch her high-maintenance family for a few hours.

"No problem," Mia said. " See you there at noon."

She tucked the phone back in her jacket pocket. As she turned to go back inside she found Hugh Wolfe standing with a white towel draped over one shoulder and a sheepish grin on his face. Mia walked up to him smiling.

"Thanks for what you did in there," Mia said. "They've been driving me crazy all morning."

Hugh grinned. "Your mother is lovely."

"Very elegant," Mia said. "You speaking French to her was the thrill of her day."

"So that's your stepdad? He's—how can I put it—meticulous. He might make a good ghost hunter too."

"Oh God, I don't think so. We try not to use the 'G' word around him. He hates what I do. He thinks the show-folk lack good breeding."

"He might have a point there," Hugh said and grinned. "Next time you go hunting, why don't you let me come with you? I promise not to scare away the ghosts."

Mia felt a warm heat sink from her spine all the way down to her toes. Hugh was so straightforward and honest, like a fresh, breezy afternoon at the beach. They'd both been so busy, it had been hard to arrange a second date. But every time she saw him and he hinted at wanting to spend more time with her, something came up. Today was already looking like a train wreck.

“I’d really like that, but for now, I have to go,” Mia said. “Something just came up at work. Would you be terribly offended if I rushed out of here with Sylvie in tow?”

“Of course not,” Hugh said. “Between Madison’s French and Daniel’s passion for authentic cuisine, I think you just brought me some of my best customers.”

Mia walked back inside to the table. Everyone was chatting happily over their French cuisine and croissants.

“Mom? Daniel?” Mia said. “Sylvie and I have to go to work.”

“What’s up?” Sylvie said.

“There’s a new location in Swampscott we need to see today,” Mia said. “Graham and Ollie said it’s time sensitive.”

“All right, make sure you check the itinerary. Catch up with us when you’re done,” Daniel said, puffing up out of habit. But Mia could see with relief they were all having a good time.

Brynn sat up straight, alarmed at Mia’s abrupt departure.

“You’re coming back soon, right?” Brynn glanced at the Middleton mob and back at Mia imploringly.

“I will,” Mia said and motioned to Sylvie. They grabbed their jackets and headed out the door.

“Where the heck is Swampscott?” Sylvie asked.

“It’s south, but the real question is *why* Swampscott?” Mia said.

“Okay, I’ll bite,” Sylvie said. “Why?”

“I’m not sure but my spidey-senses are tingling,” Mia said. “I sent a bunch of great locations to choose from, but now we’re supposed to check out a haunted house I’ve never heard of before?”

“You mean Mr. Hollywood is up to something?” Sylvie said and snorted.

“There’s only one way to find out. Let’s go get our equipment and check this place out.”

CHAPTER FOUR

Mia, Sylvie, and Tandy piled into Mia's Toyota and drove to the address Graham had texted them. The route wound down toward the ocean and as they got closer the sun seemed to grow brighter and the air was fresh and salty.

A public bus passed by with a large advertisement wrapped around the doors that read: *Own a little piece of bliss! Call Seaside Estates Realty!* The ad featured a tan woman with short blonde hair posed in front of what looked like a million-dollar estate. Tandy's head stuck out the window with his tongue and ears flapping in the wind as they passed a city marker sign:

Entering Swampscott

Est. 1629

They turned off the A1 highway and into the small town. The blocks of houses were more stately than those in Salem, but despite the sunny streets, there was still a sense of history. The wooden clapboard homes were painted the colors of autumn leaves with burnt yellow, deep orange, and sage green tones as they curved around the suburban plots, following Google maps to the haunted location.

"Looks like the Stepford Wives version of Salem," Sylvie said, looking out at the tidy neighborhoods with manicured lawns. The neighborhoods were well-maintained and lined with the early twentieth-century houses so popular in the area. Tandy saw another dog out the window and barked. He was ready to stretch his legs.

As Mia turned down Elmswood Road, she was concerned. She hadn't had any time to research the location, which meant going in blind. And even though she'd brought equipment, knowing the history of a location was important. Besides, she barely trusted Graham after some of the stunts he'd pulled in the past, like the first *Bell, Book, and Candle* show when he was caught tampering with the actual haunting. He'd sworn never to do that again, but still, she liked to keep an eye on him. Mia scanned the quiet, upper-middle-class street. It didn't seem particularly spooky.

"Can you Google the address and see what comes up?" Mia said.

"Sure," Sylvie said, fingers lightly tapping. "That's weird…"

"What?" Mia said.

"The street view is blurred in Google maps."

"Really? Let me see," Mia said.

Sylvie held the phone up and Mia glanced at her screen. There was a blur where the house was supposed to be located.

"Google does that sometimes when something notorious has happened at the location," Mia said. "Check out the Amityville Horror house."

Sylvie's fingers typed quickly into her phone.

"Whoa!" she said, surprised. "You're right, it's a blur too."

"So maybe something bad happened at the Elmswood House?" Mia said.

"Funny, but this town is not like Salem at all," Sylvie said, scrolling through the Internet. "They don't seem to like to talk about their ghosts. And the crime rate is virtually non-existent. I do see one thing from back in the eighties. The Browder family murders took place on Elmswood. Looks like a whole family was killed there."

"I guess we'll find out the hard way," Mia said.

"According to the blur, the house should be just ahead," Sylvie said.

The driving directions app started blinking and a voice said—*You have arrived at your destination, on the right.* Mia pulled over and pointed to a long driveway extending out of a patch of massive greenery. A large For Sale sign was planted in the yard. She inched the Toyota forward until the house came into view.

They stared in surprise. Hidden behind the overgrown yard, peering out from behind a tangle of dead tree branches, was an old Victorian-style house, surrounded by what looked like a dilapidated park. The once stately, turn of the century home had a steeply pitched roof, with pointed arches and front-facing gables, but the wooden slates were in disrepair and part of the delicate verge-board trim was broken. The peeling paint had become stained and blistered, stripped by the salty wind blowing in from the sea. A few of the windows were cracked and broken.

Mia and Sylvie stood, unable to take their eyes off the old mansion.

"That is one creepy house," Sylvie said. "Talk about a wreck."

"Yes," Mia said. " How can this place even be *for sale*?"

"The fixer-upper from hell," Sylvie said.

A strange feeling lodged itself in Mia's gut. The house looked unhealthy, unsavory, diseased. She knew that wasn't a very logical way to think, but she couldn't help herself. Mia felt a little queasy just looking at the place.

Mia and Sylvie stepped out of the car, followed by Tandy, who immediately started acting squirrelly. He growled and ran to the nearest patch of grass to mark the new territory. As he sampled all the brand-new smells, he looked up at the house and made a huffing sound.

"There you are," Johnny said, cheerfully, coming around the corner of the house, followed by the crew and the producers. He was dressed in jeans and a dark shirt with a distressed leather jacket. As he got closer, he met Mia's gaze with his dusky hazel eyes. Despite her better instincts she felt a wave of attraction. *Not a good idea,* she told herself. Getting involved with her co-host, when she was already practically dating a great guy, could only lead to trouble.

"Hey, Johnny," she said nervously and broke eye contact with him. "What a place, huh?"

Tandy ran over to greet Johnny who petted his head. A lock of dark ashy hair fell across his forehead. He smiled at Mia and she felt another jolt of electricity pass between them. She acted like nothing had happened.

Then Graham Stone and Ollie Cooper came around the corner, deep in conversation, while Jake, the cameraman, calculated exterior shots, closely followed by Will, the boom operator/intern who was making notes.

Will whistled to Tandy, who trotted toward him but stopped abruptly and whimpered, slowly backing away.

"What's wrong with him?" Will said, confused. He walked Tandy all the time, so the dog's refusal to come closer to him was strange. Mia looked at the house. Maybe Tandy sensed there was something wrong with the place too?

"Maybe he knows something you don't," Mia said, looking up at the house.

"Great, isn't it?" Johnny said, excited. "You can feel there's something haunted about the place."

"I don't know, I haven't had time to research it," Mia said.

"It's ugly, I'll give you that," Sylvie said.

"Someone's coming to show us around," Johnny said.

The two producers stopped and smiled. Ollie wore a relaxed windbreaker and checkered shirt with dark slacks. Graham was dressed in a peculiar safari suit combo, with four patch pockets on the front. His shirt was a psychedelic paisley with a wide collar. Mia supposed this was his ode to dressing down or maybe he had themes?

"Well, what do you think?" Graham said. "Looks the part, doesn't it? Very scary stuff."

"You mean it looks like it should be condemned and torn down?" Sylvie said. "That is true."

"I don't get why we're here exactly," Mia said. "I sent you some great locations. Why this house?"

"Because this one is *exclusive* and it's on the market," Graham said, pointing to the For Sale sign. "It's time sensitive. We have to act now. You'll see as soon as Cindy gets here."

"Your other locations are very good, Mia," Ollie said. "Thank you for all the research. We will revisit them."

"Here's Cindy now," Graham said.

At that moment, a white Lexus pulled up the driveway. A woman got out of the car and strode up the incline, legs thrusting powerfully as she walked. She was dressed in white heels, a pale cheetah-print skirt that hugged her knees, topped with a powder blue leather suit jacket, a silver sateen shirt, and chunky gold jewelry. Mia recognized her immediately. This was the real estate agent from the bus billboard, the one from Seaside Estates.

"Graham? You are right on time. I knew you would be," the woman said.

"Guys, this is Cindy Moore," Graham said. "You already know Ollie. Let me introduce our film crew, Jake and Will. Sylvie is our film and sound editor. And the stars of the show, Johnny Astor and Mia Bold."

Cindy thrust out her hand, weighed down with heavy rings and a gaudy charm bracelet that sparkled as she shook each hand vigorously.

"So you're the *Bell, Book, and Candle* group? So good to meet you, really, it's an honor," Cindy said. "I love psychic shows like *Manhattan Medium*. Love, love, love! Which one of you is the psychic?"

"Actually, we're ghost hunters, Cindy," Johnny said and smiled. "We use science to investigate the paranormal, right, Mia?"

Johnny smiled at Mia and her knees went a little funny, He was being so sweet, it was making it hard to concentrate on work.

"Oh my gosh, you are adorable!" Cindy said. "Isn't he cute, Graham?"

"Why don't you tell our stars about this place, Ms. Moore?" Ollie said.

"Well, as I told Graham when we met at the sports bar," Cindy said in a gossipy voice, "this is the location of the Elmswood Horror."

The moment she said the words, Mia felt a sense of dread. The Elmswood Horror? It sounded familiar.

Was that why she felt so bad? Had she read about the place?

"What happened?" Johnny said.

"The Browder family murder, that's what!" Cindy said.

Mia and Sylvie glanced at each other. They were right.

"The one from the eighties?" Sylvie said.

"That's right. The Browder family moved into the house," Cindy said. "Donnie Browder, his wife, Angie, and their two boys, Bobby and Todd. As you can see, the house is laid back from the street. So, Donnie Browder starts acting crazy, like talking to himself and fits of anger. One day the kids don't show up for school. The next morning the police find the whole family dead, except Donnie, he survived. Now he's in the loony bin."

"Donnie Browder murdered them?" Mia said.

"That's right, hon. He gassed them. He drove his car into the garage and left it running. The carbon monoxide filled the house and the next day the whole family was found dead, scattered around the house. He gassed himself too but they found him still alive."

"So the murdered family is haunting this place?" Johnny said.

"That's what they say," Cindy said. "After the tragedy my client, Connie Carol, bought the place cheap. She moved in with her hubby, Dean. They were going to renovate. That's when they started seeing and hearing things."

"Like what?" Mia said.

"Thuds in the night, footsteps, loud bangs, ghosts, you know, creepy stuff! Within a month Dean died of a heart attack and Connie moved back out again. Now she's all alone in the word, poor thing."

"And get this," Graham said. "The rumor is that a ghost killed Dean."

Mia frowned. Ghost sightings were rarely violent.

"Is Connie Carol available for an interview?" Mia said.

"I doubt it. She's very private," Cindy said.

"Too bad," Graham said.

That was strange, Mia thought. Usually, people wanted to talk about their ghostly encounters. Sometimes anonymously, but still…

Cindy flashed a smile with glossy peach lips at Graham.

Sylvie gave Mia a funny look. Were Graham and Cindy having a thing?

"Why is this place such a wreck?" Mia said.

"We've had a couple of big storms and no repairs done. The neighborhood kids try to break in now and then. They vandalized the windows and the verge board. Now that the property tax has skyrocketed Connie just can't hang onto the place any longer. Now, who wants a tour?" Cindy said.

"That would be great," Johnny said.

"You go ahead," Graham said. "Ollie and I have some business to discuss."

Cindy motioned for the crew to follow her. Then she walked up the driveway to a weathered set of steps which led to a wide porch.

Concerned, Tandy lowered his head, but when he saw Mia was going inside, he crept cautiously beside her. The way he was acting made Mia even more nervous. Worse, she couldn't account for *why*. She'd been to a dozen places worse than this, but she'd never had such an aversion to a place. She looked up at the shuttered windows and the peeling paint, took a deep breath, and tried to bury her trepidation.

Cindy walked up the front steps. The wood creaked under her white heels as she stepped onto the veranda. She took a skeleton key out of her handbag and opened the door.

"We've had some trouble with kids breaking in," Cindy said. "All hours, day and night."

Mia, Johnny, and Sylvie mounted the steps, with the rest of the crew just behind. There was a loud creak as Cindy opened the door.

On the top step, Mia took a deep breath and hesitated. What was it about this place? For some reason, she did not want to go inside. Tandy whimpered, sensing her feelings. Mia could see he felt the same way she did.

"It's okay, boy," she whispered, not wanting her fellow crew members to see that she was having a case of nerves, especially Johnny

Astor. For the first time in her career as a ghost hunter, she felt resistance to walking into such a place.

Why? What was that sense of dread she felt? What was waiting for them inside the door?

CHAPTER FIVE

One by one, they entered the house. The moment she was inside, Mia felt the fine hair lift on her arms and the back of her neck. Her head felt heavy, as if there was a sudden pressure drop. Tandy stuck close to Mia's fingers, his furry shoulder pressed against her thigh as the crew followed Cindy into the dark house.

The entry hall had a rounded cathedral ceiling, but chunks of plaster had fallen down and scattered on the floor. There was a window set above the door gable, obscured by a layer of dust that made the light streaming through appear gray and dismal. The house was furnished, but in a decaying state of disrepair with peeling paint, stained wallpaper, and a faded carpet. An old-fashioned credenza faced the door and Mia jumped when she saw a person standing in the mirror. Then she realized she was looking at her own reflection.

Get a grip, she told herself.

"The Browders left all their furniture," Cindy said as she swept through the alcove. "The Carols were planning to redecorate. But then you know what happened. They never had a chance, After Dean died, Connie could barely afford the property taxes, let alone a renovation. The place is pretty much the same as when the Browders lived here."

"Creepy," Sylvie blurted out.

"We're trying to find a buyer who will restore the property. It's turn-of-the-century, you know." Cindy grabbed the handle of the door to the left and turned to face the small group.

Jake and Will hung back, arms crossed, discussing technical issues.

Johnny stepped up, eager to see the house.

"This door leads to the library," Cindy said.

Mia tried to hide her uneasy feelings and took her EMF reader out of her bag. She clicked the device on and measured the area.

"What is that thing?" Cindy said.

"An electromagnetic field reader," Johnny said. "Mia is the scientific one. She's going to see if there are any energy fields afoot."

“We should really create an energy map of the house and measure ions and geo activity,” Mia said. “But this is the best I can do on short notice.”

“Well,” Cindy said as she opened the door. “Let’s see what your gadget does, shall we? This is the room where Donnie Browder was found.”

They entered a rectangular room that ended in a hexagonal bay window. The room would’ve been beautiful if it wasn’t covered in cobwebs and dust. It was also brighter than the entryway and Mia looked up to see a circular skylight. The furniture in the room was neglected. The tall bookcases were filled with crumbling books. Something scrabbled in the walls.

“I think you’ve got mice,” Sylvie said helpfully.

“Those little pests,” Cindy said. “First the neighborhood kids try to break in, and now the mice.”

“Must be a tough sell,” Sylvie said.

“You have no idea,” Cindy said and pointed to an old leather chair.

“What does your gizmo say about that chair?” Cindy said.

Mia swept the area.

“I’m getting some spikes,” Mia said. “A slightly higher field.”

“That’s where they found Donnie Browder, lying in this chair with a book open, unconscious. At first, they thought he was dead, but no such luck.”

Mia held the EM reader over the chair. The magnetic needle swung up, but just barely.

“Not very impressive,” Johnny said, looking over her shoulder.

“True,” Mia said. “These readings are within a normal range.”

“Maybe you gotta be dead to spike that thing,” Cindy said. “Donnie’s just in the nut house. This way.” She led them all through a dining room to the kitchen.

“The house is built in a spiral,” she said. “See that small alcove? That’s the mud room.”

“Mud room?” Sylvie said.

“At the turn of the century, people took their muddy boots off there. The right door leads to the yard, the one on the left to the garage. She pushed open the garage door. Tandy bristled immediately, ears flattening.

“This is where Donnie Browder left the car running,” she said. “He made sure all the windows were closed in the house. Then he left this door wide open and went to read his book. They say there is a very effective duct system in the house that moved the carbon monoxide up into the bedrooms."

Mia held up her EMF reader and the needle moved, spiking. She rotated the reader to test all directions. As Mia looked into the garage, she felt sick, her stomach queasy and her legs weak. The garage was pitch-black, like a sucking wound in the center of the house.

Suddenly, Mia felt dizzy and began to sweat. She touched her forehead, surprised at her own reaction. Tandy nudged her hand with his head and nipped at her heel, trying to move her away from the dark space.

"Are you okay?" Johnny said, noticing something was off about Mia's demeanor. "You look pale."

"I'm fine," Mia lied. The whole thing seemed impossible. She stared at her EMF reader and the needle spiked higher. She'd been exposed to higher EMF readings than this without such a terrible reaction.

What the heck was causing her to feel so much dread?

"I can't wait to see what happens when we get upstairs," Cindy said, staring at Mia. She led them through the kitchen and up the main staircase.

Cindy stopped at the first door on the left.

"This is the master bedroom, where Angie Browder was found," she said. Inside the room was a double bed, flanked by two bedside tables and a vanity.

Mia took a reading but the EMF was relatively quiet.

Next, Cindy walked them across the hall and opened the door to what was obviously a children's room. There was a bunkbed and the wallpaper was decorated with trains and cars. The room seemed heavy and Mia felt that strange pressure again. The curtain in the window fluttered softly from a draft.

Then Tandy faced the window and growled.

"What is it, boy?" Mia said, inching toward the window.

In answer, Tandy growled and placed his paws on the window ledge.

Mia checked the EMF reader. The electromagnetic energy jumped. She walked over to the window. The needle spiked again. Then she saw something down in the yard. A small figure stood at the very edge of the woods, dressed in a cloak. *That's weird,* she thought, trying to get a better look. *Who is that?*

The window was covered in a film of grit. Mia rubbed the glass, trying to clear a visual patch. Was that a child? It looked like a little girl. The figure looked up directly at her, eyes black and haunted. The fear came rushing back, almost knocking the wind out of Mia.

"Do you see that?" Mia said, pointing at the child standing in the dry grass. Tandy whined and started to lick her hand as Sylvie walked over and looked out the window.

"I don't see anything," Sylvie said. "Where?"

Mia looked again, but the little girl was gone.

"A kid," Mia said. "She was there a second ago."

Johnny walked over to the window and looked out. The backyard was wide and seemed to merge into the old abandoned playground. There was a rusty swing set and an old metal merry-go-round, turning slowly in the wind.

"There's nothing there, Mia," Johnny said and looked at her with concern. "Come on, I think you need to get some air."

They headed back down the steps and outside into the yard where Graham and Ollie waited. Tandy ran down the steps, trotting as far away from the house as he could manage while still keeping an eye on his human tribe.

Mia glanced back toward the spooky playground. The old swing set stood with a rusted swing twisting in the wind. *Where did that kid go?*

"Come on," Johnny said and pulled Mia away from the house. "Let's take a break, that energy was intense."

Mia looked at Johnny and immediately felt better.

"Well, what did you think?" Graham said, rushing over. "Isn't it great?"

"I think it'll make a solid show," Johnny said.

"Mia?" Ollie Cooper said. "You look a little faint, is everything okay?"

"I'm fine," Mia lied. "Are you sure you want to film here?"

It wasn't something she wanted to admit to her coworkers. But the truth was she wanted to get away from the house and never come back.

"It's a great location," Graham said. "Super scary and exclusive. No other ghost hunting show has ever gotten access to this house. We'll scoop them all."

"But I need more time to research," Mia said, desperate to come up with a reason to back out of the situation.

"When can we film, Cindy?" Graham said.

"Let's see, I have a potential buyer coming tonight, Mr. Fat Cat. After that, the place is all yours."

"So, does that answer your question, Mia?" Graham said. "You've got all day tomorrow to do your research, then we regroup."

"Great," Mia said, desperate to get away from the place. The real mystery was how she was going to get anything done with her family in town. When would she find the time? Maybe late at night once they retired for the day?

"Meeting adjourned," Graham said, happy that he'd gotten his way.

"Sylvie? Can you come back to the office? I want to go over the scene list," Jake said and headed for the van with Will and Johnny.

"No problem, just a second." Sylvie pulled Mia out of earshot. "Listen, what just happened? Did you see something in there?"

Mia nodded reluctantly. "I can't talk about it here."

"Meet me at Café Noir in an hour," Sylvie said.

"Okay, see you then," Mia said and walked with Tandy to the car.

The further away from the house she got, the better she felt. It was like she had been exposed to some kind of dark radiation. And even though EMF could cause all kinds of strange symptoms, she hadn't seen a sustained spike that would account for the feelings of aversion she just experienced.

Mia opened the door for Tandy and walked around to the driver's side. The house drew her attention back like an awful magnet. She looked up and there, on the second floor staring at her from the window, was the little girl from the abandoned playground.

That's impossible! Mia thought and began to tremble. She climbed into her car and drove away as fast as possible. How was she going to manage her family with an investigation like this going on? If feelings were anything to go by, the Elmswood House was the most extreme place she had ever investigated before in her life. The idea of coming back to this terrible place took her to a deep well of primal fear. She wondered if this was what people who experienced hauntings felt like; this sick, awful feeling. How would she survive this episode of *Bell, Book, and Candle*?

CHAPTER SIX

Mia walked into Café Noir with Tandy. The restaurant was in that twilight time between lunch and dinner, so she picked a quiet table for two by a green ficus tree and sat down. She felt a deep sense of relief to be back in the spacious, familiar room after being in that creepy house. She wasn't sure why the Elmswood House had brought up such uncomfortable feelings, or how to tell Sylvie about what she experienced. Had there been something about that house that affected her senses? Something other than EMF? No one else had seen the child in the cloak. Could she have hallucinated? Mia wondered. The thought was unnerving. Her phone buzzed. It was Brynn again.

Daniel and Reynolds on a rampage.

If I see another colonial house, I will scream.

When are you coming back?

Mia texted back as quickly as her fingers could manage.

One more hour...

Hang in there!

Mia really wanted to decompress with Sylvie before the next round of Middleton madness. Sure, her family was busy antiquing now, but eventually they would come up for air.

Tandy settled at her feet, relieved to be away from that place too. Mia reached down and rubbed his floppy ears, reassuring him as he rested his head on his paws to nap. Becca came over and Mia ordered a coffee and eased back, enjoying the cheerful atmosphere and the soft murmur of conversation.

Across the room, Hugh Wolfe spotted Mia as he polished a glass. He made his way over to where she was sitting, his apron dusted with flour. When he smiled his eyes were warm and inviting. The minute he was within distance of the table Tandy jumped up and greeted him. Hugh petted Tandy and smiled at Mia.

"So, your family was interesting," he said.

"Oh, good grief," Mia said. "I am so sorry about that scene this morning. The Middletons can be high maintenance."

"Oh, believe me, I'm used to it," Hugh said. "Going to chef school in Paris was incredibly demanding. I felt right at home with their vibe, actually."

"Well, you were wonderful." Mia smiled.

"So, what's the story? Daniel's your stepdad?"

"Yes, my real dad, Frank Bold, left when I was a kid." The moment Mia said his name, a wistful memory rose up in her mind. She was just a kid the last time she saw her father. He used to take her on outings along the Jersey Shore. She could still remember playing games with him at the booths, tossing bean bags through the clown's mouth to win a prize, or riding on the Ferris wheel overlooking the sea.

"Frank, huh?" Hugh said. "What was he like?"

Mia took a deep breath and sighed.

"He was funny, charming, and he did some strange things I'd really like to ask him about sometime. He used to pretend to be other people, nothing ever too serious, but he would tell people he was a spy or a Scottish lord."

"A mystery man," Hugh said.

"You could say that. He used to take me down to the Jersey Boardwalk on the weekends."

Hugh nodded, taking in what she was saying with interest.

"Well, even if Frank was a little odd, there's nothing like spending time with your dad," he said. "It's almost mystical." He rubbed Tandy's ears and looked up at Mia with his deep, brown eyes and handsome, rugged face. "Hey, Mia, speaking of spending time with someone, I was wondering—"

"Mia? Is that you?" said a low masculine voice.

Mia looked up, and a wave of shock rolled through her body.

Standing in the middle of Café Noir was her ex-fiancé, Mark Harris. Tall and athletic with light blue eyes and short, tightly curled hair that reminded Mia of a Roman sculpture, he sported the relaxed grin of a man who was used to getting a lot of attention.

What was Mark doing in Salem? Tandy seemed surprised too. He knew Mark and sniffed his hand, but not with the enthusiasm he reserved for Hugh Wolfe. Mia supposed that this was the dog version of keeping his social obligation but not being very impressed.

"Mark? Well, this is a surprise," Mia said, at a total loss.

"A good one, I hope," Mark said and grinned.

Out of all the places in the world to run into Mark Harris, Salem was the last place on earth she expected to see him. The spooky, eclectic town of Salem was diametrically opposed to Mark's personality. He was ambitious and practical. He aspired to live in New York, to get ahead and climb to the top of the heap. Mia knew his stringent social standards, because she'd run afoul of them in the past. Why would he show up here in Salem?

"Didn't you always make fun of the Witch City?" Mia said. "You used to call this place Wacko City."

"I've developed some new interests," Mark said and sniffed.

Hugh Wolfe stood back and stared at Mark curiously. Tandy wagged his tail and watched Hugh, eternally hopeful that someone would take him for a walk.

"Brynn said you might be here," Mark said. "It's good to see you."

"I—the thing is that I'm actually meeting my friend Sylvie," Mia said, horrified at the way Mark was barging into the conversation.

Hugh extended his hand to shake.

"I'm Hugh Wolfe," he said and glanced at Mia, confused as to who he was greeting. "This is my place."

"Nice. Mark Harris. A pleasure to meet you."

As the greetings were exchanged, Tandy decided to settle back down. He laid his head in his paws waiting for the human ritual to complete.

"How do you two know each other?" Hugh asked.

"We went to college together," Mia said.

"Oh, we were closer than that," Mark said. "After all, I was your *fiancé*."

Mia's cheeks flushed red and she glanced at Hugh in abject horror. This was like one of those nightmares where you were naked and the whole room was staring at you. She shook her head back and forth trying to signal to Hugh that she had no idea why Mark was here.

"I see," Hugh said, taken aback.

"Hey, buddy, no offense but Mia and I need to catch up here—" Mark said and slipped into the seat opposite Mia.

"Oh no, I told you my friend's coming," Mia said uncomfortably. "This is just a strange coincidence."

"Didn't you say you owned this place?" Mark said and turned to Hugh. "I'll have a cappuccino, please."

Mia cheeks blazed red with embarrassment, but Hugh didn't miss a beat.

"Coming right up," Hugh said. "Listen, Mia, I'll catch you later."

Mia recognized the look on Hugh's face. He was hurt and she couldn't blame him. Mia was utterly embarrassed as Hugh disappeared behind the counter.

She had a horrible sinking feeling and a dawning realization at the same time. Her family was capable of the most ridiculous social behavior. They were impressed by status and now that she thought about it, so was Mark. Everything Mia had ever done was eventually picked apart and examined in the context of whether it was acceptable to society.

Just like his ridiculous itinerary, Mia's stepfather, Daniel, had a list of professions he thought were acceptable. Mark Harris, who worked in the finance sector, was the epitome of acceptable. They had made their feelings clear that they thought Mark was an excellent choice for her.

Was this whole "Middletons coming to Salem" thing some kind of set-up? Did Daniel and Madison arrange a trip to ambush her with her ex-fiancé?

Mia's embarrassment started to turn to anger.

Seated across from her, Mark smiled.

"You look great, Mia," Mark said. "Still working out. Listen, why don't we have dinner—"

"Why are you here? Did my family have something to do with this?"

"Of course not! I only found out they were here when I texted Jeffrey."

Mia cringed at the mention of Jeffrey, her brother-in-law, the guy who always gave her a hard time every chance he got.

"I haven't heard from you in a year and suddenly you just show up?"

"Why not? You're overreacting, Mia. Come here, boy," Mark said and patted his thigh, trying to get Tandy to come over. But the dog was wary and just looked at him without moving.

"Listen, Mark, we broke up. Remember?" Mia was livid at this point. "You thought my ghost-hunting podcast was ridiculous."

"I might've been a little hasty; at the time the whole ghost-chasing angle sounded kinda crazy. But things have changed."

"Changed? What do you mean?"

"Well, I hear your little podcast is going to be a TV show now and that's not silly at all."

What was Mark's game? Mia wondered. Were success, money, and status so important to him that now that Mia might be on a TV show, he was back? At that moment, she realized she didn't know Mark at all. When they were at university, he'd always seemed so funny. Now he just came off as sneaky and calculating.

"Nothing's changed, Mark. I'm still doing the same thing I did before. Whether or not you approve of my career is immaterial to me."

Mark laughed out loud. "I love when you get all crazy like this."

Mia felt the heat rising to her face. What was that supposed to mean?

At that moment Becca Wolf came over with Mark's cappuccino. Mia looked up to see Hugh behind the counter polishing glasses. He gazed over at Mia with a forlorn expression and a wistful smile. Mia wanted to go and apologize to him but she was trapped. The minute Becca left, Mia leaned in toward Mark.

"Look, Mark, I have a new life now. I don't know why you came here but you need to back off."

"Gosh, I missed you, Mia," Mark said, ignoring every signal.

Mia looked at him, flabbergasted. What was his problem?

"Who's your friend?" Sylvie said, sauntering up to the table, chewing gum. She blew an enormous pink bubble before popping it and sucking the gum back into her mouth. Tandy immediately leapt up, wagged his tail, and greeted his auntie with excitement. The human conversation was getting a bit heated and he was relieved to see Sylvie show up.

"Sylvie, this is Mark Harris," Mia said.

"Your ex?" Sylvie said, her eyes widening. They had shared old boyfriend stories, including how Mia lost her job and fiancé in one day. The final dinner Mia shared with Mark was legendary.

Mark looked Sylvie up and down, cocking his head as if studying a bug.

"Are the Sex Pistols in town?" he joked rudely.

"Oh, funny," Sylvie said. "So, you're the jock financial guy?"

"Mia told you about me, huh?" he said and chuckled to himself.

"Not everything she said was sunshine, unicorns, and rainbows," Sylvie said sweetly, chewing her gum. Tandy started to tug at Sylvia's sleeve as if to convince her to leave this awkward situation.

Mia loved Sylvie right now. Her fearless New York attitude was exactly what was needed. Mia had already had one terrible experience with Mark Harris. She certainly didn't need another.

"Listen, Mark, I have to go," Mia said and pushed her chair away from the table. She pulled on her jacket and tossed a bill on the table. Tandy danced around happily. He really wanted to get out of the bad energy zone.

Mark leaned back and looked Mia up and down.

Why did he do that? Like he was shopping for livestock. Gross!

"You look good, Mia. Great, actually."

"Why don't you run back to Daisy Weston?" Mia said, reminding him of the sorority girl cheerleader he started dating a week after their breakup.

"Daisy?" Mark said, surprised. "We dated once or twice. Is that why you're upset with me?" He sipped his cappuccino. "Jealous?"

Mia felt her cheeks blaze. First Mark broke up with her because of her work. Now he wanted to rewrite history. He had never made an effort to win her back or explain anything.

"Listen, Mark, I didn't invite you here. Got it?"

"I forgot how cute you are," he said. "Like a prickly porcupine."

Mia opened her mouth to speak but no sound came out. He was so infuriating! She turned on her heel and headed for the door with Sylvie. Tandy trotted behind, relieved to be getting out of the restaurant.

"See you soon, Mia," Mark said and grinned.

"I doubt it," Mia said in a huff.

As soon as they were outside Mia got her phone out and group texted Brynn and Madison. There was no way she could let this stand. If they were going to ambush her with her ex-fiancé, they were going to get an earful.

Where are you?
I need to talk to you NOW.

After a few moments, Madison texted back.

Phillips House, dear.
Having a wonderful time.

Mia texted a reply, her fingers darting over the keyboard.

Stay there!
I'll be over in 10 minutes.

"Who are you texting?" Sylvie said as they walked to the car.

Tandy trotted alongside them, sniffing the bushes happily.

"My family, "Mia said. "Either my ex-fiancé is stalking me, or my family is meddling. I'm going to get to the bottom of things either way."

CHAPTER SEVEN

By the time Mia pulled up to the Phillips' House Historic Museum and parked, she was fuming. Ever since she could remember, her mother and stepfather had meddled in her private life. It was one thing when you were a kid, but she was a grown woman. The very first time she brought up her own podcast before she joined the cast of *Bell, Book, and Candle*, they were less than supportive. Sometimes there was a vibe of subtle disapproval. Other times, like today, they crossed the line into plain manipulation. Mark appearing out of nowhere and showing up in Salem was not a coincidence.

"What are you going to do?" Sylvie said, blowing a pink bubble.

"Give my mom and dad a piece of my mind," Mia said. "You want to stay in the car?"

"And miss a family feud, are you kidding?" Sylvie said.

They got out of the car and Tandy ran along the grass.

The Phillips House was a federal-style house built in 1806, with a symmetrical façade in the style of the Georgian period. The three-story, dove-gray house with black shutters had passed through a number of hands, including those of Captain Nathaniel West. This was just the kind of historic location Daniel Middleton would find exhilarating.

As if on cue, the Middleton family and Reynolds appeared, walking around from the side of the house, admiring the structure.

"There they are," Mia said and whistled for Tandy, who trotted beside her as they crossed the street. As Mia drew closer, Brynn spotted her and waved. Then she recognized the determined expression on Mia's face and tapped her mother's shoulder in warning. Mia walked up to her sister and mother.

"Okay, you two, time for a chat," she said and walked them off to one side. Daniel and Reynolds were deep in a conversation about the house's Palladian windows and hipped roof, oblivious to Mia's arrival.

"I'm going to play some fetch with Tandy," Sylvie said and winked at Mia.

"What's up, Mimi?" Brynn said, looking at Mia warily.

Madison fished around in her handbag. She had always been a terrible liar and she looked guilty.

"What is Mark Harris doing here?" Mia said testily.

Madison turned and looked at her with a demure expression. Anyone would think she was completely innocent of all sin.

"Well, he was coming to Salem *anyway*," Madison wheedled. "So we invited him along."

"Good God, Mother, what were you thinking?" Mia said, incredulous. "What kind of business could Mark possibly have here?"

Madison pouted her lip the exact way Brynn always did, which was weird because Brynn was her stepdaughter. But from their Chanel suits down to their pearl earrings they were so alike, it was spooky sometimes.

"You really don't have to take that tone with me, Mia," Madison sniffed.

Brynn was looking off at a chestnut tree in front of the house as if it were the most interesting thing she had ever seen in her life. Then a thought hit Mia. What if Jeffrey, Brynn's husband, started this fiasco? Her brother-in-law always created havoc in her life. The whole reason she was pushed to take the job in Salem was because of Jeffrey! He'd kicked her out of the house the same week she lost her lab job and fiancé. It wouldn't surprise her in the slightest if Jeffrey was responsible for Mark's appearance.

"Did Jeffrey have something to do with this, Brynn?" Mia said.

"What do you mean?" Brynn said coyly.

"Mark Harris shows up in Salem? Then stalks me at the local restaurant?"

"Well, Jeffy did mention Mark was coming to Salem."

"And you didn't think to tell me?" Mia said, frustrated.

"Well, I didn't think you would be reasonable," Brynn said. "When it comes to Jeffy you can get a little crazy."

"I'm warning you both," Mia said sternly. "Stop interfering in my life."

Mia walked over to where Sylvie and Tandy were playing toss the stick. At that moment Reynolds joined them.

"Hey, Mia," he said tentatively.

"Hey, Reynolds," Mia said.

"Act natural," he whispered and leaned down and to pet Tandy. "I just wanted to give you heads-up. Jeffrey arrives sometime tomorrow."

Mia froze and felt the hair on the back of her neck bristle. Within the family, her brother-in-law was her biggest nemesis. Her stepfather could be fussy, but he was a saint compared to Jeffrey, who seemed to be out to get her, stirring up drama whenever possible.

"Jeffrey's coming to Salem?" Mia whispered.

"I'm afraid so," Reynolds said.

"Thanks for the heads-up. You're a good friend."

No doubt her brother-in-law had everything to do with the fact that Mark Harris had suddenly appeared in Salem.

Daniel came over, chest puffed up, notebook open and filled with scribblings and measurements. He was always half-crazed when he went to a historic site. "Tonight we're visiting a historic pub, will you be joining us, Mia?"

"I'm going to have to pass," Mia said. "Tomorrow is going to be impossible. There's a production meeting early in the morning and our evening shoot. But after that my schedule frees up."

"Oh, I see," Daniel said. "That seems like an awful lot of work for a theatrical production."

"It's hard work but fun," Mia said.

"Well, I certainly hope you'll make time for the family."

"Just family, right?" Mia said.

"Of course," Daniel said huffily. Mia noticed that Daniel glanced toward Madison and Brynn as he straightened out his coat. Was he in on the plot to bring Mark Harris back into her life, or just uncomfortable?

"As soon as we're done with the shoot, I'm all yours."

Mia and Sylvie headed back to the car with Tandy. Mia opened the back seat and Tandy leapt inside. The minute they were alone, Sylvie started laughing.

"Your stepdad's face when you said *just family*." She waved goodbye as the car pulled into traffic and headed back toward the Essex Street apartment building.

"Ugh, they better think twice before dragging Mark Harris with them," Mia said as she reached back to pet Tandy, who had his head stuck out the window. The drama of Mia's family faded behind as they drove under a canopy of trees changing color in the cool weather.

"Listen, the whole reason you and I were meeting got sidetracked by Middleton mania," Sylvie said. "What happened back there at the Elmswood House? You looked pretty upset."

"I saw something." Mia said, and the fear suddenly flared up again.

Sylvie looked at Mia hard.

"Okay then, what did you see?"

"A little girl in a cloak," Mia said. "She was outside in the wooded area and standing at one of the windows when we were leaving."

"Like those people in period clothing you saw?" Sylvie said.

"Sort of," Mia said, feeling uncomfortable about the topic. Sylvie was referring to the terrible incident where Mia had seen mysterious figures in period clothing at the Howard Street Cemetery. At the time, she was being hunted down by a psychotic maniac named Arthur Crippen, the previous owner of Charnel Tours before Albee Abernathy took over. Johnny and Sylvie were convinced she'd seen a pair of ghosts, but Mia wasn't so sure.

"Maybe the little girl is a ghost?" Sylvie said.

"I also got a really bad feeling in the house."

"A feeling?" Sylvie said. "Now don't get me wrong, I have bad feelings all the time, I just never thought I'd hear Mia Bold say that she got a bad feeling about a haunted house."

"I know, it's ridiculous," Mia said. "I didn't want to say anything in front of Graham and Ollie, let alone Johnny. But that house made me feel sick."

"The place could use some work, for sure. But I didn't feel anything. Maybe you have psychic powers? Like that white witch Hazel?"

"That's ridiculous," Mia said.

"I'm serious, Mia. Even you admit there's such a thing as ESP."

"I wish we were filming at another location. Maybe I can convince Graham and Ollie to choose another place."

Suddenly there was a text on Sylvia's phone and she looked down.

"Too late, the shooting schedule just came through."

She held her phone up and Mia glanced at the schedule.

Cast and Crew Call
Bell, Book, and Candle: The Elmswood Horror House
Call Time: 1700 Hours
Location: 555 Elmswood Drive—Swampscott

Mia had to admit, she was more than just nervous about going back to that house; she actually felt ill and overwhelmed at the thought. Fear was building up in the pit of her stomach as if something awful was going to happen. The fate of the Browder family made her cringe. And there were some well-documented haunted houses like the Amityville Horror and the Indiana Demon House that had caused measurable physical symptoms in the investigators. As far as Mia was concerned, knowledge was power. She needed to better understand that house on Elmswood Road before she walked back inside the scariest place she'd ever encountered. She pulled into the parking lot behind the building. As they got out of the car, Sylvie yawned.

"I have to admit, your family has exhausted me," she said and grinned. "I think I'm going to take a nap before I meet Johnny. We're going to a Love Addicts Anonymous meeting tonight. Wanna come? Maybe it would help with Mark?"

"Believe me, I'm so over Mark," Mia said. "Besides, I really need to research tonight. Usually, I have weeks to investigate a site, not twenty-four hours!"

"Okay, later," Sylvie said.

Mia watched Sylvie disappear into her apartment. Both her friends had bonded over their recent bad romances. Sylvie had broken up with Dexter, the lead singer for Amplitude, a New York City rock band. And Johnny had been dumped by the beautiful but toxic Salem lifestyle blogger, Vicki Carlyle.

Mia and Tandy stepped into the hurricane of her apartment. Tandy and Rose took one look at each other and ran off to play while Mia started cleaning.

An hour later, Mia squeezed the mud out of her mop and finished the last patch of floor in the kitchen. No more muddy boot and paw prints. Books were back on the shelves, papers were filed, maps folded and put aside. Tandy and Rose watched her work like she'd gone crazy.

"Okay, you two," Mia said as she put the cleaning supplies away in the cupboard. "We're ready for inspection." Now, if her family showed up, she could pass the white glove test.

It had been a long, busy day, but Mia was finally alone.

After taking a shower and putting on her favorite black, silk pajamas, Mia poured herself a glass of wine. Then she opened her computer and settled down to research the Elmswood House. An incoming message pinged. When she saw who the email was from, she sat bolt upright. All her plans dissolved in an instant.

CHAPTER EIGHT

Mia stared at the unexpected email from Suzy Sharpe and a nervous flutter erupted in her stomach. Suzy, a local news reporter for the *Salem Star*, had almost derailed Mia's last investigation. But eventually they made an uneasy truce after Mia agreed to give her an exclusive interview. In return, Suzy had agreed to help Mia find her real father, Frank Bold. As Mia read the subject line, she felt a thrill.

Subject: *Possible cell phone number for Frank Bold.*

Mia sat bolt upright. *Had Suzy Sharpe found her dad's number?* She opened the email, eager to see what Suzy had discovered.

Hey Mia,

I have a source who looked at cell phone data for calls made at Salem Athenaeum the night your dad was there.

Every number could be easily attributed to someone except one, a pay-as-you-go number: 555-555-0194.

I called but there was no answer and the voicemail was just a recording with some music.

My source traced the same number to calls made from the Hawthorne Hotel. For Salem, that's pretty fancy. So, if it was your dad, looks like money isn't a problem.

—Suzy Sharpe

Mia looked at the number and felt a thrill. Could this be her father's phone number? She often thought of the warm, sunny days they'd spent together along the Jersey Shore boardwalk. Mia was too young to understand at the time, but Frank was a confabulator. To this day, she had no idea why he had told so many stories—to amuse himself or was there a deeper reason? Mia could remember distinctly Frank having half a dozen supposed jobs, from international journalist to explorer. She didn't believe he was a grifter or a con man, but he told tall tales to nearly everyone they had ever met. Frank Bold was last seen only three months ago at the Salem Athenaeum dressed as a wealthy Scottish laird or landowner, listening to a reading of Robert Louis Stevenson.

What was Frank up to that night? Mia wondered. Had he really stayed at the Hawthorne Hotel?

She opened her phone to dial the number, filled with anticipation. Her hand hovered over the keypad, torn whether to call him or not. What should she say after all this time? What would he say? How could he possibly explain his long absence?

Frank had been missing for years, since Mia was a little kid. Everything her mom had ever said about him rumbled through her mind. That he was a dreamer without a practical bone in his body, a rambler, a loner, a lost cause.

Mia took a deep breath. For all she knew, this was just another disappointing clue that pointed to a dead end.

There was only one way to find out. Slowly, she dialed the number and held the phone to her ear. After a moment there was a click as the line picked up.

"Hello?" Mia said. But instead of a voice on the other end of the phone, a song began to play "Drive," by The Cars.

Mia was so shocked, she nearly dropped the phone.

That was her dad's favorite song, part of the era he'd grown up in and had a moody quality. As Mia listened to the lyrics, she longed to connect to her dad.

Who's going to drive you home tonight? Who's going to pay attention to your dreams? Who's going to pay attention to your schemes?

There was a loud beep indicating she was supposed to leave a message.

Her heart beat faster and her throat shut down.

"Um, hello, this is a message for Frank—I mean, *Dad*. I'm not sure if this is your phone? But if it is, could you call me? It's your daughter, Mia."

She recited her cell phone number and hung up. The whole thing was probably a dead end. But The Cars song haunted her. It had to be him, didn't it? She reread Suzy's letter. The Hawthorne Hotel? Mia fought the urge to run over to the hotel and question the staff. Instead, she went into her files and retrieved the article that had appeared in the *Salem Star* and spread the paper across the table.

Scottish Lord visits Salem Athenaeum

Residents of Salem, Massachusetts, were treated to a rare visit from royalty when Laird Frank Bold of Aberdeenshire paid a visit to our very own Salem Athenaeum. The Scottish lord enjoyed an evening of readings featuring a native son of Scotland, Robert Louis Stevenson...

The picture in the center of the page was definitely Frank Bold. That night he had posed for a group photograph wearing a formal kilt and fitted argyle jacket draped with a plaid mantle. He looked handsome and sported a benevolent smile. Mia had already questioned the other people in the picture including Winifred Brumley, one of the librarians at the Salem Athenaeum. No one knew a thing.

Frank had mysteriously shown up that night, and just as mysteriously disappeared. Mia had been a kid when Frank had pulled these kinds of stunts. In her child's mind they were just playing, but was there something more? Was there something to Frank's disguises? And would she ever solve the mystery of why he had disappeared completely and never contacted her again?

Mia felt a swell of emotion threaten to overwhelm her. Her eyes teared up and she wiped them away. She needed a distraction to clear her head.

Time to get back to her research. *What did she know about the Elmswood House? What happened there? Who was haunting the place and why?*

Mia began to search the Swampscott news archives. After a few tries, she found an article.

Tragedy on Elmswood Road

A Swampscott family was found dead after the children did not show up for school and the parents could not be reached. Swampscott PD Detective Charlie Waite investigated the house and discovered a car running in the garage. The autopsy found that carbon monoxide had poisoned Angie Browder and her two sons, Bobby and Todd, during the night. Donnie Browder, the father, survived and was taken into custody on suspicion of murder.

Next, Mia checked the court records; Donnie Browder had pleaded not guilty by reason of insanity and was sent to Bridgewater State Hospital.

As Mia dug deeper, she found that the haunted activity began soon after the tragedy. People reported seeing members of the Browder family in the upper windows of the house. Despite the rumors, Connie and Dean Carol bought the Elmswood House and, after moving in, reported haunted activity; footsteps, doors opening and shutting, ghosts. Eventually Dean died of a heart attack and Connie moved out.

Mia started to piece the timeline together.

So, the haunting had started with the Browder family tragedy and continued once the Carol family moved into the house.

But one account made her skin crawl. Connie and Dean had reported seeing a particular ghost—a little girl.

Mia scoured the Internet for stories of the ghost.

The little girl was rumored to be a dark entity, the one who killed Dean Carol. That fact sent chills down Mia's spine.

Mia glanced at the clock. It was getting late and she needed to be up early. She finished her wine and climbed into bed with a copy of Hans Holzer's book *Ghost Hunter.* Tandy jumped up to sleep at her feet and Rose delicately made her way across the sheets to snuggle in the crook of her arm.

Holzer was the famous Austrian-American ghost hunter who had investigated the Amityville Horror House. There was an echo of that famous haunting in the Elmswood House. Mia usually relied on hard research, but there was something to be said for just absorbing the experience of someone in her profession. Though Hans Holzer often used mediums and other psychics to explore haunted houses, he was levelheaded *and* scientific in his approach.

Mia knew how hard it was to thread the needle between those two points. But the longer Mia worked in the field, the more she had to keep an open mind. Still, a thread of fear gripped her heart. What had she seen at Elmswood? An apparition? Was there a vengeful ghost in that terrible house? And if so, who would it try and kill next? Just before she dozed off with the book open across her chest, she glanced out the window. The sky was crisp and clear with the stars shining down. The full moon was so bright, it seemed to fill up the sky.

Slowly, she drifted into sleep.

Mia found herself standing in a field of snow. A wave of fear overwhelmed her as she looked up to see the Elmswood House. The old mansion loomed against a gray sky, emanating a terrible energy, with its broken shutters and filmy windows. Then out of the corner of her eye, Mia saw a young girl in a dark hooded cloak. The girl waved to her and turned on her heel, feet silent in the snow as she disappeared around the corner. Mia felt a stab of fear, but followed the girl as she turned the corner and stood by a fence.

As Mia approached, the girl pointed toward an open field. Across the snowy expanse was an American colonial house, snowbound and isolated. Icicles had formed along the eaves and two dormer windows protruded from the roof. The front door was slightly obscured by a gnarled old tree.

That must be the way Swampscott looked in the nineteenth century, Mia thought.

I must be dreaming! Mia realized.

She looked at the girl. Her eyes were a deep slate gray and her dark hair fell along her shoulders. She seemed sad and lost.

"What's your name?" Mia said.

"Lydia," the girl said. "You need to leave before you get hurt."

"Leave? Where?" Mia said.

But instead of answering, the girl slipped through the fence rails and ran across the field.

"Wait," Mia cried out. "Lydia? Come back!"

Mia ran to the gate and pulled it open. Then she followed the girl out into the field, feet kicking up white powder. She tried to catch up, but suddenly she was back where she started, standing before the dilapidated Elmswood House. The heaviness of the house weighed down on her. Then her eyes were drawn to the second floor.

What she saw made her blood freeze. A woman with hollow eyes stood at one of the upper windows. Beside her were two children with vacant expressions. Slowly, the woman traced a message on the glass. *HELP US.*

Mia tried to scream but her throat was silent.

CHAPTER NINE

Mia snapped awake and rolled on her side, breathing hard, trying to shake off the dream. Rose and Tandy sensed her distress. Tandy climbed along the bed rail and licked her face with concern, while Rose purred and stared at her with mystical eyes.

Mia checked the time. It was just before sunrise. She tried to fall asleep again but she was too shaken up. She cuddled with Tandy until she felt better and petted Rose's bunny fur. Then she got up and decided to make coffee.

As the sun rose, she started to shake off the ominous feeling the dream had stirred up. The Elmswood House had really gotten to her. As soon as she calmed down, she texted Sylvie.

Ready for the meeting today?

Almost immediately, Sylvie texted her back.

As ready as I'll ever be.

Pick you up in an hour.

Mia opened her computer and searched for "Lydia" and Elmswood, but there was nothing. Then she opened the article she'd read last night and stared at the image of the Browder family. A chill moved through her body.

Angie, Bobby, and Todd looked exactly like the people in her dream.

I guess I buried all this in my subconscious mind, she thought.

Still the dream had shaken her down to her core. What about Donnie Browder? He was still alive. *There must be a police interview,* she realized.

She searched YouTube. With such a notorious murderer, it didn't take long to find the police interview. She pressed play.

Donnie Browder was lying in a hospital bed being questioned by Detective Charlie Waite, a typical cop, heavyset with short-cropped hair. The detective had ruddy skin and a serious demeanor. There was something confident in his presence. After administering the Miranda warning, he began his questions.

"So, Donnie," Detective Waite began. "You left your car running in the garage. Did you mean to do that?"

"Yes, sir. It seemed the right thing to do," Donnie said.

Almost immediately, his attention drifted away.

"Did you know the carbon monoxide would kill your family?" Waite said.

Donnie Browder nodded.

"Can you speak up for the camera now, Donnie?"

"Yes sir, I knew. I wanted to save them."

"From what exactly?"

"Lydia," Donnie Browder said and there was terror in his eyes.

Mia sat bolt upright, shocked. The name *Lydia* had just come out of Donnie Browder's mouth.

"What did Lydia tell you?" Waite said.

"Save them," Browder said as he pressed his hands against his temples. He shook his head over and over. "Lydia was there, in the snow."

The snow? Mia stopped the video nervously. What were the chances of that? She'd dreamed of the name, the family, and the snow?

"Save them from what?" Detective Waite said.

"Lydia is the devil," Charlie said and started weeping.

A horrible thought occurred to Mia and her heart thudded in her chest. Was she going crazy like Donnie Browder? Why was she dreaming about the same entity Donnie had just confessed to seeing? She tried to rationalize how Donnie Browder had seen Lydia in the snow too. An explanation eluded her. Suddenly her phone pinged. Madison was texting her.

Honey? Sorry you got upset about Mark.
You never did like surprises, dear, even when you were little.
But don't you think you should give him another chance?

Mia stared at the text, stunned. That was practically an admission that Mark's appearance was no coincidence! The Middletons were interfering with her life as usual. Mia frantically texted back.

Give Mark another chance?
He blew me off, Mom! Now he wants to come back?
I don't have time for this today!

Love you but stop trying to help!

Being mad was better than being scared, Mia realized. Maybe she should thank Madison for getting her mind off of the strange, unsettling dream. She had a busy day ahead of her. First there was the production meeting and in the evening, filming would start. After showering, she towel dried her hair and picked out an outfit that was professional, but practical; jeans, her best urban hiking shoes, and a fitted black dress shirt. Her damp hair fell in waves down her back.

After feeding Tandy and Rose, she put on her watch and grabbed her messenger bag and jacket, piling them on the table by the front door, ready to leave. Tandy sensed a new adventure and pranced excitedly while Rose groomed her long tail. Another text came in. It was her mom again.

Brynn should be there by now.
Try to be reasonable.
Mark did come a long way to see you.

Mia stared at Madison's text. *What? Brynn is coming here now?*

She typed back frantically.

Mom! I have to work today!

At that exact moment Tandy ran over to the door wagging his tail with excitement. There was a knock. It wasn't even 8 a.m. yet! Mia was amazed. Her family was incorrigible when it came to interfering.

She opened the door to find Brynn standing in the hallway, dressed fashionably in designer jeans, heels, a silk blouse, pearls, and a knitted jacket. Her hair was swept up with long tendrils falling down. But even though Brynn looked perfectly coiffed, there was a hint of dark circles under her eyes.

Exhibit A of why I spent hours cleaning up, Mia thought. You never knew when a Middleton was going to arrive at your door.

Tandy danced in a circle greeting his favorite auntie.

"Hi, pup-pup," Brynn said, bending down and kissing Tandy's nose.

"Hey, Brynn," Mia said. "Mom just said you were coming."

"Your apartment looks great, Mimi," Brynn said and smiled. "Too bad Mom and Dad didn't see it like this."

"Coffee?" Mia swept her arm in the direction of the kitchen.

Thanks," Brynn said as she stepped inside.

They headed for the kitchen. Mia knew exactly how her sister liked her coffee, so she made it to her taste with milk and one sugar. Then she poured herself a cup. They both sat down at the kitchen table.

"Did you get enough sleep?" Mia said. "You look a little tired."

"Now that you mention it, I didn't sleep too well," Brynn said, rubbing the back of her neck. "There were some strange sounds in my room last night."

"Like what?" Mia said.

"You know, creaking boards, footsteps. It's an old building."

"Well, I hope Jeffrey isn't coming to stay with you," Mia said, knowing full well Jeffrey was due to join her, thanks to Reynolds.

"Why?" Brynn said suspiciously.

"Because Katherine, the ghost that haunts Room Seventeen of the Salem Inn, doesn't like men, remember?"

Mia didn't believe in Katherine the ghost but she couldn't resist teasing her sister.

"Mimi! Why are you always trying to scare me!" Brynn said, flustered. Mia could see that she had really encountered something strange last night. Maybe it was best to change the subject to something more down to earth.

"Don't you get sick of the Middleton madness?" Mia said.

"Sorry, Mimi, you know how Mum gets. I just wanted to see you before you rushed off to your meeting. Honestly, I know you have a life."

"Please don't tell me you're here to pitch Mark to me," Mia said.

"I would never do that," Brynn said. "Even though Mark does check quite a few boxes."

"What boxes?" Mia said, baffled. "The dumping his girlfriend when she gets to be too much trouble box? Or the show up when you're getting a cable show box?"

"Come on, Mimi, you have to admit you were acting pretty crazy when you two broke up."

"You mean because I quit my job?" Mia said.

"Addendum," Brynn said, touching a finger to the air. "You mean you quit your prestigious, high-paying job and left—for *Salem.*"

"What's wrong with Salem?" Mia said.

"Oh, come on, Mimi. It's just a little bit, shall we say, *lurid.*"

"Lurid? Have you been playing Scrabble? You sound like Daniel."

"You know what I mean. Do you really want to raise kids in the middle of a Halloween store?"

"Raise kids? What are you talking about? I have a job in Salem, that's all."

"The clock is ticking, Mimi. I can't help it if I think it's a little crazy you threw away your life for this place."

Mia cringed at Brynn's words. She was used to a sisterly dressing down now and then, but this was different. It was as if Brynn was touching on her secret fears. Was she throwing her life away? Maybe her old life had offered her safety and security, but at what cost? Mia steadied herself. Now that she had a job she loved and real friends whom she could count on, there was no going back. She'd chosen her path.

"Listen, Brynn, tell me the truth. Did Mom and Daniel arrange for Mark to show up here?"

Brynn looked at her shoes and turned her ankle as if to check for scuff marks. Then she spread her fingers and checked her French manicure. After that she took a deep breath and released it in a long sigh.

"I think it was Mark's idea, but yes, they encouraged it."

"Thanks for being honest with me," Mia said, fighting the urge to say something mean that she would later regret.

There was a knock on the door and Sylvie walked in.

"Hey, Brynn," she said. "Mia, are you ready?"

"Ready," Mia said and clipped on Tandy's lead. "Listen, Brynn, Sylvie and I have to go to a production meeting."

"I'll walk with you," Brynn said.

"Okay," Mia said. " I just have to make one stop on the way."

"Where?" Brynn said.

"The Ascension Bookshop," Mia said.

"I love bookshops!" Brynn said.

Mia and Sylvie exchanged knowing glances. The Ascension Bookshop was no ordinary shop. It belonged to long-time Salem residents and local power couple T.G. Prophet and his wife, Hazel, who just happened to be a white witch. If anyone could give Mia insight into the Elmswood House and Lydia, it was Hazel Prophet.

CHAPTER TEN

Salem was just waking up as Mia, Brynn, Sylvie, and Tandy stepped out onto the street. Being out in the fresh air felt great after Mia's spooky dream. Tandy's retractable lead gave him a little more freedom and he trotted ahead to sniff the wares of the various vendors. Each booth was filled with occult items and spooky treats. There were witch hats, wizard capes, crystal balls, magic wands, touristy keychains, T-shirts, and souvenir "witch city" cups, along with all kinds of delicious treats from candy apples and brownies to lollipops shaped like ghosts.

Brynn and Sylvie walked just ahead. They were an odd pair with Brynn dressed like she just stepped out of *Vogue Paris* and Sylvie attired like a punk princess, in pink combat trousers and a cropped jacket covered with vintage pins.

Mia's wardrobe was quite toned down in comparison to them both.

Tandy trotted up to Mia before going back to his doggie business.

"Oh look, they're having a sale on Dracula fangs," Sylvie pointed out.

"Lucky I remembered to bring mine," Brynn said and giggled.

"Down that road is the Witch City Side Show. There's a guy who pounds nails into his head. Your dad might like that, I know mine would."

"Oh Sylvie, you're incorrigible," Brynn said. "My dad would lose his mind. But I'll tell Jeffy about it. He might like that sort of thing."

"Jeffy?" Sylvie said.

"My hubby, he's a lawyer. Which is handy with Mia around," Brynn said pointedly, referring to Mia tendency to get mixed up with the law.

"I've never once called Jeffrey for help," Mia said, little disgruntled.

"So, your dad doesn't like circus performers?" Sylvie teased.

"He despises performers in general," Brynn said.

"You mean, like the hosts of podcasts and TV shows?" Sylvie said.

"Oh no, I didn't mean—" Brynn said.

"Yes, exactly like that," Mia said and winked at Sylvie.

"Well, it's true, he's not too happy about your show," Brynn said.

Mia sighed. Even though her stepdad was a snob and her family were busybodies, she loved them. They were oddballs but good people.

The food stalls were firing up their grills and the smell of heating oil and spices filled the air. The locals were rolling out of their apartments and heading out for morning coffee with their bulldogs, poodles, and mutts.

Tandy lifted his head into the air and flared his nostrils, savoring the fascinating array of scents along the street, sniffing other dogs and nibbling on outcroppings of grass. Despite the cheerful atmosphere, Mia found her thoughts straying back to her dream of Lydia.

There must be an explanation, but Mia was at a loss to account for how she managed to dream of the same entity Donnie Browder had described.

Up ahead was a peculiar storefront—even for Salem. A large plate glass window was set between two wooden pillars, painted in a delicate shade of lilac. The sign hanging above the arched doorway was printed in gold and white calligraphy with butterflies and hummingbirds swirling through letters set against a blue sky with a bright sun rising in the background.

The owners of the shop, T.G. Prophet and his wife, Hazel, were out in front, washing the large, front window with squeegees. Inside the window, a display of books was nestled between large crystals of amethyst and citrine.

"So this is the Ascension Bookshop?" Brynn said, surprised. "Where are all of the bats and witches and creepy stuff?"

" Didn't you just tell me Salem was lurid? I thought you'd be relieved," Mia said.

"I am!" Brynn said. "This shop isn't like Salem at all."

"And why is that exactly?" Sylvie said.

"Well, just look at the window! There are crystals and candles and self-help books by Eckhart Tolle and Deepak Chopra. This place looks like Oprah's reading club come to life."

"I'll introduce you to the owner," Mia said.

"Watch out, Hazel's a white witch," Sylvie teased.

"Really?" Brynn said. "Now that seems more like Salem."

"Think of her more as a light worker, as Oprah would say," Mia said.

Tandy wagged his tail and ran over to greet Salem's most perfect couple.

T.G. greeted Tandy and waved as he recognized Mia and Sylvie walking toward them. He was tall and elegant with blond, almost white hair and penetrating blue eyes, dressed in a pea coat and plaid scarf.

After greeting T.G., Tandy beelined for Hazel.

"Hey, Tandy," Hazel said, leaning down to ruffle Tandy's floppy ears. She had delicate features with striking, moss-green eyes, and was dressed in layers of flowing Boho artisan knits. Her long red hair was loosely tied up in a colorful scarf and she wore dozens of amulets and beaded bracelets.

"Hey, Mia," Hazel said and smiled.

"I wanted to introduce my sister, Brynn," Mia said.

"Your shop is so adorable!" Brynn said. "Oh, is that Deepak Chopra's latest book? I love him!"

"Let me show you around," T.G. said and escorted Brynn inside the shop.

"What are you two up to?" Hazel said, leaning her squeegee against the window.

"We have a production meeting for our ghost hunt tonight," Sylvie said.

"How exciting," Hazel said. "Where?"

"The Elmswood House in Swampscott," Mia said.

"Where the Browder murders took place?" Hazel said in a low voice as her cheeks drained of color.

Tandy stood beside Hazel quietly, gazing up at her in deep concentration. Her long tapered fingers petted his head and the dog's eyes seemed to close at half mast, completely relaxed as Hazel stroked him.

"Yes," Mia said, surprised Hazel knew about the place. She glanced at Sylvie. They had both developed a superstitious awe of Hazel, who seem to be able to predict things before they happened. On more than one occasion Hazel had given Mia an object that actually saved her life. Mia had thought long and hard about how that was even possible. How could Hazel know just the thing someone would need in the future? What she finally decided was that Hazel had some form of precognition. ESP was a well-studied phenomenon with many credible scientific studies. So whenever Hazel spoke, Mia listened.

"Did you dream about her yet?" Hazel said.

A chill went down Mia spine. "Who?"

"Why, Lydia," Hazel said.

Mia stared at Hazel, astounded. How could she possibly know about her dream?

"You know about Lydia?" Mia managed to say.

"Uh, what are you two talking about?" Sylvie said.

"Remember the little girl I saw? Well, I dreamed about her last night," Mia said. "She said her name was Lydia."

"No way!" Sylvie said, looking at Hazel superstitiously.

"I saw the Browder family too. They asked me for help," Mia said.

"The family that got killed in that house?" Sylvie said, eyes wide.

"What else happened in the dream?" Hazel said.

"Lydia pointed out a weird house with two windows in the roof and a gnarled old tree in front."

"She's trying to tell you something," Hazel said casually.

"So, you think Lydia is a ghost?" Sylvie said.

"Yes," Hazel said. "They can't communicate directly, so they'll send signs to guide you."

"Guide me?" Mia said. "About what?"

"I'm not sure," Hazel said. "There are number of ghosts in that house."

Tandy watched the conversation with a strange expression on his face as if he understood it. He was very sensitive to people.

"Donnie Browder mentioned Lydia," Mia said. "That she spoke to him."

"Yes," Hazel said. "They say he was driven mad by her, but I'm not so sure. Sometimes people blame ghosts for their own evil. One thing to remember about ghosts, fear binds them to the earth and makes them manifest more easily."

"I wish Johnny Astor was here right now," Sylvie said. "He loves ghost talk."

"I don't believe in ghosts," Mia said and shook her head.

"Well, they believe in you," Hazel said. "This isn't the first time you've had an encounter. You saw something strange in the Howard Street cemetery too."

"She's got a point," Sylvie said. "You could be a ghost magnet, Mia."

"Come on, that's crazy!" Mia said.

Hazel took Mia's hands in her own.

"Don't be afraid, Mia. Keep the light of your consciousness steady, so the ghosts can find their way home."

"How am I supposed to do that?" Mia said.

"Fight the fear," Hazel said. "You're a truth seeker, and that means you serve the light."

Suddenly the shop door opened, and Brynn and T.G. Prophet stepped outside. Brynn had a paper bag filled with books, and she was giddy and happy, utterly charmed by the little shop. The lovely atmosphere, the aromatherapy, and the wind chimes and positive vibrations had done wonders for her. Tandy trotted over to greet Brynn as she stepped out onto the street.

"Hello, pup-pup," Brynn said in a sweet voice, refreshed and radiant.

"Guess where Brynn is staying?" T.G. prophet said to his wife, knowingly. "*Room Seventeen* at the Salem Inn."

Hazel's eyes widened and she took a deep breath.

"You don't say? So you're bunking with Katherine?" Hazel said. "Wait here, I have something for you."

Hazel disappeared into the shop in a flurry of flowing skirts. A second later she was out again, carrying a small braided bracelet with a tiny goddess with upraised arms carved in alabaster. She tied the bracelet around Brynn's wrist.

"Keep this on your wrist while you're in Salem," Hazel said and smiled. "You'll get a good night's sleep from now on."

Brynn hugged Hazel and kissed her on the cheek.

"Thank you!" she said.

"There is one little side effect," Hazel said. "The goddess energy sometimes attracts acolytes."

"Well, that's a good thing, right?" Brynn said, waving goodbye.

Mia, Sylvie, and Brynn headed down the street to the production office. Tandy was happy to be on the move again. He had taken the route a hundred times and was busy reading the news of the day via his olfactory receptors.

Up ahead, Graham Stone stood on the front steps of the production office, talking on his phone. He wore one of his signature outfits, a silk shirt unbuttoned halfway down with an abstract pattern, topped by a white linen jacket with a wide lapel and mustard-colored brushed corduroy flares with a thick belt with circular brass holes. A few gold chains peeked through the gap in a shirt. Lately he had also taken to trying to grow facial hair. Mia did not need to be a psychic to predict a mustache was on the way. He looked like a holdover from the '70s.

As they drew closer, Graham saw Brynn and stiffened like a hunter in the forest seeing an elk.

"Call you back later," he said and sauntered down the steps, eyes fixed on Brynn. Sylvie grabbed Mia's jacket and tugged on it; they both could see what was coming.

"Who is *this*?" Graham said, rubbing his chin where stubble was growing. Brynn looked at Mia with concern, not sure what to do.

"This is Graham Stone, one of our producers," Mia said reluctantly. "And this is my sister, Brynn."

"So good looks run in the family?" Graham said. Mia and Sylvie watched in alarm as he kissed Brynn's hand.

"So, you're Mimi's producer?" Brynn said. "She's mentioned you before."

"All good, I hope. Are you in town for long?"

"Not long. My *husband* will be joining me soon. We're staying for just a few days," Brynn said.

"That's a shame," Graham said, strangely undeterred.

"I better go, Mimi," Brynn said, looking at her watch. " You know how Dad gets when he has a full day planned."

Brynn turned on her heel and disappeared back toward her hotel. Graham looked after her longingly.

"What a knockout!" he said in a faraway voice.

"Cool off, Graham," Sylvie said. "She's married!"

"What?" Graham said, lingering for a moment, staring at Brynn's retreating figure as she disappeared around the corner. "Hey, Mia, I'd like to take you and your parents, and of course your lovely sister, out to dinner."

Tandy made a strange throaty sound.

Mia stared at Graham as if he'd gone quite mad, but he was deadly serious.

"You don't need to do that—" Mia said.

"I insist," Graham said. "It's the least I can do for my star. And I can admire your beautiful sister while we dine."

Mia wondered about Hazel's warning. As a skeptic she could not believe the bracelet Brynn wore could possibly have an effect, but Brynn certainly did have an acolyte now.

As Mia prepared to walk into the meeting, she was nervous. Usually, she relied on facts and skepticism to guide her through an investigation. But for the first time in her career as a ghost hunter, she had more questions than answers. She was full of dread. Every instinct she had told her to run from the Elmswood House, and this meeting was the first step in walking back inside that awful place.

CHAPTER ELEVEN

As Mia entered the office, she felt heartened by the sight of her coworkers. The *Bell, Book, and Candle* offices were buzzing with energy. Ollie Cooper was on the phone with one of the show's sponsors, Jake the cameraman and Will the intern checked equipment and piled bags by the door to take to the location for the evening shoot. You'd never know from the busy, professional atmosphere that they were all preparing to walk into a notorious haunted house.

"Where's Johnny?" Mia said, noticing the conspicuous absence of her co-host. Ever since she'd known him, Johnny had a terrible habit of making a dramatic entrance to every occasion.

"He's running late," Graham said, sliding into his seat at the head of the conference table. He stared at his phone intently. "Just making reservations, Mia. I'll email you."

Mia looked at Sylvie, who just shook her head in amazement. Graham was absolutely tone deaf when it came to picking up on social cues.

Will rushed over to Mia. He was getting taller every day, his long limbs poking out of his clothing. He had turned into a good-looking kid, Mia thought. Handling the boom microphone had built his muscles up and he looked lean and athletic, even if he was still an awkward teenager. Will greeted Tandy and roughhoused with him a little bit, which Tandy loved.

"Do you want me to put up that cat run for you?" he asked.

"That would be great," Mia said. "You have a key. Just let yourself in whenever it's convenient."

"Cool," Will said.

Ollie Cooper got off the phone and stepped over to the conference table.

"Okay, let's get the schedule nailed down," he said and pointed to a stack of papers. Will rushed off to grab schedules and place them around the table as everyone took a seat.

"We'll be blocking the show late in the afternoon. This is a one-day shoot with only one additional day for pickups, so we have a tight schedule. We can't afford to have any major goofs, so bring your A-game."

"Also," Graham added, "we've hired Albee Abernathy to give us a little history lesson."

Mia groaned internally. *Please, not him,* she thought. Albee Abernathy, the local warlock who ran Charnel Tours had a *thing* for Mia. But she had to admit, he did know Salem's history.

"Are you sure Abernathy is the right guy for the job?" Sylvie said. "Isn't he in his coffin during daylight hours?"

"Very funny," Graham said. "Nobody knows Salem like Abernathy."

The door opened and Johnny Astor stepped inside. He was dressed casually in jeans, a black T-shirt, and a leather jacket. His ashy hair had grown to his shoulders and a lock fell across his forehead. Tandy ran to him and butted his head against him like a billy goat until Johnny kneeled down to greet him. He looked up at Mia and she was struck, as always, by his intense hazel eyes and long, dark lashes. He smiled when he saw her and Mia felt a flush of heat in her body. Being attracted to Johnny was extremely inconvenient for two reasons.

1. Johnny Astor was her co-host.
2. She had started dating Hugh Wolfe.

She tried to ignore Johnny and think of something boring, like a detergent commercial; *whites are whiter, colors are brighter, removes grass stains*.

"Hey, Mia," Johnny said. "I heard your family's in town?"

"True," Mia said. "They've been keeping me busy."

"I'm taking them out to dinner," Graham said, pleased with himself. "Why don't you join us?"

Mia stared at Graham like he was crazy. He just grinned. The thought of Graham and Daniel Middleton in the same room together was like matter and anti-matter. If it actually happened, something would blow.

"Sounds good," Johnny said. "I'd love to meet them."

Mia blushed, completely thrown off her game by Johnny's presence.

"Okay, listen up," Graham said. "We're all meeting back here this afternoon to be briefed by Abernathy. Then we head for the Elmswood House."

"Are we all clear?" Ollie said.

Everyone mumbled their agreement. Mia picked up the schedule.

Clipped to it was a picture of the Elmswood House. The moment Mia saw the house again, an awful shudder of dread moved through her body. The place seemed to scream death and decay. She stared at the rotting boards and dead vines that shrouded the house and her heart beat faster.

Mia stood up abruptly and swayed, feeling queasy and faint.

"Are you okay?" Johnny said, stepping by her side.

"I think I need some air," Mia said. The feeling she'd had in the dream erupted inside her mind. She felt a rush of adrenaline. Her breath huffed out of her chest as if she'd been punched.

Johnny led her outside into the bright sunlight with Tandy trotting behind. They sat down on the steps together.

"What's going on with you? Are you sure you're well enough to do this?" he said, concerned.

"Of course," Mia said, "I'll be fine. It's just my family being here and—"

"And what?" Johnny said.

"Nothing, the place just creeps me out," Mia said, annoyed with herself. How was she supposed to be a ghost hunter if she got overwhelmed and emotional at a haunted house? At that exact moment she realized she couldn't live like this any longer. She had to face her fear.

"We can always call it off," Johnny said, sweetly.

"No," Mia said. "I can do this."

"I loved your locations," Johnny said. "But next time you run off to the Devil's Swamp, you should call me. Please?"

"I didn't think you were the swamp type," Mia joked.

"I could be for you, Mia," Johnny said and met her eyes with that deep, intense gaze. For a moment Mia felt herself falling into the depths of his gaze and wondering what if—

Then the door to the office flew open. The meeting was over and the crew were headed their separate ways.

"Don't forget this," Sylvie said and handed Mia her bag. "I'll meet you back here. I've gotta take the production laptop to the computer store. FYI, Johnny, you missed some great stuff with Hazel Prophet and Mia's creepy dream."

"Creepy dream?" Johnny said.

"Mia saw the ghosts of Elmswood House," Sylvie said, "in a dream."

"Really?" Johnny said, impressed. "It isn't uncommon for sensitive people to start experiencing dreams and phenomenon around a haunting."

"I know you guys are trying to help, but sometimes a dream is just a dream," Mia said, and checked her watch. She'd started to formulate a plan. She glanced at the contact sheet. Everything she needed to investigate was right there on the sheet. Cindy Moore's number and the address of her real estate company, Seaside Estates. She could easily get to Swampscott and back before the Abernathy debrief and the shoot started.

"Listen, I've got to do something before we film tonight," Mia said.

"Can I help?" Johnny said.

"Not with this," Mia said. "This is something I have to do myself."

Johnny nodded and they all parted ways. Tandy jumped up, ready to accompany his mistress to the ends of the earth.

"Come on, boy," Mia said as they headed back to the apartment to pick up her car. She'd already made her decision. There was no way she was going to be a victim of fear. And she couldn't risk having a meltdown in front of Johnny and the crew. In order to face her terror, she had to go to Elmswood House and walk through the place on her own. That way she could confront her phobias before she had to be on camera. It was just an old house, after all, she thought. But to get inside, she needed to find one person—the real estate agent, Cindy Moore. And she needed to find her ASAP.

***

Mia and Tandy pulled up in front of Seaside Estates, a tidy and busy real estate office close to the beach in a bright and sunny section of Swampscott.

The moment they were out of the car, Tandy smelled the cool sea air and looked toward the ocean, his whole body lengthening as he took in the intoxicating scent of seaweed, fish, and brine.

Through the plate glass window, Mia could see a reception desk and some offices. The bell jangled as she opened the door.

The receptionist looked up and smiled. She was wearing a sunny yellow blouse with black polka-dots and a white-fitted jacket.

"Oh, cute doggie," she said in a sing-song voice. "Can I help you?"

"I'm looking for Cindy Moore?"

"And you are?"

"Mia Bold, from *Bell, Book, and Candle*," Mia said.

The woman pressed a button on the office phone.

"Yes?" said a man's voice through the intercom.

"I have a Mia Bold here to see Cindy Moore. She's from that show."

"I'll be right out," said the man.

A moment later the door opened and a tall man dressed in light khakis and a blue shirt with a red tie walked into the room. He held a hand out and they shook. Everything about him was trim and tidy. He had manicured fingernails and was wearing an expensive gold watch on his tanned wrist. His clothing was crisp, and he was sporting a broad salesman's smile with teeth that looked capped.

"So, you're from that spooky show, huh?" the man said.

"I guess I am," Mia said. "I've been trying to reach Cindy, but I keep getting her voicemail."

"I'm Doug Tanner, Cindy's junior partner. We haven't seen her all morning, right, Beth? She's probably out with a client. Is there anything I can help you with?"

"I actually need to see the Elmswood House. It has to do with the show," Mia said. "I just drove up here early to have a look at the property."

"You're filming there tonight, right? That place is a real eyesore. And the owner has a lot of stipulations. I keep telling her to sell to a developer."

"I'm sure it's a tough sell," Mia said. "Any idea where I can find Cindy?"

"Well, let me see. The last time I spoke to her was yesterday afternoon. She was going to Elmswood to meet a client. She's been trying to unload that house for the last six months. Hold on a second here."

Doug went back to a corkboard covered in hooks with dangling keys. He rifled through the keys and plucked one off its hook, an old skeleton key.

"You don't see these too much anymore," he said. Then he fished a card out of his wallet. Cindy Moore's mobile was on one side and

Doug Tanner's was on the other. "Why don't you just go over there and have a look around?"

"Thanks," Mia said, taking the card and the key.

"I'd take you myself, but I have a client arriving in thirty minutes. If you need anything call me."

Mia dug through her pocket and pulled a *Bell, Book, and Candle* card out of her pocket and handed it to Doug.

"That's my mobile," Mia said.

"Great, if Cindy turns up I will have her call you," Doug said. "Nice pooch you have there." He patted Tandy's head.

Mia walked back to her car, put Tandy in the backseat, and slid behind the wheel. The thought of going back into that house was terrifying. But she was determined to face her fears. As she drove toward the house, a terrible foreboding filled her body. She couldn't account for why she was having such a strong reaction. After all, she had investigated a dozen haunted places, why was this place burrowing so deeply into her subconscious mind?

She gripped the steering wheel tightly and kept driving, winding away from the beach area. As she turned into the curving streets, the atmosphere shifted. There was something about the old houses and the trees that created a more ominous feeling. She turned onto Elmswood Road.

There was the house, like a giant wound on the street. Even in the bright sunlight everything about it seemed dark and decayed.

She looked for Cindy Moore's car—the white Lexus. But the street was empty and eerily quiet. She parked and stepped out of the car, letting Tandy out. This time when he sniffed the air, his reaction was very different. The hackles on the back of his neck rose and he made a growling sound.

Mia steeled herself and walked up the driveway. The age-old question of psychic phenomena was whether terrible events could imprint themselves on a place. Was it possible for a location to become infected with the malevolent energy of the people who had lived in that place? Until now, Mia had not believed that was even possible, but every instinct in her body was telling her to run.

"It's just a house," she told herself. "I need to face my fears."

But as she looked up at the house, she felt like something bad was going to happen. As she walked to the front steps, the house loomed over her. The wind blew and the dead tree branches rattled and groaned. Tandy followed, slinking by her calves. The rotting steps creaked under their feet as the pair made their way to the porch. Mia was horribly nervous. She tried to steady her breath as she stood in front of the weathered door, working up the nerve to walk into the house.

Maybe I should try calling Cindy Moore one more time before barging inside, she thought nervously. She pulled the card Doug Tanner gave her from her pocket and dialed Cindy's number. Her own handset buzzed, and then Mia heard a faint ringing. She looked around, trying to locate the noise before realizing where the sound was coming from—inside the house.

CHAPTER TWELVE

So Cindy Moore was in the house? Mia thought, surprised. Where was her car? Mia stepped up to the weathered door and knocked. The wood rattled with a hollow thud. A part of her wanted to keep quiet as if not to wake up whatever malevolent energy existed inside, but her rational side realized that was crazy. *That's why I need to do this,* she thought. *I won't be ruled by fear.*

Tandy whimpered and kept looking at Mia, trying to convince her the whole thing was a bad idea.

"Cindy?" she called out. But there was no response. She realized the phone had gone to voicemail and held it up to her ear.

This is Cindy, I can't come to the phone right now—

"Hey, Cindy, this is Mia Bold," she said. "I'm standing out front. Your partner Doug Tanner gave me a key so I'm going to let myself in. I just need to take a look at the house." As the recording finished, Mia's phone went dark.

With a shaking hand, she pulled out the skeleton key and turned it in the lock. There was a dropping sensation as the tumblers turned and with a groan, the door opened.

The house was pitch-black.

"Darn it," Mia said and reached into her pocket to pull out her flashlight. The house seemed to swallow the thin beam of light. The floor creaked under their weight as Mia and Tandy entered the dark house. The bad feeling she had was just getting worse. Tandy growled again and Mia remembered the mirror above the credenza on the far wall. She swept the flashlight up and caught her own reflection. The fear in her eyes was obvious and she took a deep breath, glad Johnny Astor wasn't there to see her like this.

"It's okay, boy," she said, feeling Tandy's hackles rise as they entered the house. Even though it was the afternoon, the house was like a tomb, cold and dark. She swept her light over the peeling paint, tatty wallpaper, and faded carpet in the shadowy hallway.

No wonder Cindy couldn't sell this place, Mia thought, trying to imagine what a potential buyer would think of such a creepy house. She tilted her flashlight up at the rounded cathedral ceiling. Since yesterday, spider webs had formed around the high window set above the door gable, which barely illuminated the entrance with a dingy light.

"Cindy?" Mia called out, her voice muffled by the damp walls. She listened for an answer but the house was wrapped in silence. She stepped past the credenza and into the rectangular room that ended in a hexagonal bay window. Then she pointed her flashlight at the old leather chair where Donnie Browder was found, still alive. Somehow, the room seemed even gloomier than before. If this was an exercise in defeating her fear, it wasn't working.

Mia looked up through the circular skylight and saw that the sky was gray and overcast. There was a rustling sound and she nearly jumped out of her skin. Tandy growled and sniffed at the floorboards. Then she remembered the place had mice. The little creatures must be traveling through the walls.

"Cindy?" she called out again. Her own voice echoed for a moment before the empty silence returned. Maybe she had forgotten her cell phone? Mia wondered. That seemed strange since for a real estate agent.

Suddenly, there was a rush of footsteps across the ceiling. Her heart started to pound. That must be her, she realized.

Funny, she could have sworn the rustling sound was closer.

Didn't Cindy say the house was built in a spiral? Maybe that created auditory illusions? She turned and headed for the main stairs with Tandy trailing behind. She called up into the gloomy silence.

"Cindy? Are you up there? Where are you?" Her voice echoed into the stairwell. She started up the steps cautiously. The wood creaked as she climbed to the second floor. One by one, she checked each room for Cindy Moore.

They were empty.

Tandy crept behind her, hackles raised. She could have sworn she heard something running up here. Didn't she?

If Cindy was downstairs, who ran across the ceiling? Mia thought with a chill. She felt a little bit dizzy. She walked over to one of the windows and leaned against the frame, looking into the overgrown yard. A wave of nausea threatened to overwhelm her.

She looked down at Tandy and patted his head for reassurance.

"What's wrong with me, boy? What is it about this place?"

Maybe she would find out tonight when they conducted a proper investigation. There could be an electromagnetic field that was affecting her. After all, the physical symptoms were often reported at sites where the EMF readings were high.

Tandy whined and scratched at the window. Something moved outside. She glanced at the yard adjacent to the little plot of land. Something was there, moving in the wooded area near a tangle of bracken and dead trees. Then she saw the little girl in a dark cloak run across the yard. A rush of adrenaline shot through Mia's system. *What if the girl was real?* If she could just talk to her that would prove there was no ghost. Mia knocked on the window and the little girl stopped and looked up at her. Then she disappeared through the bushes and was gone.

Darn it, Mia thought to herself. Cindy must know the kid. She needed to find her. Either the Realtor was somewhere in the house or she'd left her phone behind. She tried dialing Cindy's number again.

A sharp ringtone echoed from downstairs. She hurried down the steps with Tandy at her heels. The ringing seemed to be coming from the kitchen.

"Cindy? Where are you?" Mia called out as she stepped into the room and swept her flashlight over the counter. "I can hear your phone."

Ring, ring, ring. Then the ringing stopped and there was just a low hum.

She halted in her tracks. The humming sound was coming from the mud room, the small alcove where Cindy had explained people took their muddy boots off. A few steps led down to a wide landing with two doors, one leading to the yard, the other to the garage. The garage door was open and the humming was coming from there. She took a step down and saw Cindy Moore's white Lexus inside the empty bay.

The motor was running.

Tandy crouched down and started to growl.

Mia swept her flashlight around and gasped. Cindy Moore was slumped over on the built-in bench, skin a livid shade of pink. The phone in her pocket lit up, then suddenly went dark.

Mia stumbled back, horrified. She felt as if she was going to pass out. Her muscles grew weak and numb as she realized what she was seeing.

Mia rushed down the last few steps and over to Cindy and shook her.

"Cindy! Wake up!" she said frantically.

She felt for a pulse, but there was nothing. Cindy Moore was dead, cold to the touch, lifeless.

CHAPTER THIRTEEN

Mia's heart pounded and she felt a wave of shock rush over her. Tandy whined and backed up the steps. Mia stared at Cindy's body, surrounded by muddy footprints. This could not be happening.

She just saw the woman yesterday! She'd been so full of life!

Mia stumbled back until she pressed against the wall and fumbled for her phone. She dialed 911 and got a recording asking her to hold for an operator.

As the recording played in her ear, she stared at Cindy Moore's lifeless body. She was dressed in a pristine suit and heels as if she were meeting a client. Mia glanced at Cindy's shoes. They were clean, with only the usual scuff marks. That was odd, Mia thought. Someone had tracked mud inside but it wasn't her.

Mia looked closer at the footprints, trying to identify if they were male or female, large or small, but they were so thick with mud and smeared she couldn't tell. They just looked vaguely foot shaped.

Then the low purr of the car engine caught her attention again.

Why was her car running in the garage?

Then it struck her, the running car and the bright pink skin—Cindy must have died of carbon monoxide poisoning.

Exactly like the Browder family.

"Nine-one-one, what's your emergency?" the operator said.

"I'm at five-fifty-five Elmswood Road, a woman is dead here," Mia said, her voice shaking. Her body tried to recoil from the reality of what she was seeing. Suicide? Had Cindy Moore left her car running on purpose? Why would she do that?

"Please stay on the line, ma'am. We're sending someone to your location. Can you tell me—" But even as Mia heard the words, her stomach twisted into a knot, cramping. She doubled over and felt sick.

Tandy started to bark, agitated. Mia looked at her dog's face and suddenly realized: carbon monoxide was colorless, odorless, and tasteless. If Cindy died of carbon monoxide poisoning, she had been breathing the same fumes for the last thirty minutes. No wonder she felt sick and lightheaded! The symptoms were headache, nausea, dizziness, blurred vision, and eventually loss of consciousness. Mia realized she was being poisoned, and Tandy was too!

Tandy barked again.

Mia ran to the garage door and gripped the handle with both hands, but her muscles suddenly felt weak. She pulled as hard as she could but the door wouldn't budge. She ran to the car to switch off the engine, but the Lexus was one of those keyless cars. She tried the handle, but it was locked. She would have to search through Cindy's bag and pockets to find the key-fob. But as Tandy started to bark louder and louder, Mia realized she needed to get out now before she passed out.

She ran back toward the front door and burst out of the house, before sinking onto the grass, out of breath. The moment she took a deep breath, she felt better. Slowly, her head started to clear.

Tandy sat down beside her and started licking her.

At that moment, an ambulance pulled up.

A pair of EMTs jumped out. They were both young, athletic, in their twenties; a man with a beard and a woman with dark hair pulled back into a ponytail. Mia pointed to the garage. Tandy stayed beside her as if on guard.

"She's dead," Mia said. "Her car is running in there."

"You were inside the house?" said the woman.

"Yes, but only for about thirty minutes," Mia said. "I'm fine."

"I'm going to check you out anyway," the woman said and retrieved some portable oxygen and an oximeter.

"It's okay," Mia said and petted Tandy as the EMT strapped the mask around Mia's face and read the numbers. Her partner put on a mask and disappeared into the house. After a few breaths of oxygen, Mia's residual dizziness and headache dissolved.

"Your blood oxygen level looks good," the woman said. "Just keep breathing through the mask for a few minutes."

"What about Tandy? Is he okay?"

The EMT check the dog's heartbeat and stroked his side.

"He's fine," she said. "You will be too. It's just a precaution."

The garage door opened and the male EMT stepped outside. Then a blue and white police Ford Explorer pulled up in front of the house and parked.

A tall middle-aged man climbed out of the car. Mia thought he looked familiar. She squinted into the sunlight, trying to figure out where she'd seen him before. He was heavyset, wearing a leather jacket and a white IZOD shirt over baggy jeans. A police badge hung around his neck, plainly visible. Despite his stocky build, he walked with a swagger. His hair was cut military style and peppered with gray.

"Hey, Janey. What've we got here?" the detective said, pulling on a pair of latex gloves. The EMTs and the cop conferred for a moment and disappeared back inside the garage. A few minutes later, the low hum of the white Lexus's engine shut off and Mia realized they'd found the key.

Mia suddenly knew where she'd seen the man. This was the detective on YouTube who interviewed Donnie Browder all those years ago—Detective Charlie Waite. He was older, heavier, but she recognized him just the same. He reemerged from the garage and approached Mia. He pulled off his gloves, revealing a wedding band.

"How's she doing, Janey?" Charlie Waite said to the EMT.

Janey walked back, checked Mia, and removed her mask.

"You'll be fine," she said and started packing up her equipment.

Mia took a deep breath, relieved to be given the all clear.

"She says she was only in there for thirty minutes," Janey told Waite. "It takes longer exposure for CO to reach a critical level."

"All right then," Charlie said. He petted Tandy, who accepted his presence readily. "I'm Detective Charlie Waite of the Swampscott PD, and you are?"

"Mia Bold." She got to her feet and brushed off her jeans. Tandy got up too and started acting less stressed, sniffing the lawn and getting back to his usual pursuits.

"Is that your car in there? The white Lexus?" Waite said.

"No, that belongs to the woman inside, Cindy Moore," Mia said, shaking her head. She felt an urge to cry and swallowed hard. "I guess she's dead?"

"Oh, she's dead, all right," Charlie Waite said. "This is a small town. Everyone knows Cindy. Anyone who doesn't has seen her posters. They're all over town. You aren't from around here, Ms. Bold. Are you a client of hers?"

Mia shook her head. "I work for a podcast. We're supposed to be filming here tonight."

"A podcast, huh? Have I heard of it?"

"*Bell, Book, and Candle*, out of Salem."

"Out of Salem, huh? Isn't a podcast like a radio show?"

"Yes, but we're filming a sample episode for a cable network," Mia said.

"What's the show about?" Waite said.

"We investigate haunted phenomena," Mia said.

"Ghost hunters, I see," Waite said. "So you're here to film a haunted house? I guess you picked this one because of the Browder incident?"

"Yes." Mia nodded. "Actually, I'm familiar with your history on the case."

"Then you know the gruesome details," Detective Waite said. "So what does that make you, Ms. Bold? Some kind of *tragedy tourist*?"

"No!" Mia said, shocked that Detective Waite would accuse her of such an awful thing. "My show, we investigate hauntings, that's all."

Listen, Ms. Bold. I'd like you to come down to the station for an hour or so to help me with my report."

"But I have to get back to—" Mia began to say.

"Maybe I phrased that wrong. I need you to come to the station *now*, so cancel your plans. Are we clear?"

"Of course," Mia said, alarmed by the way the detective was acting.

At that moment, the forensics van arrived. The technicians stepped out of the vehicle, dressed in disposable crime scene coveralls.

"Just wait here for a moment," Detective Waite said and disappeared to speak with the technicians. Mia petted Tandy and when she looked up again, Waite was making a phone call. He was in a heated exchange for a moment before hanging up.

Suddenly, Mia's predicament cut through the fog of shock. She had just been found alone with a dead body. That meant she was about to be dragged into a situation with the Swampscott police. And the Middletons were in town. After a few moments, Detective Waite headed back to Mia.

"Are you okay to drive?" he said.

"I think so," Mia said, feeling numb. She went to her car and let Tandy in the back. But as she slipped into the driver's seat and placed the key into the ignition, she realized she was shaking. The image of Cindy Moore erupted in her mind, eyes closed in her clean and pressed suit and heels.

Had she seemed like the type who would kill herself?

Then Mia remembered the muddy footprints.

Had someone else been there with her? Maybe someone had killed her? But why did they murder a real estate agent? And why did they use the same method as the Browder family?

Detective Charlie Waite pulled up beside her and flashed his lights, signaling her to follow him. As Mia pulled behind him, she knew that she was in deep trouble.

***

Mia pulled into the Swampscott Police Station next to Detective Waite's Ford Explorer. The station was exactly what you'd expect in a quiet little seaside town. The old building was made of brick and wood with the upper wooden siding painted a pale gray blue. The neighborhood was quaint, you could even say sleepy. An American flag was hoisted high on a flag pole in front of the building where a display of autumn gourds and dried corn stalks decorated the front entrance. The place looked more like an old city building than a police station. Mia checked her makeup in the mirror and wiped away a little smear of mascara as Charlie Waite approached her old Toyota.

"Go ahead and bring your dog in with you," Detective Waite said. Tandy's ears pricked up as Mia opened her door, stepped out, and pulled the seat forward. Tandy ran around the front of the station sniffing and marking his territory.

As Mia followed Charlie Waite inside, she checked her phone. There was a flood of texts and messages from Sylvie, Brynn, and her mother. But before she could read them, Detective Waite stopped her.

"Turn that off, please," Detective Waite said.

Mia did as she was told and switched off her phone.

Detective Waite held the door open and Mia walked inside the foyer.

"Come on, boy," Mia said and whistled for Tandy, who slipped through the door. Their footsteps echoed against the gray tiling as they passed the intake window where a cop was leaning back in her chair.

"Hey there, Charlie," a thin woman in uniform said.

"I hope you're having a good day, Ruthie," Waite said.

"Same old, same old," Ruthie said and buzzed them inside.

Mia heard the lock click into place behind her. Waite led her down a corridor and into an office with a lot of security cameras and a pair of officers monitoring them. The officers petted Tandy as he walked past, wagging his tail. Waite tossed the keys to the Ford Explorer onto the desk of a fellow officer.

"Thanks, Tom," Waite said, steering Mia toward his office.

"So, what happened?" Tom said, glancing at Mia with interest.

"Cindy Moore's dead," Detective Waite said. Mia caught out of her peripheral vision that something passed between them.

"That's a shame," Tom said, suddenly losing all curiosity while keeping an eye on Mia, who was growing more uncomfortable with every step.

Detective Waite must have been on the phone to his people while we were driving to the station, Mia realized. Even she had to admit, Cindy Moore dying the same way as the Browder murders was incredibly suspicious. And once the police checked Mia's Google search history, they'd find all her research centered around the Browder murders and Charlie Waite.

Tandy looked up at her with big eyes as if he were reading her thoughts.

Yes, boy, we're in trouble, she thought. Mia prayed she would get through this police report without the unnerving possibility of being tangled up with the police while trying to cope with Middleton madness.

Detective Waite led Mia into an office and offered her a chair before slipping behind his desk. There were pictures of his family covering every spare space. Mia sat down and Tandy settled down beside her.

"Are those your kids?" Mia said, pointing to some picture frames with little children on the beach playing.

"My grandkids," Detective Waite said. "My kids are all grown. You?"

"Kids? No," Mia said. "At least not yet."

Waite slipped a sheet of paper down in front of her.

"Do you mind writing down what happened?" Waite said. "I'll just go get us some coffee."

"Sure," Mia said and scribbled out what she remembered from the moment she arrived at the Elmswood House.

Charlie returned with two coffees, but instead of settling at his desk he nodded toward one of the interrogation rooms.

"Do you mind if we discuss this in a conference room?" Waite said. "Officer Brent here will watch your dog, won't you, Tom?"

"Sure," Tom Brent said and called Tandy over to pet him.

This was a sign that things were taking a turn for the worse. Interrogation rooms had one-way glass where suspects were brought for observation. They also had hidden camera to record every word and reaction during an interview. That was where you took someone when you thought they may have committed a crime.

Detective Waite let Mia into the interrogation room. Then he settled heavily in a chair facing Mia across a white expanse of table. He pushed a coffee over to her and Mia pushed her statement across the table.

He read the statement with interest, as Mia looked at the one-way glass and wondered who was watching them. Maybe Tom Brent, the cop he'd given the weird look to. The interrogation room was bleak and designed to put pressure on the suspect.

"How do you know Cindy Moore?" Detective Waite asked.

"One of my producers arranged for us to film at the Elmswood House. I just met Cindy yesterday," Mia said.

"Did you arrange to meet her today?"

"No, I mean I was trying to find her. We were supposed to be filming tonight."

"So why'd you show up early?" Charlie Waite said casually. But when Mia looked at his eyes, they were hawklike, steady, and piercing.

"Pardon me?" Mia said. "You mean to the Elmswood House?"

"That's right. It says here you were going to film in the evening. So, why'd you show up in the afternoon?"

"Well," Mia began reluctantly, "I was confronting my fears."

"Your fears?" Charlie said gruffly. "What kind of fears?"

"We visited the house before and I had a bad reaction. So I wanted to get that reaction under control before—"

"Before you started your ghost hunt? What are you going to be hunting exactly? The poor dead wife and kids of Donnie Browder?"

Now Mia's discomfort moved up an octave. The questioning was borderline hostile. Was this a knee-jerk cop thing, or did Detective Charlie Waite believe she was involved with the death of Cindy Moore?

The phone rang and Detective Waite picked up the phone.

"Uh-huh, really? I see. Well, what time? Ballpark is fine. Okay." Waite hung up the phone and stared at Mia. "I've just had some interesting news."

"Yes, what's that?" Mia said.

"Cindy Moore died last night, around eleven p.m."

"Oh my God," Mia said. "Her body was in the house all that time? That's awful."

"Where were you last night, Ms. Bold?" Detective Waite said coldly.

Mia felt her stomach drop. There it was. Waite wanted her alibi. She thought back and realized she was home alone the entire night. There were no witnesses and no record of her whereabouts. She had plenty of time to drive to Swampscott and kill Cindy Moore.

"At home—alone," Mia said.

"Did you text anyone? Email them?"

"I did some research early in the evening before going to bed."

"On what exactly?" Waite said.

"Um, my dad. And stuff I needed to know for the shoot," Mia said.

"What stuff?" Waite said, leaning forward and staring at her.

Mia knew there was no point hiding anything. Detective Waite was going to find out one way or the other. She looked him in the eye and folded her hands.

"The history of the Elmswood House," Mia said matter-of-factly.

"How much do you know about the Browder family murders?" Waite said.

"I know that Donnie Browder killed his wife and children by carbon monoxide poisoning."

"Yep. The exact same way Cindy Moore died," Waite said.

"Yes, it does seem strange," Mia said.

"Anything else you want to tell me?" Waite said.

Mia turned her coffee cup in a circle.

"I saw you interview Donnie Browder on YouTube," Mia said.

"Huh," Waite said and scribbled something in his pad. "What did you do after all that research?"

"I went to bed and read a book." The moment the words came out of her mouth she recognized the weakness in her alibi.

"Strange? Do you want to know what I think? I think you have an unhealthy fascination with the history of this house. Now I find you at the scene where a woman has died in the exact same way as the notorious murder that took place on the premises? Tell me, what am I supposed to think?"

Mia's heart began to race and she could feel herself perspiring. There was something about the way Detective Charlie Waite looked at her that made her afraid. To him, she was just some random nut job who knew way too much about that house and the Browder murders. Once they found her history of incriminating Google searches, they would have a pretty good case.

She wished she had never come near that Elmswood House.

"Listen, Mia," Waite said in a foreboding voice. "Believe me when I tell you, I'm going to find out exactly what happened here. But you could save me a lot of trouble. Now, is there something you want to tell me?"

Mia suddenly felt like a deer in the headlights. Maybe Detective Waite was just searching for answers, but she was starting to feel bullied. How could a day that started off in an attempt to face her fears spiral into such a total nightmare?

Suddenly, there was a knock on the interrogation room door. It opened and Mia looked up in shock.

"What are you doing here?" she gasped.

CHAPTER FOURTEEN

Standing in the doorway was Detective Clayton Landry of the Salem PD, a formidable cop with a razor-sharp mind. Mia was astonished at his appearance in the Swampscott police station. Then she remembered that Detective Waite had called someone while they were at the Elmswood House. No doubt he'd checked up on her during his drive to the station.

"To answer your question, Ms. Bold, Charlie here called me to verify your identity," Landry said. "He knew I'd be familiar with you and *Bell, Book, and Candle*."

"I didn't tell you to come down here, Clayton," Waite said, disgruntled.

"No, but I thought you could use my help," Landry said. "After all, Swampscott and Salem have a long-standing agreement to help each other, don't we?"

"That's true," Waite said reluctantly. "Well, since you've come all this way, have a seat."

Mia was relieved to see the familiar Salem detective. Even though she'd had brushes with the law in the past, and even been pulled in by Landry for questioning, she'd found him to be both rigorous and fair. He had always told her the truth and she trusted him. And at this point, it was clear she needed some help.

She examined Waite's reaction. He was clearly surprised to see Detective Landry too, which Mia supposed was a sign in her favor.

"Thanks, Charlie," Landry said and stepped into the interrogation room. He was dressed sharply in a gray fitted suit with a scarlet muffler thrown over one shoulder of a camel coat, as if he'd been caught off duty. He faced the Swampscott detective, who he obviously had some kind of history with, and smiled. His gray eyes, striking against his tawny skin, gave nothing away.

"Is that how they dress down in New Orleans?" Detective Waite said. "You look like you walked out of a fancy magazine."

"I was at a reception at the Salem Athenaeum," Landry said as the two cops shook hands. "I took an Uber over here."

"You didn't need to drop your plans and come all this way," Waite said, testily. "I just needed one little piece of information."

"No trouble," Landry said. "Mia? How are you?"

"I've been better," Mia said, hands folded in her lap. The starkness of the room had done its work. She wanted to be anywhere but the bleak, featureless box of the Swampscott interrogation room. Waite didn't realize it, but Mia wanted to find out what happened to Cindy Moore as much as he did. And to do that she needed to get out of this room. If anyone could free her, it was Detective Landry, but Mia wasn't sure of his motivation. Ironically, he had put her through similar interrogations in the past.

Detective Landry took off his camel coat and folded it carefully over a chair before taking a seat at the interrogation table. He looked at Charlie Waite like a chess player waiting for the next move.

"So, you wanted to know about *Bell, Book, and Candle*?" Landry said.

"Yes, Ms. Bold here claims to work for that outfit," Waite said.

"That's correct. Bell, Book, and Candle is a production company that set up shop in Salem a few months ago. They've filmed at a number of locations, including the Black Cat Inn and the House of the Sea Witch. Good for the tourist trade. I'm sure you already realize they're ghost hunters."

"Uh-huh, well, we've got a situation here," Charlie Waite said as he pushed his chair back from the table.

"What kind of situation?" Landry said.

"One of our local real estate agents, Cindy Moore, turned up dead today and Ms. Bold here was at the scene," Waite said.

Landry took that in for a moment. Then he glanced at Mia.

"You found her?" Landry said.

"I did," Mia said. "It was awful."

"How did she die?" Landry said.

"The labs aren't back yet but it looks like carbon monoxide poisoning," Waite said.

Landry weighed the situation, choosing his words carefully.

"Not to disrespect the dead," Landry said in a measured tone. "But carbon monoxide poisoning is a pretty common way for people to commit suicide. Is there some reason you think this death is suspicious, Charlie?" Landry said with a measured tone.

As Mia observed the two of them, she realized that Landry was treating Waite like he was a dangerous snake.

Detective Waite leaned back in his chair casually, but despite the appearance he was cultivating, Mia could sense the tension in the air. She'd already seen how tricky Detective Waite could be.

"Well, let's see, time of death is approximately eleven p.m. last night and Ms. Bold has no alibi. It took place at the old Browder house. She knows all about the Browder case. The current victim, Cindy Moore, died in the exact same manner," Waite said.

"Do you mind if I look at what you've got so far?"

"Be my guest," Waite said, sliding a file across the table.

Landry picked it up and leafed through the police report and Mia's statement. He seemed to turn the facts over in his mind.

Mia started to wonder about the relationship between the two cops. They seemed a little prickly, as if they were rivals.

Finally, Landry closed the file and stood up.

"Come on, Mia, I'll take you back to Salem."

"Hold on there," Detective Waite said. "I'm not done questioning her."

"Come on, Charlie, you've got nothing and we both know it."

For a moment Charlie Waite tensed up. Then he smiled and spread open his hands in a diplomatic gesture.

"All right, all right, I can call Ms. Bold in again. After all, you said you were going to help me on this case, right?" Waite stared at Landry, as if challenging him to answer.

"Sure I will, Charlie. Whatever you need. I'll nose around Salem for you, talk to witnesses, you name it."

"And you'll take responsibility for her? If I need to question her again you'll bring her in?"

"Absolutely," Landry said. "I'll keep an eye on her."

"Well then, I'll send you the files, Detective," Waite said. "What's that old saying about keeping your frenemies close? Anyway, let me walk you out."

Mia felt a deep sense of relief as they headed back into the squad room. Tandy ran over and jumped up excitedly, dancing in circles as Waite led them all out of the station and into the parking lot.

"Have a nice day now," Charlie Waite said as he watched them walk over to Mia's old Toyota. "And don't leave town, Ms. Bold.

Clayton here is risking his job by vouching for you. I'd hate to see him lose his badge."

"Good to see you too, Charlie." Landry saluted before walking around to the driver's side.

"Give me the keys," Landry said. "You've had a shock."

Mia tossed her keys to him and let Tandy in the back seat. Then she slipped into the passenger seat.

"Thanks," Mia said.

"It's not over yet," Landry said as he adjusted the seat. "Charlie Waite has your scent and he's not going to give up easily." He started the ignition and pulled the Toyota into the sunny street with a sense of command that put Mia at ease immediately. Tandy stuck his head out the back window so that his ears fluttered in the wind and his tongue lolled. He was happy to be on the move.

"How do you know Detective Waite?" Mia said.

"Charlie's famous around these parts. As I'm sure you know, he was the detective on the Browder family murders. He got Donnie Browder to confess."

"I saw that interrogation on YouTube," Mia said. "Can I ask why you came all the way to Swampscott to answer his question?"

"I have my reasons," Landry said mysteriously. "Why don't you tell me why you went to your haunted location early when you weren't due to film until tonight?"

Mia sank back in her seat. The silence in the car lingered until it grew awkward. She supposed it was too much to hope that she would be able to get out of explaining herself in to Detective Landry. He was detail oriented and had just made a promise to a rival cop to keep an eye on her. She decided she might as well save time and jump in feet first.

"I was facing my fears," Mia said. "It's hard to explain."

"Your fears? That's not like you," Landry said, adjusting the rearview mirror slightly. "What were you afraid of exactly"

"The Elmswood House," Mia said.

"Why?" Landry said, baffled. "When it comes to the paranormal, you're a seasoned investigator."

"This is going to sound crazy, but I had a nightmare about that place," Mia said. She looked at Landry nervously but he didn't flinch. A seriousness had crept into his demeanor.

"What kind of nightmare?" Landry said.

Mia was reluctant to go any further. She'd always been a skeptic who kept an open mind. Since moving to Salem her beliefs had been challenged by a series of paranormal encounters. But confessing her dream about dead people to a police detective was pushing her nerves to the limit.

"Listen, Mia, I'm from New Orleans, remember?" Landy said. "I'm more open to the supernatural than you think. Tell me what you saw."

Mia took a deep breath and steeled herself. Landry would know all about the Browder case so there was no way to be vague. She had to assume he'd seen all the material she had seen, and then some.

"In the dream, I was at the Elmswood House. There was an open field covered in snow. Then I saw a little girl—*Lydia*. She was trying to tell me something."

"The same entity Donnie Browder encountered," Landry said matter-of-factly.

Mia turned bright red and looked down at her hands, but Landry didn't flinch. She wondered what he was thinking. Most people would never let this kind of exchange fly, but Landry seemed thoughtful, almost solemn.

"Then I saw the Browder family. They cried out for help."

"And you being a skeptic." Landry smiled.

"I know it's probably my subconscious mind. But there's something awful about that house. So that's why I came early, I needed to face my fear."

"Listen, Mia, my great-aunt was a mambo, a fully initiated Vodou priestess. She would have said you have *Prizdezye*, the ability to 'see.' So why go there alone? Why ignore your instincts?"

"I didn't want people to see me scared."

"You mean your co-host, Johnny Astor?" Landry said.

That observation was cutting things a bit close. Was she that transparent? The truth was, she often tried to measure up against Johnny Astor. He was always so calm and collected and charming. And for some stupid reason, she cared what he thought about her.

"I suppose so. He's so good on camera, I wanted to get past my own reaction."

"Do you mind if I see the house for myself?" Landry said, turning down Elmswood without warning.

"Go ahead," Mia said and sank down into her seat. A feeling of dread rose up in her immediately.

Landry turned onto Elmswood Road and pulled up in front of the house. Tandy growled. The forensic crew was gone but the crime scene tape was still up across the garage. Landy stepped out of the car and crossed the street. Mia let Tandy out and followed him.

They stood side by side as the Elmswood House loomed above them.

"So, this is the place?" Landry said, staring up at the steep angles, the crumbling wood, and the peeling paint. Everything was very quiet, no sound of birds or squirrels, just silence. Mia felt fear seep in like a fog. The urge to leave was overwhelming.

"I see what you mean," Landry said. "This place scares me too."

Mia realized she had better get back to Salem ASAP.

"Would you mind taking me to the Bell, Book, and Candle production office?" Mia said. "I need to warn them not to come here."

"You do that," Landry said, eyeing the house as if it might move. They both got back in the car and drove away as fast as they could.

CHAPTER FIFTEEN

The *Bell, Book, and Candle* crew was bustling in and out of the production office building, packing equipment in the van. Tandy stared at his friends across the street and started to wag his tail.

Detective Landry parked Mia's Toyota and turned off the engine. Mia was relieved to be back in Salem after such a shocking morning.

"Thanks again for getting me out of there," Mia said.

"Are you sure you're going to be all right?" Landry said.

"Why wouldn't I be?" Mia said.

"Maybe because you're in shock?" Landy said.

"I'll be fine, really," Mia said, scanning her latest message from Brynn incredulously. She'd pulled her phone out of her jacket and switched on the ringer. A dozen notifications appeared on the screen. Sylvie had tried to reach her and Brynn had left half a dozen texts.

The Middletons were in full pest mode.

Graham Stone made reservations for tomorrow night.

Mom can't wait to meet him!

Mia stared at the message in shock. How had Graham gotten their number? Any hope of squirming out of his ridiculous dinner was fading fast. She shoved her phone back in her pocket and shook her head.

"I think you are avoiding things," Detective Landry said.

"It's just—my parents are in town. Being hauled into the Swampscott police station was the last thing I needed."

"Listen, Mia. Don't give Charlie Waite a reason to focus on you, okay?" Landry said and held out the car keys. "You have no alibi, so things could get dicey."

"If you say so, Detective," Mia said. She reached out to take the keys, but Landy pulled his hand back.

"Now that I have your full attention, I want you to promise me something." Landry stared at her with cool, gray eyes.

"What?" Mia said.

"I know you'll try and investigate Cindy Moore's death, so don't deny it,"

Mia bit her lip. Landry knew her only too well. In order to protect herself and the production company, she needed to find out what happened.

"I might dig around a little," she said finally.

"Listen, Mia, you're very independent, I get that. But the fact is you've come pretty close to getting yourself killed in the past."

"I'm listening," Mia said, knowing full well every word he said was true.

Landry looked at her with a serious, steady gaze.

"If you get any leads, I want you to tell me, understood? Text me, ring me, whatever. Even though Charlie has invited me to work on this case, I have to tread carefully. Understand? But I can look into it in a limited way and I can advise you."

"Fair enough," Mia said. "Anything else?"

"Next time you go to a graveyard or the Devil's Swamp, don't go alone."

"How did you know I went to the Devil's Swamp?" Mia said, startled. "Besides, I had Tandy."

"I have my ways," Landry said. "And one more thing. Listen to your instincts. Supernatural or not, your instincts are always trying to tell you something. People who ignore their instincts end up dead."

Detective Landy tossed her the keys and stepped out of the car.

"Okay, Detective," Mia said. "And thanks."

"We'll be in touch," Landry said and walked down the street.

Mia watched him disappear around the corner before getting out of the car. She held the door open for Tandy, who jumped out and sniffed the area.

Jake, Will, and Sylvie were packing equipment in the production van for the night's shoot. Graham Stone and Ollie Cooper were on the front steps on their cell phones. Johnny Astor was MIA as usual.

Sylvie spotted Mia and waved.

Tandy waited for Mia at the curb. She looked both ways and crossed the street. "Come on, boy," Mia said.

"Where have you been? I was trying to reach you all afternoon," Sylvie said. Tandy rushed up to greet her and she petted his furry head.

"The cops made me switch off my phone," Mia said quietly.

"*The cops?*" Sylvie whispered. "What now?"

"I better tell everyone at the same time," Mia said.

Tandy trotted over to his familiar pack of people, greeting Jake and Will, who were running up and down the steps.

"Come on, Proctor! Time for your workout," Jake said, handing him a heavy case. Mia hated to interrupt them, but it had to be done.

"Hey, guys? There's something I have to tell you," Mia said.

But instead of listening, Graham and Ollie stared at their phones and Jake and Will started bickering over some lights and how to fit them in the van.

Suddenly a sharp whistle cut through the air. Tandy sat up straight at attention, followed by every member of his human tribe.

"Listen up!" Sylvie said. "Mia has an announcement!"

The office door swung open and Albee Abernathy stepped out of the production office, dressed in his gothic Charnel Tours outfit. Mia cringed; she had totally forgotten about the fact he was going to brief the entire crew about the Elmswood House. For once she actually wanted to hear what he had to say, even though his attentions made her crazy.

The moment Albee saw Mia, he broke into a grin and waved at her.

"Hey, Mia," he said, enthusiastically.

"I don't have all day here, what did you want to tell us?" Graham said, covering his mouthpiece. "I'm on the phone to LA!"

"Hush," Ollie said. "Let her speak."

Mia really did not want to explain the whole awful story of finding Cindy Moore. Not only was her death sad and horrifying, but the fact Mia found her was tricky to explain, especially with both the Swampscott police involved and now Detective Landry. She would just have to keep it as brief as possible.

"The shoot is off," Mia said loudly.

They stared at her as a hush fell over the group.

"For goodness' sake, why?" Ollie Cooper said.

"Yeah, why?" Graham said.

Jake and Will put down the equipment they were carrying and everyone stared at her, waiting. Now she would have to tell them everything.

Tandy looked from person to person, aware that they were all acting a little odd. Mia took a deep breath and braced herself. "Well. Because—"

"*—Cindy Moore was found dead*," said a silky, masculine voice.

To Mia's surprise and relief, Johnny Astor stepped up out of the shadows. Tandy trotted over to him and licked his hand.

"*Dead?*" Graham said, stunned. "Listen, I'll call you back." He hung up the phone and stared at Johnny. "She was fine yesterday. Are you sure?"

"I just got a call from a Swampscott detective named Charlie Waite," Johnny said. "He wanted to know where I was last night. Apparently, they found Cindy dead at the house—carbon monoxide poisoning."

"I'm so sorry, Graham," Mia said. "I know she was your friend."

Mia was relieved Johnny had just saved her from telling everyone the gruesome details of what happened, and that she had found the body. He had just bought her some time.

"I can't believe Cindy is dead," Graham said, stricken and confused. He looked down at his feet, not sure what to do. Even his cheerful, powder blue leisure suit couldn't lift his mood.

"That's the same way the Browder family died," Albee noted.

"All right," Ollie said, shaking his head. "Unpack the van. We have half a dozen advertisers who've bought time on the show. I don't know what we're going to do now."

"Poor Cindy, she didn't seem like the type," Graham said. "We were so close to a deal, everything depended on this episode." He trudged back up the office steps and disappeared inside.

There was a flurry of activity as Jake and Will started to unpack the van and haul the equipment back inside the building.

Johnny stepped closer to Mia until his arm brushed against hers. A tingling sensation passed along her skin as she looked up into his deep, hazel eyes.

Oh my gosh, he knows! she realized.

Detective Waite must have told him everything, about how she had found the body. This wasn't a coincidence—Johnny was protecting her.

"Thank you," Mia whispered, leaning against him.

"I've got your back," Johnny whispered. "They'll find out you discovered her body eventually, but maybe I can help you."

Seeing the secretive whisper between Mia and Johnny, Sylvie walked over and joined the cabal, leaning in close and petting Tandy.

"Okay, you two, what's going on?" Sylvie whispered.

"I went to the Elmswood House today," Mia said. "I found Cindy *dead*, it was awful."

"No way!" Sylvie said. "Why would you go there?"

"It's a long story, I'll tell you later."

"Listen, Mia, that detective asked a lot of questions about you," Johnny said. "I think you're a suspect."

"Oh no," Sylvie said. "Not again!"

"I was at the scene and I have no alibi for last night, when she died," Mia said. "I only got out of there because Detective Landry kind of rescued me."

"Detective Landry saved you?" Sylvie said. "How ironic."

Mia didn't want to alarm Sylvie, but Landry had only managed to buy her some time. If she didn't solve Cindy's murder soon, she might end up in jail herself. Whether or not the supernatural was involved in Cindy's tragic death, she had to dig deeper, starting with the Elmswood House. And she could think of one person in Salem who was likely to know everything about that house—the biggest history nerd of all—Albee Abernathy.

"Listen, I'll tell you everything, but first we need to see what Albee Abernathy knows about that house."

"I thought you hated that crazy warlock," Sylvie said.

"I don't *hate* him, he just seems—"

"—lovesick?" Johnny said.

"According to Love Addicts Anonymous, he has all the signs," Sylvie said.

At that moment Albee Abernathy walked down the steps, his eyes bright, heading directly for Mia. Tandy's hackles rose slightly and he lowered his head, suspicious of Albee.

"Bummer about the shoot," Albee said. "I was really looking forward to the briefing. See you guys around—"

"You can't leave," Mia said.

"I can't?" Albee said, confused.

"I was so looking forward to your presentation," Mia said.

"You were? *Wow.*" A smile spread across Albee's pasty face as he stared at Mia, hope rekindled.

They all walked back into the office. Tandy sidestepped every time Albee moved in a suspicious way. Inside the office, the conference table was clean and ready to be used. Albee opened up his bag and took out some sheets of paper before passing a map to Johnny and Mia.

"What are you doing?" Graham said.

"We want to hear Albee's presentation," Johnny said.

"What's the point?" Graham said. "With Cindy dead, we can't access the property."

"Not necessarily," Johnny said. "After all, someone owns the Elmswood House. We can contact them. But first, let's see what we're dealing with."

"All right," Ollie Cooper said. "Let's hear what Albee has to say. Jake, can you set up the cameras? We might as well film this in case we ever do the show."

Jake and Will set up the cameras, lights, and sound equipment as Sylvie placed her computer on one of the desks and leaned back in a chair with a pair of headphones perched on her head. Tandy sat next to Sylvie. He was used to waiting while the crew filmed. There was a sense of relief, to have something to do instead of trying to figure out their next move. They all retreated out of the shot leaving only Mia and Johnny facing Albee.

Sylvie gave a thumbs-up to Graham, who was acting as the director.

"Action," Graham said.

"The Elmswood House has an unusually high number of ghosts," Albee began. "A terrible tragedy occurred there in the 1980s. But the area has an even darker history, which I will reveal to you now."

CHAPTER SIXTEEN

The cameras rolled as Albee Abernathy cleared his throat and tugged at his gothic sleeves. For some reason Mia wasn't nervous. Being filmed paled in comparison to the earlier events of the day. A steely calm stole over her. One camera was recording a steady shot of Albee, while Jake was poised, ready to zoom in on Mia's and Johnny's reaction shots. Sylvie was engrossed in her monitor as they filmed

"These maps illustrate the haunted areas of the Elmswood House," Albee said, pointing to the drawings sitting on the table before Mia and Johnny.

Mia kept her eyes slightly turned down so that her reaction was a little muted. She had to admit, she didn't really trust herself. Even though she was far away from the Elmswood House, the place had a way of getting to her. The last thing she wanted was the camera to catch her at a moment of weakness.

Out of the corner of her eye, she saw Tandy lying with his head on his paws, keeping watch over her.

"The first thing people think of when they tour the Elmswood house is the infamous Browder family murders," Albee began. "I've placed red X's where the bodies of the wife and two boys were found—and blue X's for the ghost sightings. As you can see, the locations match."

"Most of the sightings are in the upper bedrooms," Johnny said.

"And in the yard and woods around the house," Albee said. "There's an old abandoned playground, grown over to one side of the house."

Mia struggled to keep her breathing measured. She tried not to think about Lydia and all the unanswered questions she brought up.

"Most of the sightings were recorded by the Carol family," Albee said. "The couple that moved into the house within a year of the tragedy."

"Connie and Dean Carol?" Mia said.

"Yes, Dean reported seeing a number of ghosts and even took a famous photo of a child peeking out from behind a hedge."

He passed the photo around the table. Mia picked up the photo and felt a creepy sensation waft through her limbs. The ghostly face of Lydia looked out from behind some bushes. She felt her heart speed up.

"But this isn't Todd or Bobby," Mia said. "Who is she?"

"An older ghost," Albee said and grinned, giving his face a sinister appearance.

Mia stared at the ghostly young girl with a growing sense of dread.

"How much older?" Johnny Astor said.

"There are only theories," Albee said, tracing a bony finger over the picture. "I believe this is a seventeenth-century ghost—Lydia Humphrey."

Mia immediately recognized the name. Finally, all that research she'd done was paying off.

"Are you talking about one of the daughters of John Humphrey?" Mia said. "The first deputy governor of the Massachusetts Bay Colony under John Winthrop?"

"The same," Albee said. "The governor was one of Swampscott's most prominent citizens. He built a house in sixteen forty that still stands to this day."

"The oldest house in Swampscott, located on Paradise Road?" Johnny said. "What does the Humphrey House have to do with the haunting on Elmswood?"

Mia had to admit she was impressed with Johnny. He had really held his end up on the research lately.

"An excellent question." Albee grinned, flicking back his dark hair.

The more Mia got to know Albee, the more she realized he was less of a warlock and more of an occult nerd.

"Well?" Mia said, frustrated by his theatrics. "What *is* the connection?"

"The Humphrey house wasn't *always* located on Paradise Road," Albee said. "The house was moved in eighteen ninety-one."

"*Moved?*" Johnny repeated. "How is that possible?"

"When Swampscott developed the Olmsted District, they wanted to preserve the town's history so they used a wide, flat platform pulled by a team of horses to move the Humphrey House to Paradise Road."

"Where was the house originally located?" Mia asked.

"*Elmswood Road*," Albee said and held up a photocopy.

Mia stared at the picture in shock. The fear she had felt earlier roared back to life. In the center of a snowy field stood the house Mia had seen in her dream. The one Lydia had pointed to through the fence. The house that stood alone in a field of snow behind a gnarled old tree.

"You think Lydia Humphrey is haunting the original site of her family home?" Mia said. "Why would she do that?"

"John Humphrey abandoned some of his children in the colony. The story goes they were preyed upon by the unscrupulous. Lydia Humphrey, who was baptized in Salem, went slowly mad. She disappeared from history, but legend has it she wandered into the snow and was never seen again. Right here, on Elmswood Road." Albee held the picture up for the camera.

Suddenly Mia felt sick. Was she seeing ghosts? Or maybe she was going mad like Donnie Browder. She felt overwhelmed, unable to let go of her skeptical side but also unable to deny that she'd seen a little girl in a cloak on the property, or that she had dreamed of the Humphrey House and Lydia.

Mia put on a brave face and tried not to think about her fears.

"Amazing work, Albee," Mia said. "What do you think, Johnny?"

"I say it's time we explore the Elmswood House," Johnny said.

"Cut!" Graham said. "That was fantastic!" He turned to Ollie. "We've got to find a way to get onto that property. Did you see how great that was?"

"I'll see if I can track down Connie Carol," Ollie said, nodding in agreement. "Good work."

Mia pushed her hands against the table, fighting back the sick feeling. Tandy darted over to where she was sitting and started licking her hand and arm.

"Mia? Will you step outside with me?" Johnny said.

"Yes, thanks," Mia said. Johnny was clearly aware she wasn't feeling well.

Sylvie nodded toward Johnny. "I'll be out in a minute," she said, concerned for Mia.

Johnny took Mia's arm and guided her through the front door with Tandy trotting behind. Outside the sun was setting as Mia sank down on the stone steps. Tandy sat on one side of her and Johnny on the other.

"What happened in there?" Johnny said. "I saw the way you reacted."

"I'm not sure," Mia said. "Some of the things he said got to me."

"I've seen you like this before," Johnny said. "That night at Howard Street Cemetery and the day we went to the Elmswood House. What happened that day anyway?"

"I saw something I can't explain," Mia said.

Johnny reached over and tipped up her chin until she was looking at him.

"You have to trust me, Mia," Johnny said. He looked at her with a strange intensity that both thrilled her and made her feel like she was being pulled into something against her will. But there was also something in the way he looked at her that cut through her fear. She did trust Johnny, so as hard as it was, she was going to be honest with him.

"Okay then, I saw her," Mia said.

"Who?" Johnny said.

"Lydia Humphrey."

"You saw the ghost in the picture?"

"Yes," Mia said. "And I'm afraid I'm going to see her again."

***

Johnny, Sylvie, and Mia walked back to the Essex Street apartment building. Tandy was happy to be in familiar territory and was delicately cataloguing each scent along the path to Hatter's Emporium. The streets were filled with tourists buying mementos of their witchy stay in Salem and the air smelled of popcorn, syrup, and almonds.

"Hold on a second," Sylvie said. "I have to get some caramel corn."

As Sylvie got in line, Mia glanced at Johnny. He was deep in thought, brows knitted slightly together.

"I know you don't want to admit it," Johnny said, stepping closer to Mia. "But I'm starting to think you're a sensitive."

"A sensitive?" Mia said. "What do you mean by that?"

"Someone who can sense the astral plane, you know, like Hazel Prophet."

"Me? Are you kidding?" Mia said, shocked. "I'm a skeptic."

"Listen, Mia, this is the second time you've *seen* ghosts."

"Just because I saw a kid running through the backyard into an overgrown area," Mia said, "it doesn't prove she was Lydia Humphrey. The whole thing could be a coincidence."

"What local kid wears a cloak?" Sylvie said, holding a bag of fresh caramel corn. She offered some to Mia and Johnny and they each took a handful of the salty sweet crunchy concoction. "You've got to admit, Mia, the fact you keep seeing things is weird. And the girl in your dream called herself Lydia."

"Yes," Mia said. "But I might have read about Lydia Humphrey somewhere. My mind could have pieced it all together."

"At least be open to the possibility you're sensitive," Johnny insisted, protectively. His voice unleashed a flock of butterflies in her stomach.

"I promise to keep an open mind," Mia said, trying to ignore the nervous sensation Johnny always seemed to ignite in her.

"Being a skeptic in Salem is hard work," Sylvie said. "Why don't you just cut to the chase and say yes, ghosts exist and you're psychic."

"Are you insane? And abandon all reason?" Mia said. "Never!"

"Never say never," Johnny said and they all laughed together. It felt good to be with her friends after such a horrible and shocking start to her day.

"It was so awful to find Cindy at that rundown house," Mia said. "She was dressed in a suit, skin bright red, not breathing, and her car was running in the garage. Who could have killed her?"

"Well, I don't believe it was a suicide," Johnny said.

"Did she have enemies?" Sylvie wondered.

"We should find out," Mia said. "According to Detective Waite of Swampscott PD, everyone in town knew her. He wasn't buying the suicide angle either. The day we walked through the house, Cindy mentioned she was going to meet a client who would solve all her problems—Mr. Fat Cat. Remember?"

"Oh yeah, how can we find out who that was?" Johnny said.

"I actually have an idea about that," Mia said and pulled a skeleton key out of her pocket. "Cindy's partner Doug Tanner gave me this key. I think I should return it tomorrow and try to take a look at Cindy's appointment book."

"I'm in," Sylvie said. "Let's do it."

Tandy jumped up and wagged his tail, just before Mia's phone rang.

"Good boy, look who's psychic now?" Mia laughed as her sister Brynn's picture lit up the screen. "I better take this. Brynn? Sorry I didn't get back to you sooner—"

"Mimi! Where have you been? Something terrible has happened." On the other end of the phone, Brynn was nearly breathless and clearly upset.

"What?" Mia said, disturbed by the intensity in her sister's voice. "What's going on? Where are you?"

"I'm at the Salem Inn," Brynn said. "Jeffrey's been attacked!"

CHAPTER SEVENTEEN

"Attacked? By whom?" Mia said. She could tell Brynn was in a state because her voice always went up an octave when she was stressed out.

"By this stupid room! I need you here now," Brynn said frantically.

"All right, we're just down the block," Mia said. "We'll be there in five minutes." Mia shoved the phone in her pocket as Tandy started jumping around.

"What's going on?" Sylvie said.

"Brynn's in trouble. She's staying at the Salem Inn—Room Seventeen."

"*Room seventeen?*" Johnny said. "But that's the haunted room."

"That's just down the block, let's go," Sylvie said, shoving the caramel corn into her bag. Then Sylvie started running and all Johnny and Mia could do was try and keep up. Tandy couldn't believe his luck and sprang after Sylvie, leaping over any obstacle. They passed Hatter's Emporium and Tom Hatter, the owner and Graham Stone's father. The old man waved as they ran past.

"Where's the fire?" he called out from the doorway.

"We're meeting Mia's sister," Sylvie yelled.

"Will is upstairs putting up that cat run," he yelled.

Mia gave a thumbs-up as they shot past the Emporium and another half a block. By the time they reached the red brick building with white columns, they were all breathing hard. The black sign hanging above the door featured a golden pineapple surrounded by gold letters which spelled out *The Salem Inn*.

Sylvie held the door open as Mia burst into the sleepy inn and ran up to the desk where a clerk looked up, startled. He was dressed casually, sleeves rolled up, sorting through a stack of mail. Mia skidded to a halt in front of him.

"I'm here to see Brynn Middleton," Mia said.

"There's no one by that name here," the clerk said.

"I mean Brynn Middleton *Costa,*" Mia corrected herself. Until this moment, she had thoroughly forgotten all about her brother-in-law.

Jeffrey Costa was a slight man, not very tall, with a short man's complex. He would have been handsome if he weren't so mean. He was someone Mia didn't like to think about. She was convinced he was out to get her.

"What room?" the clerk said.

"Room seventeen."

At the mention of the haunted room, the clerk raised his eyebrows.

"Oh dear," he said. "There's been an incident." He picked up the phone and covered the mouthpiece. "You must be the sister?"

"I am," Mia said, concerned.

"She said you were coming," the clerk said and spoke into the phone. "Ms. Costa? Your sister's here. I'll send her up."

"What kind of incident?" Mia said.

Johnny, Sylvie, and Tandy walked up to the desk behind Mia.

"You better go up and see for yourself," he said and turned his attention to Tandy. "We're pet friendly! Yes, we are! Good boy! Straight up the stairs and around the corner." He pointed to the main staircase.

Mia, Johnny, Sylvie, and Tandy headed up the stairs and down the hall to Room 17. They knocked, and as if on a spring, Brynn opened the door. She was impeccably dressed, as usual, wearing a short jacket and gold jewelry with her hair tucked behind one ear. But despite her superficially tidy appearance, Mia could see the stress in her eyes.

"Brynn? What happened? Are you okay?"

"Mimi! Thank God you're here," Brynn said, upset. She swung the door open wider. It looked like a cyclone had moved through the room. Papers were scattered everywhere. Brynn's luggage was already packed and waiting by the door. Mia was relieved to see she was still wearing the bracelet Hazel had given her the day before. But Mia's brother-in-law, Jeffrey, was another matter.

He was pale and disheveled, seated on a love seat by the end of the bed, holding a damp cloth against his head. In the center of the room was an open briefcase, half filled with papers. Jeffrey glared at Mia and when he moved, Mia saw that he had a goose-egg-size lump on his forehead.

"Ouch! What happened?" Mia said.

"Nothing happened," Jeffrey spat out. "Just a stupid accident."

"It started an hour ago," Brynn said. "First there was a thumping sound, like a ball bouncing on the ceiling. I called downstairs and they said, 'Don't worry, that's the *ghost boy.*' Can you imagine! Then the door handle started to rattle. The sound got worse and worse. You wouldn't believe how loud the noise got, like a train! All of a sudden the TV flipped on, you know, gray static. Then it flipped off again. Anyway, Jeffy was resting on the bed, so he got up to adjust the TV, all grumbly and annoyed, and he tripped on his briefcase and bumped his head. Papers flew everywhere, like a rush of wind blowing everything into the air."

"That's awful," Mia said, but it occurred to her that Brynn's description sounded less like a ghost and more like Jeffrey just being clumsy.

"Then I heard it…" Brynn said, her face recoiling in terror.

"Heard what?" Sylvie said.

"A woman laughing," Brynn said, her eyes wide and her cheeks drained of color. "She was laughing at Jeffy!" She straightened her jacket nervously.

Mia realized the last time she'd seen Brynn this wired was when she was waiting to see if she'd made the cheerleading squad. Mia glanced at Sylvie, who had slapped a hand over her mouth, trying not to laugh.

"So, the ghost pranked you?" Sylvie said.

"Pranked?" Brynn said.

"The ghost made you slip and then laughed," Sylvie said.

"But it wasn't funny!" Brynn said.

"Sounds like you ran into Katherine," Johnny said. "She's haunted this room for a century. Apparently, she doesn't like men."

That was the second time today Mia was impressed with Johnny. He had been doing some serious research lately.

"Bullshit!" Jeffrey said. "There is no such thing as ghosts."

Mia ignored Jeffrey and took her EMF reader out of her bag. She flicked it on and walked around the room, testing.

As she moved toward the bed, the meter spiked.

"Look at this," Mia said, nodding her head toward the bed.

Johnny came close and saw how high the meter was spiking. He swept his hand across the head of the bed.

"There's a cold spot," Johnny said and grabbed Mia's hand. As he swept it through the cold spot, Mia felt her skin tingle, but she suspected it was from Johnny touching her rather than the temperature drop.

"I feel it," Mia admitted.

Johnny turned to Jeffrey. "I don't think you should stay in this room. This ghost can get pretty aggressive."

"There is no ghost," Jeffrey growled. "And I'm not leaving this room!"

"Suit yourself," Brynn said. "Mia? Can I stay with you?"

"Of course," Mia said.

"Fine," Jeffrey said. "You're getting just as crazy as your sister, you know that?"

"Don't speak to me that way, Jeffy!" Brynn snapped and grabbed her luggage.

"Let me get that for you," Johnny said and rolled the luggage into the hall.

"Don't you dare leave, Brynn!" Jeffrey said as Mia, Sylvie, and Tandy followed them out and the door slammed. They all walked downstairs, leaving Jeffrey to nurse his lumpy head.

Once they were outside, Johnny placed the roller case on the sidewalk and handed the handle to Brynn, who was trying not to cry.

"Come on, Brynn," Mia said. They all walked to the Essex Street apartment. Brynn kept sniffing as they walked down the block. When they arrived, Johnny took Mia's key, opened the downstairs door, and held it for them.

Are you two going to be okay?" Johnny said.

"Yeah, me and Johnny have a Love Addicts Anonymous meeting tonight," Sylvie said.

"We'll be fine," Mia said. "I think we'll have an early night,"

"I'll pick you up in the morning," Sylvie said and winked. "You should get a pizza." She pulled a menu out of her bag and handed it to Mia. "This place is awesome."

Even though the circumstances were strange, Mia was looking forward to spending time with Brynn. There seemed to be a deep tension between her and Jeffrey. Maybe she could find out what was going on between them.

***

As Mia and Brynn reached the top of the stairs, the door opened. Will was standing there with a toolbox, which he put down. Tandy jumped up and greeted him excitedly.

"I finished the cat run," he said. "Rose loves it!"

As they stepped inside, Mia saw a flash of white fur leap from a longboard set high in the living room wall, to another board, set at an artistic angle. She looked at Mia, tail up in the air, yellow eyes flashing with excitement. Then Rose the cat ran along the outside of the wall, leaping from perch to perch before landing on the mantelpiece and hopping down to the floor. She rushed over to greet Tandy, touching her pink nose to his before rubbing against him. Tandy sank down on the ground, smitten by his kitten.

"Amazing job, Will! Thank you," Mia said. "Will, this is my sister, Brynn."

"A pleasure to meet you, Will," Brynn said.

Mia got out her wallet and slipped Will a couple of bills.

"As agreed," she said.

"Thanks, Mia," Will said, excited and happy. He disappeared out the door.

Mia ordered a pizza while Brynn disappeared into the bathroom for a while, supposedly to unpack her stuff. But the way Tandy stared at the bathroom alerted Mia to the fact Brynn was more likely trying to gather her composure on the other side of the door. When she came out, her eyes were red and Mia could tell she'd been crying.

Darn that stupid Jeffrey, making her cry! Mia thought.

She'd never seen her sister so upset, which was strange because her brother-in-law, Jeffrey, was one of the most annoying people on earth. Every encounter with him frayed Mia's last good nerve

Brynn had always been incredibly patient with her husband, which Mia found amazing due to the fact Jeffrey's temperament was similar to a wolverine's. The last thing she wanted to do was upset Brynn further, so she was not going to bring up the Elmswood House or Cindy Moore's death.

Mia had been saving a good bottle of cabernet sauvignon, with deep notes of plum and black cherry and a peppery undertone. She opened the bottle and let it breathe. Then she poured a glass and handed it to Brynn.

"Here," she said. "You look like you could use a drink."

"Thanks, Mimi," Brynn said and sank down in a kitchen chair. Then she chugged the glass of wine like it was orange juice.

"Are you sure you're all right?" Mia said.

"Fine, fine," Brynn said, taking the bottle. She poured herself another glass, which disappeared just as quickly.

"Maybe slow down a bit until the pizza comes," Mia said, watching her sister carefully.

When the pizza arrived, Mia set it down on the kitchen table and got out two plates.

They each took a slice of New York style pizza, with gooey mozzarella and Romano cheese, topped with pepperoni, Italian sausage, spicy roasted vegetables, portobello mushrooms, and a hint of buttered garlic.

"What's going on with you two?" Mia said, taking a bite of pizza. The spicy, sweet flavor was amazing. Sylvie was right.

"We've been having some problems," Brynn said.

"Like what?" Mia said.

"Remember the apartment building he bought, where you lived for a while?"

"Sure," Mia said.

"Well, the buyer backed out, then his overseas investors dried up and he was forced to sell at a loss," Brynn said. "His mood has been just awful."

"He's kind of controlling, so I see how that would upset him," Mia said.

"I'm sorry he dragged Mark into town."

"So am I," Mia said. "I figured it was him."

"At first when he interfered with your life, he always said he was worried about you and I believed him. Now, I'm not so sure."

"Do you love him?" Mia said.

"Honestly, Mimi, I don't know," Brynn said. "He's not the guy I married."

Mia had not expected that. She looked at Brynn's eyes welling up with tears and felt terrible. Her sister was in crisis.

"Listen, Brynn, I know it must be hard on you, always trying to be what Mom and Daniel expect of you. Most of the time you do an amazing job. You're classy, elegant, the lady of the manor, wife to a successful lawyer. But it sounds like you need to think about your feelings."

Brynn nodded, wiping away tears.

"You're right," Brynn said. "I do."

Mia went to the closet and got out some extra sheets and a pillow.

"You take the bed, I'll take the couch. Stay here tomorrow and hang out with Rose. I'll be back before that silly dinner. We'll go together."

"Oh, Mimi, you're such a good sister," Brynn said and threw her arms around Mia's neck. After they hugged, Brynn changed into her pajamas and crawled into bed. She was immediately joined by Rose, who walked up to her chest and snuggled in the crook of her arm.

"See you in the morning," Mia said, fluffing her pillow. Then she changed into sleep shorts and a tank top. Tandy looked up at her, not sure where to go. "Go on, you can sleep with Auntie Brynn."

Tandy padded over to the bed and jumped up, joining Brynn and Rose.

"G'night," Brynn said, burrowing under the covers to cuddle with Rose and Tandy. After a moment there was a little, ladylike snore.

Brynn was fast asleep.

Mia stared at the ceiling. Her mind was racing. She was worried about Brynn. She was dreading the family dinner with Graham tomorrow night. She was also worried about her job, now that filming at the Elmswood House was on hold. But most of all, she was concerned about her investigation into the death of Cindy Moore tomorrow. She hoped she had time to make some progress before Detective Charlie Waite came for her. Mia tried to quiet her thoughts, but it was no use. She knew she wouldn't be getting much sleep.

CHAPTER EIGHTEEN

Mia and Sylvie drove toward Swampscott while Tandy rode in the back catching the breeze. Mia had quietly crept out of the apartment to let Brynn catch up on her sleep. She left a note for her sister saying she was doing some research for the production company and left a spare key. Rose cuddled up on Brynn's pillow and the two were both softly snoring when Mia gently shut the door. Mia felt a little guilty sneaking out after everything that happened the night before. But the family drama would just have to wait. Right now, she needed to figure out what happened to Cindy Moore before Detective Charlie Waite came looking for her. Sylvie pointed to one of her favorite food trucks on the side of the road.

"This place is amazeballs," she said enthusiastically. "Breakfast burrito?"

"Sounds delicious," Mia said and pulled over.

Sylvie darted out of the car and ran over to the truck. A few minutes later, she came back with a paper bag. A delicious aroma wafted throughout the car as she handed Mia a burrito wrapped in yellow paper. Mia's stomach growled as she realized how hungry she was and unwrapped the grilled flour tortilla stuffed with scrambled eggs, avocado, black beans, cheese, spinach, chunks of bacon, and topped with green salsa and fresh cilantro. Mia took a bite and sighed.

"OMG that is so good," she said.

"I get super cranky if I don't eat," Sylvie said.

"You think?" Mia said and they both laughed.

As soon as they were done wolfing down the food, Mia pulled back onto the road. Along the way, they caught little glimpses of the sun rising as they followed the coast to sleepy Swampscott. They cruised down the long road in light traffic and eventually wound closer to the beach. Sylvie pulled one of her laptops out of her bag and plugged it into the charger in Mia's car. The small computer had a tough case around it covered in stickers and cartoon logos. She started tapping keys.

"Whatcha doing?" Mia said.

"Checking Cindy's Facebook while I charge up," Sylvie said as she scrolled through Cindy's stream. "Her last post was the day before her body was found."

"Good idea," Mia said. "What did she say?"

"*Five-fifty-five Elmswood needs a facelift but she's got good bones! Prime location in a lovely neighborhood. Message me if you still want a tour!*" Sylvie said and clicked on the post. "There's a bunch of pictures of the house."

"That's going to end up in a creepy Google search one day," Mia said.

"I'm going to check Seaside Estates web site," Sylvie said, typing. "Looks like they've got an online forum where they answer questions and talk about properties and local real estate issues." Sylvie's fingers flew over the keys. "Check it out! Cindy was talking to someone named Fat Cat. Pushing them to buy!"

"Fat Cat? That's the name she mentioned on the tour!" Mia said. "I'm sure it is. She was going to meet Mr. Fat Cat."

"Hold on, let me trace Fat Cat's IP number," Sylvie said. "Nuts, that's a dead end. Fat Cat is using a VPN."

"What's that?" Mia said.

"Virtual Private Network, an intermediary server that encrypts your connection to the internet and hides your IP address. Why would Fat Cat do that?"

"I don't know but I'd be careful," Mia said. "The cops are all over anything connected to Cindy right now. I'm sure that includes the forum."

"Got it," Sylvie said, closing the browser window.

"Listen, I need to make a quick stop before Seaside Estates."

"All right, I'm game. Where?"

"Paradise Road," Mia said as she turned down the curving street and cruised past the manicured lawns.

Midway down the block she reached a dark brown American colonial house tucked behind a split rail fence. An American flag was flying on a high flagpole in front of the property and a brown hanging sign stood in the front yard.

"John Humphrey House?" Sylvie read the plaque. "So, this is the house where Lydia lived?"

"Yes." Mia stopped the car in front of the house. Then she got out and let Tandy out to run around. He darted straight to the fence to sample the scents of the area as Mia looked up at the old house. A creepy feeling moved along the back of her neck. She'd seen the house before, in her dream.

Sylvie got out of the car and joined her.

"Well?" Sylvie said, noticing Mia's intense concentration.

"This is the same house from my dream," Mia said.

"How can that be?" Sylvie said, gazing through a pair of petal-pink, perfectly round sunglasses at the dark brown colonial homestead.

"I have no idea," Mia said. "In the dream, the house was lighter and there was a big, gnarled tree in front, but the windows and roof are exactly the same. It's identical."

"Weird. Should we go inside?" Sylvie said.

"It doesn't open until this afternoon," Mia said and looked at her watch. "But Seaside Estates opens in ten minutes."

Mia whistled for Tandy and they all climbed back in the car and drove to the beach. The sun was just above the ocean now, bright and golden, streaking the morning clouds with color. Mia pulled into the parking lot of the small real estate office. Last time she'd parked on the street, but this vantage point gave them a clear view of the office. There were two desks; one had flowers set in a vase.

"That must be Cindy's desk," Mia said. "Now we just need to wait for Doug Tanner to show up." Through the open door she could see the receptionist bustling about, getting ready for her day.

"So, what's the plan?" Sylvie said.

"We'll improvise, just follow my lead," Mia said.

"You really think Cindy was murdered?" Sylvie said.

"Charlie Waite seems to think so," Mia said. "And there were muddy footprints in the stairwell. The day before, those floors were old and dusty, not muddy."

"Good point," Sylvie said. "Now that you mention it."

Tandy stuck his head between the two seats for a pat just as an electric blue BMW X3 SUV pulled into the parking lot. Doug Tanner stepped out and walked around the car admiring the paint job. Then he pulled a handkerchief out of his pocket. He carefully rubbed out a scuff mark until the finish was shining before folding the cloth and putting it back in his pocket. He stopped to check his reflection in both the side mirrors, smoothing his hair. Satisfied, he locked the vehicle from his phone and headed into the office.

"There he goes," Mia said.

"Wow, I'm not sure who he's more in love with, himself or his ride," Sylvie said, mesmerized. "Wasn't he Cindy's partner?"

"Yes," Mia said. "He doesn't seem too broken up about her death."

"Maybe she did have an enemy after all," Sylvie said.

"Listen, once we're in that office, we'll need a diversion, so we can look around without Doug Tanner breathing down our necks," Mia said.

"Leave it to me," Sylvie said and typed furiously into her computer. Screen after screen popped up as she looked at strings of code. "Okay, that should do it." She grinned and left her computer open on the front seat.

"What are you going to do?"

"You'll find out," Sylvie said. "Trust me, it'll work."

Mia, Sylvie, and Tandy headed around the front of the building and into the Seaside Estates office. Behind the desk, the receptionist seemed stressed and barely holding it together. When she looked up, her eyes were slightly red. Cindy had obviously been important to her.

"Can I help you? Oh, I remember you, the girl from the podcast," she said. "I'm sure you heard about Cindy—"

"I'll take care of this," Doug Tanner said, standing in his office door. "Good to see you again, Mia."

"I have your key," Mia said.

"Why don't you come into my office," Doug said. "We can talk there." He eyed the receptionist warily, as if she was an emotional timebomb.

Mia, Sylvie, and Tandy walked past the reception desk and into Doug Tanner's office. The window by his desk had a wide view of the parking lot, with his blue BMW framed perfectly. The desk across from him was clearly Cindy Moore's. There was a vase of flowers in the center and feminine touches including a Cloisonné Porcelain Fountain Pen balanced on a stack of pink envelopes. To one side of the desk was a large appointment book decorated with wildflower paintings. Mia glanced at Sylvie and she nodded. That was where they would find Cindy's last client. Tandy walked over to her desk and sniffed before whimpering and lying down with his head on his paws.

"It's okay, boy," Mia said.

"Wow, your dog is perceptive," Doug said. "Cindy's death has been rough on everyone." He motioned for Sylvie and Mia to have a seat.

They slipped into one of the chairs facing his desk and Mia pushed the skeleton key to the center of the desk.

"Thanks for lending me the key," Mia said.

"No problem," Doug said. "Detective Waite contacted me. Sorry you had to get involved. What happened to Cindy was a real shame."

"Finding her was pretty shocking," Mia said. "How are you holding up?"

"Cindy was a great partner," Doug said, leaning back in his chair. "But she was under a lot of stress."

"What makes you say that?" Mia said.

"Well, she kept trying to sell that house, for one thing," Doug said, a look of exasperation on his face. "You saw it, you couldn't get the Addams family to move into that place. Not to mention the commission structure was *impossible.* That house isn't even worth representing." He smoothed out his blue silk tie over his striped starched shirt. "A place like that can destroy a company's reputation."

Mia glanced at Sylvie, amazed by Doug Tanner's admission.

So Doug thought Cindy had dragged down his career? Was that the motive? Had he killed Cindy Moore?

"Speaking of the house, my friend here is looking for a fixer upper."

"Well, I have a number of places—" Doug Tanner began and eyed Sylvie. "Can I ask what you do?"

"She's a very successful musician," Mia said.

"I'm releasing an album next year," Sylvie said in a bored and haughty voice. "Sylvie Payne and Radio Forever. I used to tour with Amplitude."

"Wow," Doug said, getting excited. "I have several wonderful homes I can show you."

"What about that Elmswood House?" Sylvie said, looking over her rose-tinted glasses.

"Well, that's tricky," Doug said, his energy suddenly dropping. "As I said, that house was Cindy's project. I'm not planning to take over representing it. The owner is very stubborn about a number of things. She has certain stipulations."

"Can I talk to her?" Sylvie said bluntly.

"Connie Carol?" Doug said sourly. "I'll see if I can dig up her number."

"Are there any other interested buyers?" Mia said.

Suddenly Doug Tanner stiffened in his chair. "Well, funny you should mention it, the police asked me the very same question. They're coming by today to pick up Cindy's things. I'm really not at liberty to say."

Sylvie slowly slipped her phone out of her bag and looked at it casually.

"Excuse me. I'm expecting an important text," she said.

Then she glanced at Mia as if to say now? In return, Mia nodded almost imperceptibly. Sylvie's fingers flew across the surface of the phone.

Then, with a high, keening noise, the SUV's car alarm went off.

We-ou! We-ou! We-ou! We-ou! We-ou!

Tandy leaped to his feet and started whining before barking at the window. Doug Tanner leapt from his seat as if he'd just been hit with a red-hot poker. He ran to the window and pressed his nose against the glass.

The receptionist poked her face in the room.

"Is everything okay?" she said, concerned.

"Will you excuse me for a second?" Doug said and rushed out of the room followed by the receptionist. He reappeared in the parking lot and ran to his car, looking desperately in both directions, trying to find out who had set off the car alarm.

Tandy ran over to the window and wagged his tail, thinking this was a fun game as Doug rushed around the parking lot.

"Better find out what's in that book before the cops show up," Sylvie said.

Mia slipped over to Cindy's desk and opened the appointment book. She ran her finger along the entries and found the date of Cindy's murder.

There were two names listed.

1. Howard Angler

2. Mr. Fat Cat

Howard's name had an address scrawled beside it.

But Mr. Fat Cat was still a mystery. *Who was he?*

Mia opened a drawer, grabbed a slip of paper and a pen, and copied the names and addresses. She glanced out the window to see Doug frantically running around his car trying to shut off the alarm. Finally, the alarm stopped and Doug stood framed in the window, one hand on his head and the other on his hip clearly confused why the alarm had gone off in the first place.

Tandy watched him, tail wagging.

"How did you do that?" Mia said, impressed.

"Well, I didn't technically hack his car, just the Wi-Fi network," Sylvie said.

Mia glanced out the window to see Doug Tanner run his fingers through his sandy blond hair. Then he started to walk back to the front door.

"I need another second," Mia said, examining the book.

"You got it," Sylvie said. "Can't have the cabana boy come back too soon." Her fingers danced over the keyboard. Suddenly the car radio blared. The song "Gangnam Style" blasted over the speaker and the lights flashed on and off.

Eh Sexy Lady!
Oppan Gangnam style

Doug took his phone out and frantically pressed every button. He opened the door and turned off his radio. The music finally died and he stared at his car, puzzled. But just as he started to walk back to the office, the song blasted again.

Eh Sexy Lady!
Eh, eh, eh, eh, eh, eh

As Sylvie distracted Doug Tanner, Mia tried to decipher Cindy's handwriting. There were some hastily written notes in the margin concerning the owner of the house, Connie Carol.

Tell Fat Cat to stop trying to reach Connie or else!
Next step, restraining order!

According to this, Fat Cat was pushy, maybe even aggressive.

Was Cindy planning to confront Fat Cat that night? Did that lead to her death? Maybe Connie knew something? Mia searched the book for Connie Carol's address, but there was nothing in the book. *Darn it!*

"Okay, let's go," Mia said and shoved the slip of paper in her pocket.

Sylvie pressed a button and the radio and lights switched off.

Mia and Sylvie tried not to laugh as Doug Tanner stared at the car suspiciously. Then he locked the doors again and rejoined them inside.

"Sorry about that," Doug said, frazzled by his possessed car.

"Now about Elmswood House—" Sylvie said.

"Listen, the police are due here any minute," Doug said. "Can I text you that contact info for Connie Carol?"

"Absolutely," Sylvie said and smiled.

He shoved a card into her hand.

"Call me with all your real estate needs," he said.

As soon as Mia and Sylvie got back to the car, they sank into a fit of giggles. Tandy sat in the backseat, panting happily from the excursion.

"Tell me you got something out of that?" Sylvie said.

"Two people were scheduled to see Cindy the night of the murder-—Howard Adler and Fat Cat," Mia said and handed Sylvie the slip of paper.

"That sounds promising," Sylvie said and typed Howard Adler's address into her phone. He lived on Chatham Street in the neighboring town of Lynn, only ten minutes away.

Just as Mia was about to pull into traffic, a Ford Explorer belonging to the Swampscott PD pulled up in front of the Seaside Estates. Mia's instincts were to duck out of sight, but she remembered Charlie Waite already knew what her car looked like. She pulled into traffic, hoping he hadn't seen them.

Sylvie twisted in her seat to look through the rear window.

"Looks like we're about to have company," Sylvie said.

Mia checked her rearview mirror. There was Detective Charlie Waite, hands on his hips, head cocked, looking directly at Mia's car. They had a slight head start, but only barely. It wouldn't take the detective long to find out the exact information she had just extracted from Cindy Moore's appointment book. After that, he would follow the same trail. Once he found them snooping around town, Mia doubted he would be thrilled.

"We better hurry," Mia said, trying to stay calm. "I don't want to run into Detective Waite if we can help it."

"So, you think Howie here is the murderer?" Sylvie said.

"I guess we'll find out," Mia said. She couldn't help but be nervous. Whoever had killed Cindy was ruthless, and cold-blooded. If Howard Adler was the murderer, they might be walking into a dangerous trap.

CHAPTER NINETEEN

Mia drove through the back streets until they crossed into Lynn. The old wooden houses started to have a more modest look, with peeling paint, roofs that needed patching, and room air conditioners wedged into windows. Mia pulled up at the address she had discovered in Cindy Moore's appointment book.

The small, two-story house sat behind a security fence, flanked by an alley. The wooden siding was rundown and needed a paint job.

"That's odd," Mia said. "This guy wants to buy a fixer-upper in Swampscott? That's an expensive proposition."

"Yeah," Sylvie said. "Howie Adler can't even fix up his own place, let alone that Elmswood House of horrors."

Mia, Sylvie, and Tandy climbed out of the car and let themselves through the security gate. Then they climbed the wooden steps to the dingy front door and knocked. The sound of footsteps could be heard inside the house, crossing the floor. Then the door opened. Standing in the frame was a balding middle-aged man. He stared at Mia and Sylvie through glasses perched on the end of a beak-like nose and was dressed in a too tight Pinhead T-shirt from the 1980s *Hellraiser* movies over grubby jeans. Behind him, on the wall, was a vintage *Nightmare on Elm Street* movie poster, with the signature of Robert Englund, the actor who played Freddy Krueger, scrawled boldly across it.

"Howard Adler?" Mia said.

"That's me," Howard said. "I already told the last guy. I'm not buying a stupid magazine subscription. Not unless you've got *Fangoria*, which you never do."

Fangoria? Mia thought. *What the heck was Fangoria?*

"Oh no, it isn't that," Mia said. "We wanted to talk to you about the Elmswood House."

That information hit Howard's eyes like a depth charge. He squinted, looking a little closer at the two women who had turned up on his doorstep.

"You mean the Browder place," he said cautiously.

"Bingo," Sylvie said and smiled.

"What about it?" Howard said, looking nervous.

"Do you know Cindy Moore?" Mia said. "She represented that house through Seaside Estates?"

"Sure, I know her," Howard said. "Well, I've spoken to her on the phone anyway."

"Did you make an appointment to see that house the day before yesterday?" Mia continued.

"Sure I did. Say, what is this? Who are you guys?"

"We're from *Bell, Book, and Candle*—" Mia started to say.

That information made Howard Adler's jaw grow slack in amazement.

"T-the podcast? You're kidding me!" Howard said with growing excitement. "Holy moly!"

"Ten out of ten, Howie," Sylvie said. "We're the podcasters."

"You must be Mia Bold? I saw your picture at ParaCon last year! Why didn't I see it before? Come in," Howard said and led them into his living room, which was lined with display cases housing models from various horror movies. A collection of fantasy swords was displayed on one wall, hanging between framed vintage horror posters.

"Wow, Howie, you like the nasty stuff, huh?" Sylvie said.

"Go ahead, sit down," Howard said, pointing to a black leather couch with excitement. "I can't believe Mia Bold is in my house!"

"I guess I really am the sidekick," Sylvie said under her breath.

Mia stifled a laugh at her joke. *What would Johnny do in this situation?* she wondered. No doubt, he would be charming. She took a deep breath and smiled.

"Thanks," Mia said and took a seat. "Great collection, Howard."

Howard's eyes widened and he grinned sheepishly.

"You think so? Wow! So why are you guys here?" he said, thrilled. "Is Johnny Astor with you?"

"Not today, I'm afraid," Sylvie said.

"That's okay, would you autograph something for me?" Howard rushed around the room looking through stacks of magazines until he found an issue of *Fangoria* with Johnny featured on the cover. The title read: *The New Breed of Ghost Hunters!* Up in the corner was a little box the size of a postage stamp with a picture of Mia. Underneath the box were the words: *Johnny's new sidekick!*

It was obvious why no one had showed her this insulting cover!

"Sure," Mia said and took the pen and the magazine. She wrote across the front of the issue: *To Howard Adler, Keep searching for the truth, Mia Bold.*

"Wow, thanks!" Howard grinned, staring at the autograph.

"Listen, Howard, we have some bad news," Mia said. "Cindy Moore is dead."

"Whoa, are you serious?" Howard said, an expression of surprise spreading across his face.

"No one's sure what happened," Mia said.

"Crap. Was it that haunted house? I almost walked into that place."

"We aren't really sure what happened. We're trying to find out," Mia said. "When you first saw the property, did you ever feel any negative energy?"

"Not really, it just looked like a dump."

Mia wondered why no one else seemed to feel the awful energy of that house. Had her mind played a trick on her? Was her own silly fear getting the best of her? It didn't feel that way. The sensation of terror felt genuine. There must be some logical explanation for the reaction she was having, if only she could figure it out.

"Weren't you supposed to meet her that evening?" Sylvie said.

"I was, but she cancelled that appointment."

"Why did you want to see the house?" Mia asked.

Howard looked at her sheepishly. "It's haunted. I wanted to see, you know, the ghosts."

"Do you know why Cindy cancelled?" Mia said.

"She said another client had arrived unexpectedly," Howard said.

"What time was that, Howie?" Sylvie said.

Howard took his phone out and scrolled through his outgoing call record.

"Here," he said. "Cindy called me at five thirty p.m." Howard turned his phone so Mia and Sylvie could read the call log.

They stared at the date. Cindy had called Howard the night of the murder.

"Thanks, Howard, that really helps us," Mia said and stood up to leave.

"Hey, Mia? Are you going to film at the Elmswood House?"

"I'm not sure. Maybe."

"If you do, can I come and watch?"

“I’ll see what I can do,” Mia said. “One more thing. A cop is going to come by and talk to you—Detective Charlie Waite. Maybe pretend we were never here?”

Howard Adler ginned. “You got it.”

Mia, Sylvie, and Tandy walked back outside and jumped into the car, anxious to make their exit before Detective Waite appeared.

Sylvie’s phone started to buzz and she looked at the text.

“It’s Doug Tanner. He found the contact info,” Sylvie said and showed Mia the screen.

“Looks like she lives on the edge of Swampscott,” Mia said, locking her seat belt. “Let’s go. It’s time we had a talk with Connie Carol.”

***

Connie Carol lived in an apartment on the first floor of a two-story Victorian house painted a sunny yellow, just down the street from Swampscott High School. For the affluent suburb, this was about as tough as it got. There were two front doors set into the porch. After Tandy went crazy sniffing around the fence, Mia and Sylvie climbed the porch steps and knocked on the front door. The sound of a small dog came from behind the door, yapping and sniffing at the threshold.

“What do you want?” a low, rasping voice called out.

“Connie Carol? I’m Mia Bold and this is Sylvie Payne. We had some questions about the Elmswood House?”

“Is that a dog you have with you?”

“Yes, this is Tandy. He’s friendly.”

“Meet me in the backyard. My little Nutmeg could use a playdate.”

Mia and Sylvie walked back down the steps and opened the gate. Tandy leaped inside. At the side of the house, a door opened and a caramel-colored miniature poodle ran down the steps. Tandy approached, tail wagging, ears at attention. The poodle barreled toward Tandy. Just before they collided, the little dog screeched to a halt and his tail whirled in a circle. Then they sprang up in the air in a series of hops and greeted each other, sniffing, tails wagging before springing up with a burst of energy and tearing around the yard, leaping and frolicking.

The owner of the dog made her way down the steps, an older woman wearing overalls splattered with paint. She was holding a coffee cup in one hand as she settled down on the lower step to watch the dogs play.

"Connie Carol?" Mia said.

"I am, and that's my dog, Nutmeg." Connie looked Mia and Sylvie up and down. "Who are you exactly?"

"I'm Mia Bold and this is Sylvie Payne. We wanted to talk to you about your house on Elmswood Road."

Connie shook her head slowly back and forth.

"Well, if you're from Hollywood, I'm not interested," Connie said gruffly.

"Oh no, we're local," Mia said.

"That's funny. You look like those Hollywood types," Connie said. "Well, if you're newspaper people, I don't know a darned thing about Cindy Moore. I got a call from the cops, end of story."

"We actually just had a few questions about the property," Mia said.

A look of comprehension dawned on Connie's face. "Oh, I know, you're the ghost hunters, aren't you? Cindy said you were filming at the house, the poor woman."

"What happened to Cindy was tragic," Mia said. "We were all shocked to hear about it."

Connie nodded solemnly. "So why are you here?"

"We're trying to understand what happened to Cindy," Sylvie said.

"It wasn't the ghost, if that's what you're thinking," Connie said and sipped her coffee, starting at the dogs as they tumbled and played.

Mia glanced at Sylvie, eyebrow arched in surprise.

"What makes you say that?" Mia asked.

"Because I know that ghost. She would never hurt Cindy or me or anyone."

"I thought you were run out of the house by that ghost?" Mia said.

"Fake news," Connie said. "The ghost I knew would never hurt a soul."

"What ghost is that?" Mia said.

"Why Lydia, of course," Connie said.

Mia felt a clammy sweat spread across her brow.

"You saw *Lydia*?" Sylvie said.

"Sure I have," Connie said. "What's wrong with your friend? Is she okay?"

"I'm fine," Mia said, taking a deep breath. "Could you tell us about her?"

"Lydia showed up the week we moved in. She would appear on the old playground next to the house or running across the yard. Dean even got a picture of her. Hey, you don't look so good. Why don't you sit down?"

Mia walked over and sat on the steps with Connie.

"What makes you say Lydia would never hurt a soul?" Mia said.

"She told me so in a dream. She told me I needed to take my husband to the doctor. If I'd only listened, Dean would still be here."

"What about the other ghosts?" Sylvie said.

"The Browder family?" Connie said. "They were restless, but harmless."

"Listen, Connie, when you were in the house, did you ever feel something terrible, a feeling of dread?" Mia said.

"No. When Dean died I couldn't afford to fix it up, so I moved out and tried to sell it to someone who appreciates history."

"Connie, Cindy was supposed to meet a buyer the night she was killed. Does the name Fat Cat mean anything to you?"

"Fat Cat? Is that what they call themselves now? Is that a rap name?"

"Close, it's a name in an Internet forum," Sylvie said.

"No, can't say that I recognize that name," Connie said.

"Cindy made a note she was considering getting a restraining order?"

Connie slapped her knee and laughed.

"That's why I hired her! All these Hollywood types and vultures. I told her to keep them away from me. I'm surprised you two found me," Connie said. "Anyway, I've decided not to sell. I'm going to wait for someone who can appreciate the bones of that house."

"Can I ask you one more question?" Mia said.

"Shoot," Connie said.

"Where were you the night Cindy died?" Mia said.

"I was playing five-card draw at the rotary club. I cleaned them out too, " Connie said and chuckled.

At that moment, a Swampscott Police Ford Explorer pulled up in front of the house. Mia cringed as Detective Charlie Waite climbed out and spotted the little soiree in the side yard. He trudged over to the security fence.

"Well, well, well," he said, walking up to the fence. "If it isn't Mia Bold. You seem to be everywhere I go these days."

"Hello, Detective Waite," Mia said.

"You know these gals, Charlie?" Connie said.

"Sure I do," Waite said. "Ms. Bold here found Cindy dead in your house."

"You don't say," Connie said. "And I was betting you wanted permission to film."

"I think our boss is going to call you about that, ma'am," Sylvie said.

"Film away," Connie said and sipped her coffee. "Maybe I'll get some publicity."

"What are you doing here, Ms. Bold?" Waite said, leaning casually on the fence.

"The same thing you are, Detective," Mia said. "I'm looking for answers."

"It seems a little odd the way you keep turning up around town. Howard Adler swears he didn't see you but he had a magazine signed by you."

"Oh wow, a fan?" Mia said and whistled for Tandy, who was rolling in a pile of something green. He responded immediately by springing up and loping across the yard.

"Looks like they found the manure," Connie Carol said wryly.

"Thanks for talking to us, Connie," Mia said.

"No skin off my back," Connie said.

Detective Waite opened the gate for Mia and Sylvie and escorted them to their car. As soon as Mia, Sylvie, and Tandy were inside, he leaned on Mia's open window.

"So, you read Cindy Moore's appointment book, huh? I heard about your little car stunt. You're lucky I don't haul you into the station."

"For what exactly?" Sylvie said. "Accessing public Wi-Fi?"

"Listen, I'm going to give you gals some free advice. When you follow a trail blind, it sometimes leads you down a dangerous road."

"We'll be careful, Detective," Mia said and pulled out of the driveway.

As they drove away, Detective Charlie Waite watched them with his arms folded. As they pulled around the corner, Mia relaxed and sniffed the air.

"What is that smell?" Mia said.

"I think Connie Carol wasn't kidding. Tandy and Lucky rolled in poop," Sylvie said and lowered her window.

"Oh good God! I have to go to dinner with my parents tonight!"

CHAPTER TWENTY

Mia, Sylvie, and Tandy arrived at the Essex Street apartment. Before heading upstairs, Mia took Tandy around to the front of the building and knocked on the shop window. Inside she could see Tom Hatter puttering about, unpacking boxes while Will held a clipboard. Tom was counting plastic bags full of witch-key fobs and ghost shot glasses in order to replenish the supply of trinkets and souvenirs lining the shelves.

Tom Hatter saw Mia and nudged Will, who came to the front door. The older man sauntered behind him and leaned on the door frame. Old Tom was a bit of a busybody when it came to Salem.

"What is that smell?" Tom said. "Reminds me of my granddad's farm."

"Whoa," Will said, wrinkling his nose.

"I have an emergency, as you've noticed," Mia said. "Will? Want to make some money?"

Will looked toward Tom, who nodded.

"Gotta keep my favorite tenants happy," Tom said.

"I have to go out with my parents tonight," Mia said. "Tandy needs to see the groomer. And my car smells just as bad as him." She handed her keys to Will along with cash for the groomer and the two jobs.

"Great," Will said, happy. "I'll take him home afterwards."

"Just let yourself in," Mia said, handing him Tandy's lead.

Tandy's ears were down as he looked from Mia to Will, trying to work out if he was in trouble. Mia kissed Tandy's nose.

"I'll see you later, have fun," Mia said.

Will and Tandy walked down the street as passersby abruptly scattered at the approach of their pungent scent.

Mia and Sylvie headed up the steps to the second floor.

"We still don't know who killed Cindy," Sylvie said.

"Someone knows who Mr. Fat Cat is, we just have to find them," Mia said.

As they reached the landing, a group text from Graham Stone to the Middletons arrived with the signature ringtone assigned to Graham—"Funkytown" by Lipps, Inc.

The Tavern on the Green
Hawthorne Hotel—8pm

The Hawthorne Hotel? Mia smiled to herself. Maybe this dinner wouldn't be so awful after all.

"Graham booked dinner at the last place my real dad's mobile was traced to, according to Suzy Sharpe," Mia said, excited at the thought.

"Well, at least it won't be a total bust," Sylvie said. "After having breakfast with your parental units, I'm kind of afraid for you. I don't think Graham is their idea of civilized company."

"I can handle Graham," Mia said. "I think. I'm more worried about Brynn and Jeffrey."

"Sounds like you have your hands full." Sylvie grinned and headed toward her apartment. "I'm going to kick back and order a pizza. Oh yeah, and I wouldn't trust Suzy Sharpe."

"I'll keep that in mind," Mia said.

"Good luck tonight!" Sylvie said, yawning and disappeared into her apartment.

Mia walked into her own apartment. Brynn was relaxing on the couch watching *Wife Swap* on Lifetime with Rose curled up in her lap.

"Hey, Mimi," Brynn said. "This is such a funny episode! One lady is married to a biker and the other one is married to a stay-at-home husband. How did your research go?"

"I made a little progress," Mia said. "What have you been up to all day? I would have thought Mom and Daniel would have homed in on you by now."

"They've been so busy antiquing they don't have time to do anything else. Usually, Jeffy and I would be going to open houses, but I'm still mad at him. So then I thought Salem must have a decent day spa but I need a car. I've been so bored, Mimi! You wouldn't want to go with me, would you?"

"To a day spa? Why would I do that?"

"It was worth a try," Brynn said huffily.

"Do you want some coffee before we get ready for tonight?"

"I'd love some," Brynn said. "Where's Tandy?"

"He's at the groomers," Mia said. "Kind of an emergency. We had a roll in the manure incident."

"Oh," Brynn said and sniffed the air. "For you too, I think."

Rose hopped up on the edge of the couch and placed her paws on Mia, stretching up to touch her nose in greeting.

"Have you heard from Jeffrey?" Mia said.

"He's been texting me every hour," Brynn said and held her phone up for Mia to inspect. Mia scrolled down the increasingly aggravated texts from Jeffrey.

9 a.m.: Brynn? Where are you? I'm freezing.
10 a.m.: I think there's something wrong with this room.
11 a.m.: Hey, what's that sound? Is that you???!
12 p.m.: If you don't answer me I'm filing for divorce.
1 p.m.: Sorry babe! I didn't mean it. This room is messed up.
2 p.m.: Slipped in the shower and banged my head.
3 p.m.: Are you going to answer???
4 p.m.: Fine! I'll see you at dinner.
5 p.m.: Who is this Graham guy?
6 p.m.: Babe? You there or what? Ow! Covfefe...

"What are you going to do?" Mia asked. "He seems a little nervous."

Brynn looked at Mia contemplatively.

"I'm not sure. I'm sick of the way he treats me, like the maid."

"Honestly, you're too good for him," Mia said.

"Well, he's officially on notice as far as I'm concerned," Brynn said. "I guess we better get ready."

Mia took a steamy shower, slathering her body with vanilla and amber body wash. As soon as she dried off, Mia tied the towel around her torso and combed through her dark curls before lightly applying makeup, lip gloss, and mascara. Then she topped her look off with antique amethyst drop earrings, a gift from her stepfather, and slipped into a lilac Soutache sheath dress. She walked into the living room and turned her back toward Brynn.

"Can you zip me up?" Mia said.

"Of course, Mimi," Brynn said. "My, but don't you clean up good, sis."

Brynn looked perfect, as usual, dressed in a gorgeous winter floral Charmeuse dress with white flowers on china-blue and paired with pearls and navy pumps. Just as they were ready to go, Will knocked on the door.

"It's open," Mia said

Will let himself in.

"Whoa! You guys look awesome," he said.

"Thanks," Mia said. "How did it go?"

"I forgot to tell the groomer no feathers," Will said sheepishly. "But I got your car washed. It's spic and span." He handed Mia the car keys.

Tandy trotted into the apartment, freshly shampooed and smelling lovely with two blue tufts of feathers bobbing on his ears. He looked up at Mia, emanating humiliation, snorted, and sank down, putting his head in his paws.

Rose pattered over to sniff the feathers and started batting at Tandy's ears. He groaned but put up with her little white paws tossing his ears back and forth.

"Well, don't you look special," Brynn said.

"Will? Would you mind feeding the fur babies?" Mia said. "We're on the edge of being late."

"No problem," Will said. "How does Rose like the cat run?"

"She loves it," Mia said. "Thanks!"

Mia and Brynn headed for the car. As they climbed inside Mia noted that Will had done an amazing job. The upholstery smelled fresh and the vinyl was shiny and clean.

Mia started the car up and looked at Brynn.

"Time to face the music," Mia said.

"I hope Jeffy doesn't make a scene," Brynn said.

"Seriously, Brynn? You read those texts. I can guarantee you Jeffrey is going to be coiled up and ready to spring."

"I guess you're right," Brynn said. "Listen, Mimi, if I turn into a doormat, promise to pinch me?"

"Promise," Mia said.

CHAPTER TWENTY ONE

The tall and stately Hawthorne Hotel was a six-story, red-brick building and a perfect example of Colonial Revival–style architecture. Daniel would be pleased with the location at least. What concerned Mia most was Graham. His cheesy Hollywood persona embodied all of Daniel's complaints about the "tackiness" of the entertainment business. Mia knew her stepfather and he didn't suffer fools lightly.

After the valet took the car, Mia and Brynn walked into the Tavern on the Green, with its bright, garlanded windows under brown awnings. The restaurant faced Salem common and was situated on the first floor of the Hawthorne Hotel, next to the grand ballroom. Their heels clicked on the tile as they walked through the entrance and into the great room. The Tavern was paneled in warm wood and featured a fireplace and a long wooden bar with leather barstools. Scattered around a green, brocade carpet were wooden tables flanked by wing-backed chairs. The whole effect was relaxed, but traditional.

Mia and Brynn spotted Graham sitting at one of three tables that had been moved together. On seeing Brynn, Graham sprang to his feet and waved.

Brynn stopped and sucked in her breath, startled.

"Does he always dress like that?" she whispered.

"Sometimes worse," Mia whispered back.

Graham was dressed in a black shirt with an embroidered toreador pattern on each shoulder, like a suit of lights. His trousers were skin tight with flared legs and a set of odd patch pockets in the front. A gold belt divided the two hemispheres of his body, echoing the sparkling embroidery on his shoulders. His hair was a full on '70s do with a fluffy side part. Mia's worst nightmare, his Burt Reynolds mustache, seemed to be coming along nicely.

Then from the bar, Johnny Astor walked toward the table, looking absolutely stunning. He had chosen a sable-colored suit for the occasion which he layered with a deep maroon waist coat, dark silk shirt, and tie underneath. He smiled and waved when he saw Mia.

"Is that your co-host?" Brynn said. "My goodness, he is gorgeous!"

"He has a star quality," Mia said.

"You both do," Brynn said. "Are you sure you don't want to date him?"

"Shhhhhh," Mia said, alarmed as the distance shortened between them.

"You look lovely," Johnny said sweetly.

Mia felt her knees turn to jelly as the full intensity of his deep, hazel eyes took in her dress.

"And you look quite dashing," Mia said.

"And you must be Brynn?" Johnny said, turning on the full force of his smile.

"I sure am," Brynn said.

Johnny pulled out a seat for Mia by his side while Graham scrambled to greet Brynn, taking her hand and kissing it.

Brynn's eyes seemed to send out an SOS.

"This is your seat, gorgeous," Graham said and pulled out a wingback chair for her, sandwiching her between him and Johnny.

"So, this is Johnny Astor," Brynn said. "The Internet is abuzz."

"I've heard all about you too," Johnny said. "Great things."

Brynn smiled and sniffed the air before tilting her head curiously at Mia, who whispered "Axe Cologne" and inclined her head toward Graham.

Waiters began to bustle about the table setting up water glasses. The dining hall was modestly full with a low easy chatter in the background.

"So, Graham, have you heard back from the network?" Johnny said. "Any chance of a reprieve timewise?"

"I'm afraid not," Graham said. "Either the cops clear up this Elmswood House nightmare or we're in trouble. If I have to refund the advertisers, there goes our working capital."

"Ahem," Mia said, indicating Brynn with her head. The last thing she needed was her family finding out about Cindy Moore's murder or Brynn worrying about her getting involved with the police. They had no idea Mia had stumbled onto a dead body and she wanted to keep it that way.

"What do you mean, cops?" Brynn said. "Mimi? Are you in trouble again?"

"Me? Of course not," Mia said. "It's just, um—"

"Permits!" Johnny said and smiled. "We're waiting for a filming permit."

"Oh," Brynn said, impressed.

Graham stared at Johnny as if he'd gone quite mad.

"Yeah, this house we're working at is a bit of a wreck." Graham took a deep breath, ready to mansplain the situation to Brynn. "The real estate agent who showed me the place—ow!"

Graham stared at Johnny, who had just kicked him under the table.

"Pointed out some production *insurance* issues," Johnny said. "You know red tape, right, Graham?"

"Sure, I guess," Graham said, bending down and rubbing his shin.

Suddenly, Mia spotted her mother, stepfather, and Reynolds walking into the restaurant, dressed for dinner. Daniel had pulled out all the stops. Both he and Reynolds wore waistcoats. Daniel's had a pocket watch chain hanging from one of his breast pockets. Madison had dressed elegantly in a woven Chanel dinner suit in shades of linen, cream, and pewter.

They walked over to the table.

"Well, you two young ladies look lovely," Daniel said in his best huffy voice. "You must be the producer?" Daniel extended his hand.

Graham took it and began pumping his arm.

"At your service, Mr. Middleton," Graham said. "And this is Johnny Astor, the star of our show."

"A pleasure to meet you, sir," Johnny said and stood up to shake Daniel's hand. The cynical remark that Daniel was about to make dried up on his lips in response to Johnny's impeccable manners. But when he saw Johnny's waistcoat, even he had to nod his approval. He shook his hand firmly.

"My assistant, and our dear family friend, Reynolds," he said.

"Nice to meet you," Johnny said.

Daniel took his place at the head of the table, with Madison and Reynolds on either side. The maître d' led a crowd of diners across the room. Trailing behind them was Jeffrey.

Mia could not believe her eyes. Jeffrey had dressed in a tight pinstripe suit that somehow made him appear shorter. On one side of his forehead was a large purple lump that made him look like Quasimodo. But since Mia had last seen him in Room 17, things had gotten worse. He now had a black eye that had made his face seem lopsided.

"Oh my goodness, Jeffy, what happened to you?" Brynn gasped.

"I told you! I slipped in the shower. There's something screwy about that room," he said, his body coiled and tight.

"I suppose this must be our host," Jeffrey said, staring at Graham Stone. A flare of jealousy appeared in his eyes.

"Wow, that shiner looks pretty bad," Graham said and extended his hand.

"Jeffrey Costa, I'm a lawyer, by the way." Jeffrey squeezed Graham's hand until his knuckles were white.

"Quite a grip you have," Graham said, pulling his fingers away and turning his focus back to Brynn. "You are so gorgeous and classy," he said. "You could be an actress! I know some agents, if you're interested?"

"Me? An actress?" Brynn giggled at the thought.

"I'm telling you, you'd be great! Look at those cheekbones," Graham said, admiring Brynn's chiseled features.

"Don't be ridiculous," Jeffrey said, staring at Graham with daggers in his eyes.

Mia glanced at Johnny, who seemed amused by the exchange. Mia smiled back at him. It was nice to have a friend at the high-maintenance Middleton dinner. A waiter started to shove menus into the dinner guests' hands.

"Upscale pub food," Daniel whispered to Madison and Reynolds.

"How quaint," Madison said.

The waiter shuttled drinks to the table as they all ordered.

Jeffrey kept looking over his shoulder at the door, expectantly.

Mia noticed his strange behavior and looked in the direction of his gaze.

A man was approaching the table, dressed in a dark blue dinner jacket over an argyle sweater. He was tan and built like a football player. Mia gasped in alarm. She knew that blond, blue-eyed jock anywhere. It was her ex-fiancé, Mark. Despite his angelic looks, he was selfish and inconsiderate. He'd broken up with her on the same day she got kicked out of her apartment and lost her job. She didn't like to think about it because it still shook her up. And now, for some reason, he seemed to be stalking her.

Mia shot Brynn a questioning look. But her sister only shrugged and shook her head helplessly. She was obviously out of the loop. Mia had already told Mark she wasn't interested and she'd warned her family not to interfere with her new life. *How could they have invited him?* Mia's nostrils flared with indignation. She tried to hide her reaction but Johnny caught her distress.

"Everything all right?" Johnny whispered.

"Fine," Mia whispered back. "This is just a bit awkward."

Mark sat down across from Mia.

"Hey, babe," Mark said. "You look absolutely amazing."

"I thought you had to go back to New York," Mia said testily, drumming her fingers on the wooden table.

"Nah, I stayed to see my girl," Mark said and took his seat. He eyed Johnny suspiciously. "Are you going to introduce us?"

"Johnny—Mark," Mia said, annoyed and exasperated.

"Oh, the *co-host*," Mark said. "Well, I'm the *boyfriend*."

"*Ex-boyfriend*," Mia said, cheeks flaring red.

"Come on, Mia." Mark grinned. "We have unfinished business, don't we? I was thinking after dinner we could go get a drink—"

Mia could not believe this was happening. She had been ambushed again! This was getting ridiculous. She needed to find a way to stop her family from interfering in her life. The time had come to do something drastic.

"Johnny, can I speak to you for a second?" Mia whispered.

"Of course," he said.

"We'll be right back," Mia said and stood up. "I want to show Johnny a possible location."

"Great! Always on the job, that girl," Graham said and turned back to Brynn as Jeffrey stewed.

Mia and Johnny disappeared into the lobby and Mia walked over to a large ficus tree in a stone pot. She was nervous as she turned to face Johnny.

"You have to help me," she said.

Johnny held her gaze, his face serious.

"Of course, what do you want me to do?" he said, hands tucked casually into the pockets of his slacks.

"This might sound a little crazy," Mia said nervously, twisting the ring on her finger.

"You know me, I'm good with crazy," Johnny said.

"Could you pretend to be my boyfriend?" Mia blurted out.

Johnny's eyes widened slightly at the proposal, although his expression remained serious.

“Because of that Mark guy?” Johnny said.

“Yes,” Mia said. “I know it’s a lot to ask.”

“So, Mark *isn’t* your boyfriend?” Johnny said.

“No! He’s my ex and he’s stalking me at this point. I can’t stand it. And my family keeps dragging him along. I’ve already tried putting him off and here he is again.”

“Okay, I’m game,” Johnny said. “But if you really want to get rid of him, we need to make it look good, okay?”

Mia looked into Johnny’s deep hazel eyes and nodded. “Whatever you think will work, I’ll play along.”

They turned to walk back into the dining room.

“Wait,” Johnny said and stopped at the green carpet.

“What?” Mia said.

Johnny slipped his hand into hers. His fingers were cool as they twined through hers intimately and a tingle moved along her body and raced to her stomach, releasing a flock of nervous butterfly sensations.

“You’re my girlfriend, remember?” Johnny said and winked. Mia felt the full heat of his charm and nodded.

They walked back to the table together holding hands. As they crossed the carpet Mark furrowed his brow and stared at the new development with a growing look of annoyance.

Daniel, Madison, and Reynolds also noticed the body language. Daniel’s eyebrows shot up while Madison and Reynolds smiled and whispered.

Mia steeled herself. Words had not worked with Mark or her family. A performance would have to do. Jeffrey and Brynn were too distracted by Graham’s relentless attention to Brynn to notice.

Johnny pulled Mia’s chair out for her and then slid into his seat, letting his body press against hers. Just as they sat down, the waiter placed a New England cheese board with tiny slabs of goat cheese, hard cheddar, and gouda and slices of artisan bread, and small bowls of fresh olive oil and local honey in front of Daniel; crab cake sliders with arugula, tomato, and chipotle sauce in front of Jeffrey, who barely noticed as Graham attempted to get Brynn to share his nacho plate. In front of Johnny and Mia, the waiter set warm cinnamon-spiced crostini topped with melting Brie, cranberry, and crumbled pecans and drizzled with honey.

“You’re dating this guy?” Mark said, annoyed.

Johnny smiled and turned to Mia, who took a delicate bite of her crostini.

"We're more than dating, aren't we, darling?" Johnny said and scooped up her free hand. He brushed his lips against her fingertips. Mia blushed and felt her heart flutter. "We're quite involved."

"Well, Mia, this is a surprise. Why didn't we hear anything about your new boyfriend?" Daniel said.

"Honestly, Daniel, you have more important things to think about than my love life," Mia said pointedly.

"And is this young man an actor?" Daniel said with an edge in his voice.

"I like to think of myself as an entrepreneur, Daniel. I have a production company. I'm what's known as an influencer on Twitter and Instagram. I have several lucrative contracts with big corporations and I'm an associate-producer on *Bell, Book, and Candle*. Thanks to Mia, I think we have a good chance of getting a deal with a cable network. She is stunning, isn't she? Beauty and brains."

Mia's eyes widened and her cheeks flared red. Johnny was laying it on a bit thick, wasn't he? The fantasy he was creating made her tingle.

Daniel's expression shifted from haughty know-it-all to suitably impressed, while Mark's eyebrows knitted together in distress.

The main courses arrived and suddenly the air was filled with spices. The plates sizzled with their entrees. Daniel had baked haddock seasoned with sherry on a bed of sautéed spinach. Madison chose the fennel and peppercorn-crusted grilled swordfish dressed with stewed tomatoes and jasmine rice. Graham, Jeffrey, and Mark all ordered thick gourmet hamburgers while Brynn's seared salmon was garnished with winter citrus salsa and herbed butter.

Mia's raspberry flame-grilled chicken salad on mesclun greens with mandarin orange slices and spiced pecans was savory and sweet with a drizzle of crimson raspberry vinaigrette. Johnny's coconut-curry bowl was an assortment of sautéed vegetables on a bed of sticky rice topped with creamy curry sauce. Reynolds' penne pasta had a rich, red wine sauce, and was tossed with freshly shaved Parmesan. There was little conversation as each happy diner savored the delicious meal. After they finished eating dinner, the desserts came and Mia and Johnny shared a flourless chocolate torte. Johnny scooped up a spoonful of the black cherry compote with whipped cream.

"Here, darling," he said and slipped the spoon into her mouth.

The taste was absolutely divine.

"Mmmmmmm," Mia said. "Yum."

At this point a red rash flooded up Mark's neck and his cheeks flushed.

"I have to go," Mark said and threw his napkin down on the table. He stood up abruptly and stomped off.

"Mark?" Jeffrey said and turned to Mia. "What have you done?"

"Nothing," Mia said sweetly. "What have *you* done?"

After dessert, Graham paid the bill with all the bravado of his toreador shirt. Then he made Brynn promise she would call his agent friend.

"Oh, Graham, that's silly," Brynn said.

"Why not? This guy does commercials and you'd be great, I'm telling you," Graham said.

Everyone began dabbing their mouths politely and collecting their handbags and other items to leave.

"Are you coming to the room tonight?" Jeffrey said.

"No, Jeffy, that room is haunted," Brynn said. "I'm going to stay with Mia."

Jeffrey looked like he was about to have a meltdown.

"You should probably leave too," Graham said. "Brynn said you were in room seventeen. That's the one with the ghost that hates men."

"There's no such thing as ghosts," Jeffrey said. "The whole thing is ridiculous."

"Well, you look pretty rough," Graham said. "If you don't mind my saying. I didn't believe in ghosts either, but after some of the things I've seen in Salem—"

"Suit yourself, Brynn," Jeffrey said, throwing his napkin on the table. "Thanks for dinner, Stone."

"Sure, thing," Graham said as Jeffrey stormed off. He immediately turned his attention back to Brynn. "Now, promise to make that call?"

"Promise," Brynn said and giggled.

Johnny pulled Mia toward him to embrace her.

"Mark's gone," Mia said. "You don't have to keep pretending."

"We need to make it look good," Johnny said and brushed his lips against hers lightly. "I'll see you tomorrow."

Mia felt a tingling, breathless confusion sweep through her body. Then Johnny released her and left. She turned to find Brynn staring at her.

"What is going on between you two?" Brynn said.

"I'm not sure," Mia said, trying to shake off the emotional fog.

Now that the evening was over, she had one more thing to do and she couldn't let her stirred up hormones interfere. The Hawthorne Hotel was where her real father, Frank Bold, had stayed when he was in town. She needed to see if there was some clue to his existence.

CHAPTER TWENTY TWO

Mia walked up to the front desk of the Hawthorne Hotel with Brynn in tow. A young woman with dark hair drawn back in a ponytail and a gold name tag that read "Janet" was typing on a computer.

"Can I help you?" she said as Mia stood at the desk.

"I'm not sure," Mia said. "I'm looking for a guest that stayed at your hotel. He stayed here about a month ago. Maybe you could tell me whether you remember him?"

"Are you related to the guest?" Janet said matter-of-factly.

"Yes, I'm his daughter," Mia said.

"Name?"

"Frank Bold."

The moment Mia uttered his name, Brynn gasped and Janet looked up in surprise.

"Could you wait here for a second?" Janet said and disappeared into the back room. Brynn grabbed Mia's arm and squeezed.

"Your dad?" Brynn said. "I thought he'd been missing for years?"

"Well, he turned up in Salem," Mia said.

"Oh my gosh, Mimi. That's crazy!"

Through a crack in the door, Mia saw her dialing a phone and whispering into the receiver. Then she returned to the front desk.

"Is everything okay?" Mia said.

"The concierge will be right with you," Janet said.

Across the lobby, a tall, slender man appeared. He was wearing a suit jacket and a gold tag like the desk clerk. As he came closer he smiled broadly. His name tag read "Concierge: Samuel Reed."

"So, you're Mia Bold? We weren't sure if you really existed," Samuel said. "Will you excuse me? I just need to get something from the safe."

He walked past Mia and Brynn and stepped behind the desk before slipping through the office door out of sight.

Brynn tugged at Mia's sleeve.

"What's going on, Mimi?" Brynn said.

"I'm not sure," Mia said.

After a second, Samuel reemerged as Janet looked on from a safe distance.

"Do you mind if I see some ID?" Samuel said. "Just a formality, so I can be sure it's really you?"

"What's this about?" Mia said, fishing through her bag for her wallet. She pulled out her driver's license.

Samuel nodded and reached in his pocket. He extracted a pale envelope and handed it to Mia. Scrawled across the surface was her own name. She recognized the handwriting immediately. The refined cursive belonged to her father and seeing it took her breath away. *He wrote me a letter?* Mia thought, nervous to open the envelope.

"Your father said you'd turn up here and ask about him, so he left us strict instructions to deliver this message to you."

Mia looked up at Samuel in shock. Her blood seemed to freeze in her veins. Frank had known she would show up at this hotel?

"Does my father come here often?" Mia said.

"Indeed," Samuel said. "The laird visits us every year. It was a pleasure to meet you," Samuel said. "You look just like him, but prettier of course." He smiled, made a slight bow, and disappeared.

"Why would he do that, Mimi?" Brynn said.

Mia was tempted to open the envelope right there, but she couldn't trust her emotions. She tucked the letter in her bag.

"Let's go find out," Mia said and headed for the valet.

***

Back at the apartment, Tandy and Rose were excited to see Mia and Brynn. Tandy jumped up on Mia, kissing her face, and Rose did a turn around the cat run, hopping lightly from board to board before jumping onto the mantelpiece and down to the ground. Then she padded across the room to greet Mia and Brynn with little mincing steps. Mia walked to the kitchen and made two cups of hot chocolate with marshmallows. She brought Brynn her cup and they both settled down in the living room.

Mia took the letter from her father out of her bag and spread it open on the coffee table. It was written on thick, creamy stationery with the logo of the Hawthorne Hotel in one corner. Mia remembered her dad's handwriting and the sight of it made her feel deeply emotional. Her eyes stung with tears and she sucked in her breath. After all this time she'd finally gotten a message from her father, but it was so strange, she wasn't sure what to think.

"What does it mean?" Brynn said.

Mia reread the words.

Dear Mia,

When I heard you moved to Salem, I realized it was only a matter of time until you found my trail.

You were always a clever girl and worthy of the name Bold.

By now you know that the people of Salem consider me to be Laird Frank Bold. And though there is a mystery here, not all deceptions are lies.

The reason I've been gone all these years is to protect you, Mia. I will always love you and be your father, but you need to give up the search.

Forces bigger than you and I are at play here.

So, look no further.

With love, always.

Your father,

Frank Bold

Tears welled up in Mia's eyes as she read the words. Brynn scooted over beside her on the couch and hugged her. Although Mia fought the tears, they started to flow. How long had she dreamed of her father telling her that he loved her? But the words were also cryptic, and created more questions than answers.

"Oh Mimi, it's going to be okay," Brynn said. "I know it."

"It's just the shock, I'll be fine," Mia said and dried her eyes.

"He's alive though," Brynn said, patting her back. "And you're good at solving mysteries."

Brynn handed Mia her cup of hot chocolate. Mia wiped her tears away and took a sip of the warm, comforting drink. Tandy snuggled under Mia's arm, sensing her distress. She petted him while she considered what to do next. The letter was certainly strange. What did Frank mean by "*not all deceptions are lies*" and "*forces bigger than you and I are at play here*"? Why was he known in Salem as a Scottish lord? One thing had been cleared up: Frank was lost on purpose—apparently to protect her.

From what? Mia wondered, frustrated. The letter seemed to be a warning.

"I just can't figure out why he was here," Mia said. "Or what he's trying to protect me from."

"Maybe sleep on it?" Brynn said.

At that moment, Mia's phone pinged. It was a text from Johnny.

Did you get home safely?
XOXO, Your BF

Mia laughed, which was a relief after the ghost of her father had appeared.

"Who is it?" Brynn said.

"Johnny, just seeing if we got back safely," Mia said and smiled.

"So, you and Johnny, huh?" Brynn said.

"It's not what you think," Mia said.

"Look, I know you two were staging that little performance for Mark," Brynn said. "I don't blame you."

"You knew?" Mia said, surprised. "I didn't think you noticed. Graham was dominating your attention."

"Not all of it," Brynn said and smiled. "Now that I've seen you with your friends, I realize how incompatible you and Mark are. He's not the right guy for you."

"Thanks, Brynn," Mia said.

"I think he's in love with you," Brynn said.

"Who, Mark?" Mia said as she took off her jewelry.

"No, Johnny." Brynn said, sipping her chocolate.

"*Johnny?* I doubt that," Mia laughed.

"I'd be careful if I were you, Mimi. I can tell when a man is hung up on a girl, and Johnny is hung up on *you*," Brynn said as she strolled over to the hall closet. She pulled out a stack of sheets. "I'll take the couch tonight."

As Mia got ready for bed, she thought about her sister's words. If what Brynn said was true, what would she do about her romantic predicament? Every day it was becoming clearer she was attracted to two different men.

Hugh Wolfe was down to earth, charming, and handsome. But there was a magnetic pull between her and Johnny she couldn't deny. What was it about Johnny? He was sexy, of course, but there was something deeper, something soulful about him, and he always surprised her.

She pulled on her sleep shorts and a muscle T-shirt. Then she remembered to check her messages. The first one was from Ollie Cooper.

"Hey, Mia, we're calling a crew meeting for nine a.m. to discuss the next episode. See you then."

There was a beep and the next message played. A familiar, stern voice came on the phone, and Mia felt a deep sense of dread.

"Mia Bold? This is Detective Charlie Waite calling. I need you to come down to the station to answer a few questions. We've come to a dead end here. And well, all roads lead to you. I'll be in my office in the morning. Don't make me come look for you."

Suddenly, the seriousness of her situation hit Mia hard. It felt like a bucket of cold water had been thrown over her head. As much as she wanted to figure out what was going on with her dad, Mia realized there was a very real threat to her own life. If she didn't find out what happened to Cindy Moore fast, there was a good chance she could be arrested for a crime she didn't commit. A nervous dread overwhelmed her. Her dad and whatever he was up to would have to wait. She really wanted to talk to someone about the case. She thought about discussing it with her sister. But Brynn didn't know about what had happened at the Elmwood House and Mia wanted to keep it that way. She had enough on her mind with the recent problems with Jeffrey. Mia tiptoed into the living room to see if Brynn was still up. But she was fast asleep, nestled in a pile of covers, her blonde hair puddled on the pillow, with Rose curled in a ball, purring against her chest.

She just could not bring herself to drag Brynn into this situation.

Mia went back into her room and climbed into bed. Who could she call? She thought about Hugh, but he didn't know about the Elmswood House either. Mia didn't want to drag the new guy she was dating into a murder mystery where she might very well be the prime suspect. Sylvie was perfect but she was probably fast asleep.

Then there was Johnny, the night owl. The thought of him made her heart beat faster. Don't be silly, she told herself. No matter what Brynn said, Johnny Astor was just pretending to be her boyfriend. He was so popular, there was no way he could possibly be interested in her. But he knew about the case and nothing Mia said would faze him. She took a deep breath and dialed.

"Mia? What a nice surprise," Johnny said when he answered the phone. "Can't keep away from me, huh?"

“Ha, ha,” Mia said. “Thank you for being my pretend boyfriend. I think you might have fixed my problem.”

“Rescuing damsels in distress is one of my side hustles,” Johnny said.

“Listen, remember when you said Detective Charlie Waite called to get your alibi on the night Cindy Moore died? And you said he brought me up in the conversation?”

“He brought you up a few times,” Johnny said.

“Well, he left a message. He wants to see me tomorrow,” Mia said.

Johnny got quiet. Mia loved the way he always seemed to consider things before responding. He was a very thoughtful person, really.

“Well, that seems serious,” Johnny said. “I guess we better find out who killed Cindy Moore fast. What have you found so far?”

“Well, I spoke to her business partner, Doug Tanner. He didn’t know much. So Sylvie and I looked through Cindy’s appointment book.”

“How did you—” Johnny said, surprised. “Don’t answer that. I don’t want to know.”

“Anyway, we talked to the first client in the book, Howard Adler. He admitted to making the appointment, but said Cindy cancelled the showing due to another client. There was a name scribbled all over her book, the guy she mentioned to us—Mr. Fat Cat.”

“So the number one suspect is Fat Cat? What about the owner?”

“Connie Carol has an alibi. The night of the murder she was hustling seniors in a poker game,” Mia said. “And she changed her mind about selling the house.”

“So basically, we need to hunt down Fat Cat?”

“Exactly. I found his name in one of the online real estate forums. It seems he was snooping around and asking a lot of questions about Elmswood House.”

“Listen, Mia. I’ll pick you up in the morning. After the BB&C meeting, you and I can head down to Swampscott. Maybe that real estate guy knows more than he’s letting on.”

CHAPTER TWENTY THREE

Mia pulled her boots on, straightened out her outfit, combed her hair, dusted her cheeks with blush, brushed on some mascara, and glossed her lips. Why was she always so nervous whenever she was about to see Johnny? It was as if she had no control over her body. There was a friendly rap on the door.

"Brynn? Can you get that?" Mia called out from the bathroom.

"Sure, Mimi," Brynn said and opened the door.

Mia could hear Sylvie and Brynn greeting each other. She checked herself one last time. She looked casual but professional in black slacks and a silky dove-gray blouse. She completed the look with small silver hoop earrings.

"You ready?" Sylvie called out.

"In a second," Mia yelled as she fluffed her hair before walking out to greet Sylvie. Tandy danced around, happy to see her too. Rose jumped up on the table and sniffed the air with her pink nose before rubbing her flank against Sylvie as she set down her giant pack of equipment.

"What's in the bag, a way to patch into the matrix?" Brynn said, sipping her coffee.

"Oh you know, mega files of Mia and Johnny jabbering away," Sylvie said and grinned. She was forever shuttling hard drives between the office and home.

"I'm almost done," Mia said. "Johnny should be here any second."

"Johnny, huh? He's picking us up?" Sylvie said, curiously. Her hands were tucked into her bomber jacket and she wore a tartan skirt and black tights along with her customary Doc Marten boots.

"He's looking out for her," Brynn said and giggled.

"What is that supposed to mean?" Sylvie said.

"Knock it off, Brynn," Mia said, sweetly. "She's just making jokes about dinner last night."

"Did something happen at dinner?" Sylvie said.

"Mark showed up and Jeffrey had a black eye," Mia said.

"That ghost in room seventeen, huh? I heard of a guy who ended up having chunks of his hair pulled out," Sylvie said.

"Really?" Brynn said, growing a little pale. She touched the bracelet Hazel gave her. "According to Mia's witch friend, I'm protected."

"Don't worry, that bracelet Hazel gave you will do the trick," Sylvie said. "You're good."

Mia grabbed a distressed brown leather blazer off the coat rack and checked the equipment in her bag.

"Ready," she said and slung her messenger bag over one shoulder.

"Can I ask you a question before you go, Mia?" Brynn said.

"Sure," Mia said.

"Should I call that agent friend of Graham's?" Brynn said.

"Why not?" Mia said. "Graham might be a little eccentric, but he has a lot of Hollywood contacts. What would Jeffrey think?"

"I don't care what Jeffrey thinks right now," Brynn said, pouting.

"Well then, your biggest problem is Daniel. You know how he feels about showbiz. If his stepdaughter and his daughter both end up in the business, he might blow his top."

"Are you talking about our Graham?" Sylvie said, eyebrows raised in surprise. "The producer who escaped from Quentin Tarantino's wardrobe department?"

"Yep, he thinks Brynn would be great in commercials and gave her a contact to call," Mia said.

"She would," Sylvie said. "Just look at that face."

"Oh, you're sweet," Brynn said, blushing. "I'm going to meet Mom and Dad later. I'll lock up when I leave. Have a fun meeting."

Mia clipped on Tandy's lead and they headed downstairs. The minute Tandy was outside, he buried his nose in the flowers and started happily chomping on grass.

Johnny was waiting across the street, dressed in a dark maroon shirt, leather jacket, and jeans. He waved at Mia and Sylvie as they crossed the street.

"Hey there, boy," Johnny said and ruffled Tandy's ears. "Shall we?"

They started down the street toward the office.

Tandy trotted beside his human pack, sniffing each of the vendors who were out in force. As they passed Charnel Tours, there was a congregation of Salem's magical community milling in front of the building. A large sign announced there was a psychic fair and the magical readers were setting up their tables with the tools of the trade: tarot cart decks, crystal balls, crystals, scrying pendants, rune stones, and ointments. The air smelled of burning sage.

Albee Abernathy was out front overseeing the production. He spotted the three of them and tipped his hat in their direction.

Tandy growled slightly at the sight of the tour guide.

"Hey, Johnny," Sylvie began. "Any idea what's on the agenda for today's crew meeting?"

"I suspect there's a deadline with the cable network," Johnny said. "There always is. Speaking of deadlines, what are we going to do about Detective Charlie Waite?"

"Why? What happened?" Sylvie said, turning to Mia. "Is he still bothering you?"

"He called me again. He wants to see me today," Mia said.

"Hoo boy," Sylvie said. "So, you're still a suspect?"

"Looks like it," Mia said, distracted. Down the street, a man was walking toward her with purpose. His blond hair and athletic gait were familiar.

"Oh no," Mia said with a sinking sensation like she was swimming in quicksand. Of course she knew him—it was Mark. He started jogging toward her, his expression strangely deluded. Mia got the distinct impression last night's performance had barely made a dent.

"Isn't that your ex-boyfriend at twelve o'clock?" Johnny said.

"Yes," Mia said miserably. "Here we go again."

"It's showtime," Johnny said. Suddenly, he slipped his arm around Mia's waist. Mia looked up at him, startled, as her heart began to pound.

Sylvie gave Mia and Johnny a questioning glance.

"What the—" Sylvie said, surprised at their new familiarity.

"Just play along," Mia whispered to Sylvie.

There was an oily puddle on the ground in front of them.

"Hold on a second, darling!" Johnny said loudly and swept Mia up in his arms. Then he stepped across the puddle and stole a kiss before letting her down gently on the other side of the puddle. Mia blushed and Tandy leaped up with excitement.

Mark stopped in his tracks and shoved his hands in his pocket. He stared at the elaborate gesture, baffled and disturbed by Johnny's attention toward Mia. He opened his mouth as if to say something before shaking his head. Then he abruptly crossed the street to avoid them. Mia glanced back to see Mark disappear around the corner.

"My lady." Johnny bowed and genuflected with his hand. "The dragon has been dispatched."

"Very gallant, Sir Astor," Mia said and curtsied.

"Good grief! What is going on with you two?" Sylvie said, stumped by their odd behavior.

"Johnny's been pretending to be my boyfriend," Mia said.

"What?" Sylvie said. "Because of your ex?"

"Mark's been impossible," Mia said. "He won't take no for an answer."

"That should do the trick," Johnny said.

"Your dinner must have been interesting," Sylvie said skeptically. "So, you're just *pretending*?"

"Of course!" Mia said, her cheeks rosy and her heart beating fast after the excitement of being swept into Johnny's arms.

"Absolutely," Johnny said, glancing at Sylvie with an innocent expression on his face.

"Hmmm," Sylvie said and stared back at him skeptically. "The next meeting of Love Addicts Anonymous should be a doozy."

They reached the *Bell, Book, and Candle* building and headed up the steps. The crew was already there. Mia immediately noticed that Ollie looked worried and was drumming his fingers on the conference table. Graham was sitting at his desk talking on the phone. Will and Jake waited at the conference table staring at their phones. Tandy checked in with each of his human friends before finding a chew toy and settling down to give his jaws a workout.

Mia, Sylvie, and Johnny joined the others around the table.

"Well," Ollie said. "As you all know, the tragic death of Cindy Moore has thrown off our shooting schedule. We can either put our faith in the cops and hope Elmswood House is cleared in time, or we can go with another location."

"Maybe it's just as well," Mia said. "The house was creepy before Cindy died. Now the whole thing just feels tragic."

"You have to admit, Mia," Johnny said, "Elmswood House is an amazing find. It's unique. And we are in the ghost hunting business, so there is no avoiding creepiness and dark histories."

"At least someone appreciates the location," Graham said.

Sylvie nudged Mia and whispered, "Does Graham think you and Johnny are an item?"

"He didn't seem to notice," Mia whispered back. "He was too focused on Brynn."

Jake cleared his throat and put down his phone.

"Mia's right, the house is creepy as hell!" Jake said. "But as far as filming goes, it's going to look terrific. So, if what you're looking for is drama, that house is a great location."

"I agree," Will said and darted a glance toward Mia. "Sorry!"

"Okay, but with the police involved and all, I just think there are more straightforward places to shoot," Mia said, trying to remain calm but the anxiety was building. All she had to do was think of that house and her nerves were on edge. "Whatever is going on in that place is—" She broke the thought off.

"—What?" Ollie said.

"I'm not sure, just wrong," Mia said.

"Nobody else has filmed there, which makes the location pretty marketable," Johnny said. "And I have to admit I was intrigued after Albee told us about the ghost of Lydia Humphrey."

When Johnny mentioned Lydia Humphrey, Mia suddenly felt ill. Her stomach churned and she thought she might be sick, just like the day she discovered Cindy Moore's body.

"Mia?" Johnny said, noticing her cheeks drain of color.

"I just need a little air," Mia said and pushed away from the table.

"Okay, guys," Sylvie said. "While our stars are getting some air, I want to go over some points about editing—"

Mia was grateful to Sylvie for covering as she stepped outside.

Johnny and Tandy followed her as she walked over to the steps and sank down, leaning her forehead against the iron railing. Tandy settled at the step where her feet rested.

"What's going on with you, Mia?" Johnny said. "Every time we talk about that house, you get weirded out."

"I didn't tell you everything," Mia said, resting her chin on her knees.

"You mean the day you found Cindy Moore?"

"Yes, the day I found her, I was breathing in gas, so maybe that explains it. But I heard something run across the ceiling. When I looked outside, I saw her."

"Lydia?" Johnny said and sat down beside her on the steps.

"Yes," Mia said as a wave of dread washed over her.

"You know I'm here for you, right?" Johnny said. "You can always tell me about whatever is bothering you."

"I was embarrassed," Mia said.

"I know it's hard for you to admit you saw a ghost," Johnny said. "But I think there's something special about you, Mia. This isn't the first time you've seen things. You saw those ghosts at Howard Street Cemetery."

"There's no proof what I saw were ghosts," Mia said. "And when it comes to Lydia, I prefer to think the carbon monoxide made me hallucinate."

"Look, you know I believe in the supernatural," Johnny said. "And you're a skeptic. But let's both try to keep an open mind, deal?"

"Deal," Mia said and smiled.

"As soon as this is over, let's go down to Seaside Estates," Johnny said. "Do you think Cindy's business partner could have killed her?"

"Doug Tanner?" Mia said. "The day Sylvie and I paid him a visit, he seemed almost happy that she was gone. He said that having Elmswood House on the books was terrible for his business."

"Well, that seems suspicious," Johnny said. "Wasn't he the one who gave you the key to Elmswood?"

"Yes, which is how I ended up discovering Cindy's body," Mia said.

"Putting you in the crosshairs of Detective Waite," Johnny added.

"He must be trying to frame me!" Mia said. Now that she thought about it, Doug Tanner certainly had the means and the opportunity to commit the murder. All they needed to figure out was the real motive.

"Okay, let's finish up this meeting and hit the road."

They went back inside. Graham was on the phone talking loudly and everyone else was looking at him in anticipation.

"I need more time," Graham said into the phone. "This isn't a studio shoot, it's a haunted house. Do you get that? Sure, I realize you're on a schedule. But I can't wrangle the ghosts, now can I? That's what I'm being paid to do? Really? Is that so? Fine, we'll make it happen. No problem."

Graham hung up the phone looking exasperated.

"What?" Sylvie said.

"We're screwed," he said. "The network says if we don't hand the show in to them in a week, the deal is off."

Mia looked around at her friends, the crew of *Bell, Book, and Candle*. Everyone depended on the show, including her. She needed to figure out what really happened to Cindy Moore before everything they'd built up was destroyed.

CHAPTER TWENTY FOUR

Mia pulled into the parking lot of Seaside Estates. Johnny was in the passenger's seat with Sylvie and Tandy riding in the back. Doug Tanner's SUV was parked in front of the office. Through the window, they could see the real estate agent on the phone, leaning back in his chair with his feet up on the desk.

"He doesn't look too broken up over the whole thing," Johnny said.

"That's what we thought," Sylvie said.

"Come on, let's find out what he knows," Mia said and opened the door for Sylvie. Tandy jumped down and ran along the side of the building, stopping to check the interesting scents he found there. They walked around to the front of the building and strolled inside. The receptionist took one look at Johnny and stood up abruptly, dropping the papers in her hand in surprise.

"J-Johnny Astor?" she said, barely able to choke the words out. "Oh gosh, I love your podcast. I follow you on Twitter. Your new show is amazing."

As usual, Johnny seemed to have a magical effect on people. Mia was struck by the contrast between the girl's lackluster response the last time she was in the office and her current display of recognition.

"That's great," Johnny said and smiled his thousand-watt smile. "What's your name?"

"Me? Ah, I'm P-Pam," the receptionist said, her eyes as wide as saucers. Suddenly she remembered her appearance. Her hands fluttered over her jacket, straightening the seams so that she sat a little bit taller.

Johnny pulled a card out of his pocket and turned it over. Then he signed the back with a flourish and handed it to Pam. The card read: *Official friend of Bell, Book, and Candle. I hope we can count on you to bust some ghosts!*

Mia looked at the card, stunned.

Johnny had printed up cards to autograph?

"I hope you come to my next video chat, Pam," Johnny said.

"Oh my gosh," Pam said. "This is awesome." She stared at the card with Johnny's signature, blushing head to toe. Then she seemed to remember her duties. "Oh goodness, let me get Doug." Pam knocked on Doug's door.

Doug Tanner came out of his office. The moment he spotted Johnny he plastered a smile across his face.

"Aren't you the guy on that *Bell, Book, and Candle* show?" Doug said. Then he spotted Mia and Sylvie. "Any luck getting the owner to sell to you?"

"You were right," Sylvie said. "She wasn't interested in selling."

"Come on into the office," Doug said. As they all walked inside, Doug took a seat behind his desk and leaned back with his hands behind his head. "So, what can I do for you? Ready to look at some of my other properties, Ms. Rockstar?"

Johnny looked at Sylvie questioningly and she pursed her lips and shook her head, indicating not to go there.

"I'm still kind stuck on that one," Sylvie said.

Mia took the seat across from Doug and steepled her fingers.

"Listen, Doug, I have a question."

"Shoot," Doug said.

"Did you kill Cindy Moore?" Mia said sharply.

The color drained from Doug Tanner's face and his salesman's smile crumbled. He looked at Sylvie and Johnny, who just stared back at him while Tandy snorted and lay down to wait out the human business.

"What?" he said. "You think I killed Cindy? How could you think that!" He seemed genuinely shocked by what Mia was saying.

"You don't seem too broken up over her death," Mia said, watching him carefully. He was tense. But it was hard to tell if his reaction was genuine.

Doug looked down at his desk and nodded, his fists clenched.

"Look, Cindy and I had our problems," Doug said in a ragged voice. "She had a big personality and she didn't like to listen. Sure, she brought in a lot of clients, but I'm not going to lie and tell you things aren't easier now that she's gone. She argued with me about everything, that Elmswood House most of all."

"Why?" Johnny said.

"The owner, Connie Carol, was too high maintenance, a total recluse who refused every reasonable offer and wouldn't even meet with serious buyers when they asked. I begged Cindy to take that

Elmswood monstrosity off our books. But she was a workaholic, she took any commission, big or small."

"So maybe you killed her for the sake of the business?" Mia said, pushing him. Was he upset about being accused, or being found out?

Doug Tanner shook his head back and forth.

"The business? Are you kidding me? Cindy was the face of this place. With her gone, I'm in trouble! Her clients loved her. Most of them have already gone with other agents," Doug Tanner said.

"Why should we believe you?" Johnny said, glancing at Mia.

"Because I have no motive to kill her! She was a money-maker. Besides, I was at a neighbor's housewarming party with my family that night!"

"Listen, Doug," Johnny said. "We want to help you clear your name."

"Why? Do the cops think I did it?" Doug said nervously.

Johnny slid into the chair next to Mia and shrugged.

"Somebody did it," Johnny said. "You knew where Cindy was, you had a key. How late were you at that housewarming?"

"I-I'm not sure," Doug said.

"Exactly," Johnny said. "The best thing you could do is help us find out who killed her."

Mia and Sylvie exchanged glances. She'd never seen Johnny use his powers of persuasion so diabolically before. But from the look on Doug Tanner's face, Johnny's theory was working. The guy was cracking big-time

"Doug?" Mia said. "We spoke to one of Cindy's clients, Howard Adler. Cindy called him the night she was killed. Do you know him?"

"No," Doug said.

"She told him she was meeting another client. We need to find who that client was, any ideas?"

"I already told you Cindy didn't take my advice. She was a bit reckless."

"Cindy referred to the client as Mr. Fat Cat. Ring any bells?"

"Fat Cat?" Doug said. "We only had one client who was pretty loaded and was interested in that house. A guy from Salem named Greg Abbott. He owns that freak show in Salem, the one where they swallow swords and crap."

"I know the place," Sylvie said. "The Witch City Side Show. There's a guy who pounds nails into his head. I think I told your sister about it."

Doug opened up his phone and texted the contact card to Mia.

"Thanks, Doug," Sylvie said. "As soon as my record contract drops, I'll let you know about my real estate needs."

"Sure, sure," Doug said, glad to see them leave.

Johnny gave Sylvie a funny look but kept his mouth shut. As soon as they were outside he turned to Sylvie.

"Record contract? Now look who's pretending?"

Mia's phone buzzed with an incoming text from Swampscott PD. As she looked at the text, the hackles rose on the back of her neck.

We need to ask you a few questions.
When are you available to come in?

"Ugh, it's Detective Waite," Mia said. "What if he arrests me?"

"You realize a lawyer would tell you not to talk to the police," Sylvie said. "Isn't your brother-in-law a lawyer?"

"That is a last resort," Mia said and started typing out a reply.

Today is bad.
Got a few things to clear up.
Maybe tomorrow?

Mia shoved her phone back in her pocket.

"Let's go have a chat with Mr. Abbott," Mia said.

***

Mia pulled up in front of the Witch City Side Show. The outside of the building was red brick with blackened windows painted with garish circus performers eating fire and swallowing swords. Mia put Tandy on a leash so he wouldn't freak anyone out as they walked past the small line of people waiting to buy tickets for the next show. The girl behind the desk was wearing goth makeup and chewing gum. She checked in guests who had bought tickets on the Internet, and took cash from others. Mia glanced at Sylvie, who nodded. They learned the lesson of the last receptionist. Best to let Johnny handle it.

"You better deal with this," Mia whispered and pushed him forward.

"No problem," Johnny said and stepped up to the front desk. He smiled charmingly and leaned on the counter.

The goth girl looked at him and her eyes got big. She blinked her doll-like fake eyelashes in recognition.

"Johnny Astor?" she said. "The podcaster?"

"That's me," Johnny said.

"You jerk! Why'd you break up with Vicki Carlyle?" the girl said.

"I-I didn't mean to upset her," Johnny said, flustered. "Our breakup was mutual!"

"That's not what she said!" the goth girl said, indignant. "She posted that she fell out a window and ripped her clothes."

"I would never—" Johnny said, startled by her venom.

"She's a creative genius. Her clothing line Cauldron Chic rocks. You're a jackass."

He opened his mouth to defend himself but no sound came out. Sylvie stepped in to handle the situation.

"Hey, we're looking for Greg Abbott?" Sylvie said.

The girl looked at Sylvie and calmed down.

"Cute boots. Can I ask who you are exactly?" the girl said, chewing her gum behind black lips.

"Mia and Sylvie from *Bell, Book, and Candle*. Is it okay if we bring Tandy with us?"

"That cute doggie? Of course! We have a dog in the act too," the girl said and came around the desk to pet the mutt. Then she walked back and dialed Greg Abbott's extension. "There're two women here to see you. Yes, Mia and Sylvie from a *Bell, Book, and Candle*. Yeah, they seem all right." She hung up and pointed through the curtains. "Go ahead. Through there and to the left of the stage. You'll see the stairs to the office."

The goth girl glared at Johnny and started texting.

"Good work, lover boy," Sylvie said with a smirk as they walked through the curtains.

"I broke up with Vicki months ago," Johnny said. "She has an army of Instagram followers. They're always so unreasonable."

Mia and Sylvie started giggling as Johnny tried to recover his dignity.

Inside the darkened auditorium, it took a moment for their eyes to adjust. The curtains were dark and dingy and stage hands were setting up the various props onstage, including an assortment of swords. They made their way to the stairs and climbed to the second floor, then down a narrow hallway to a door marked *Office*.

Mia knocked.

"Come in," came a throaty voice. The door swung open into a cramped room. Behind the desk was an older man, with a gray beard and a waxed mustache curled up on the corners of his mouth. Greg Abbott made a welcoming gesture with his hands.

"What can I do you for?" he said.

"Doug Tanner mentioned you were interested in buying the Elmswood House?"

He stared at them for a moment as a look of comprehension dawned on his face. "Why? Is it available?" Greg said.

"I'm afraid not," Mia said. "Did you ever have a look at the place?"

"Sure I did. I was planning to buy the property."

"Were you going to live there?"

"In that wreck? No. I wanted to open a haunted attraction. You know, tours of a haunted house and once a year on Halloween make the place a serious haunted house. I could have drawn people from across the state."

"What happened?" Mia said.

"The current owner caught wind of what I was planning to do and backed out. She didn't want the house turned into a 'spectacle.'"

How far would Greg Abbott be willing to go to acquire the house? Mia wondered.

"Did you know Cindy Moore?"

"Who?" Greg said.

"Doug Tanner's partner?"

"Oh, I know who you mean. I saw her in the office a few times. But I worked with Doug. You're talking about the bottled blond with the Jersey attitude?"

"That's her," Mia said. "I'm afraid she's dead."

"Dead?" Greg said, looking surprised. "How?"

"Carbon monoxide poisoning," Mia said.

"She was found at the house," Johnny added.

"Oh good lord," Greg said, shocked. "When?"

"Two days ago," Mia said.

“Huh, the last week we’ve been working every night putting a set together. What a shame,” Greg said. “My condolences. Isn’t that house the Browder family died?”

“Yes,” Mia said and glanced at Johnny. They both knew that eliminated Greg. Unless he was lying, there would be a ton of witnesses who could account for his whereabouts.

“One more question,” Mia said. “Were you ever on the real estate forums at Seaside Estates?”

“Sure,” Greg said. “I asked questions from time to time.”

“What was your username?”

“Showman26,” Greg said. “Why?”

“Did you ever see a user called Fat Cat?”

Greg looked up at the ceiling as if trying to retrieve a thought.

“Oh wait, I remember. There was a guy who kept asking about that Elmswood property too. I can’t remember his user name. He could have been Fat Cat. I do remember he was kind of a real estate nerd, always quoting weird facts.”

Mia, Johnny, and Sylvie exchanged glances.

“Thanks, Greg,” Johnny said.

Greg handed him a card.

“Give me a call, I might want to advertise on your show,” he said.

They walked back out through the theater. The show had started and there was a smattering of audience members as a man stood on stage lowering a sword down his throat. They all crept along the far aisle and attempted to sneak out of the auditorium without disrupting the show.

As they emerged through the heavy velvet curtains and stepped into the lobby, Mia froze. Her cheeks flushed as she saw who was waiting for them.

“What are you doing here?” Mia said.

CHAPTER TWENTY FIVE

"I should be asking you that question," Detective Landry said, leaning casually against the ticket counter. "What are you doing here, Mia?"

"Um, hi, Detective Landry," Mia waffled as she stepped into the lobby from behind the curtain, followed by Johnny, Sylvie, and Tandy.

"That's them," said the goth girl said. "Like I said, the geek squad."

"Well, well, well," Landry said. "If it isn't Mia Bold and her Scooby-Doo posse. Tampering with an official police investigation, as usual." He looked directly at Mia with a mild expression of surprise before shaking his head as if this meeting was inevitable. Mia closed her eyes and took a deep breath.

How embarrassing! She was caught red-handed, investigating Cindy Moore's death. She hadn't texted him or told him anything, after he had specifically asked her to keep him in the loop.

Tandy wagged his tail in recognition before trotting over to greet the detective. Landry gave the dog a friendly stroke along his flanks.

"We just had some questions for Greg Abbott, that's all," Mia said.

Landry stepped closer to Mia. "If I were you I would consider the course of radical honesty right about now, for your own sake."

"Of course," Mia said.

"Shall we take this outside?" Landry said.

The goth girl took a picture of Johnny Astor with her phone and started to post an update.

"Really?" Johnny said as he walked out.

As they all stepped outside onto the pavement, Mia fidgeted a little. The situation was incredibly awkward. She should have texted Landry with what she'd found so far, but her whole life had been blown up by the arrival of her family and her ex-boyfriend/stalker. Not to mention, the blow-up between Brynn and her brother-in-law, Jeffrey. But Mia refused to make excuses. Instead, she stood in front of Landry and waited.

"Do you want to try explaining yourself?" Landry said with his wry southern drawl.

"Doug Tanner mentioned Greg Abbott, so we were checking him out, that's all. I don't think either one was involved."

"What makes you say that?" Landry said.

"They both have an alibi, for one thing. Doug was at a housewarming party with his family, and Greg was building sets all week for his circus show. Whoever killed Cindy needed time and privacy."

"And Howard Adler?" Landry said impatiently.

Mia's cheeks flushed red again. So Landry knew everyone she'd spoken to about the case? *Of course he did!*

"Uh, yeah, he said Cindy cancelled their appointment," Mia admitted.

"And Connie Carol," Landry said. "Don't tell me you skipped her?"

"Er, no," Mia said. "She was hustling elders at a poker game that night. She's decided not to sell."

"Well, then you and I are on the same page," Landry said. "I knew you'd look into Cindy Moore's death. I expected it. But I'm warning you—just because you're good at research doesn't mean you should investigate something this dangerous."

"Dangerous? What do you mean?" Johnny said, concerned.

"I mean that someone had a reason for killing her. In my experience, an investigation grows more treacherous the closer you get to the truth. You can unwittingly stumble into a bad situation. That's why the job is dangerous."

"He's right, Mia," Johnny said "There's a murderer out there."

"But we found a clue, Detective," Mia said. "There were a bunch of notes in Cindy's books referring to Mr. Fat Cat. That was the name of a user on the real estate forum on Seaside Estates website. Greg Abbott, also known as Showman26, was in the same forum. He said that when it came to real estate, Fat Cat was a know-it-all. He was focused on the Elmswood House."

"When were you planning to tell me all this?" Landry said.

Mia blushed again.

"I was going to text you, I swear," Mia said.

"Well, I have some news for you too," Landry said. "It seems your fingerprints were found all over the crime scene. On the car door, in the garage, on the body, and in various places around the house. There were muddy foot prints all around Cindy's body. Someone was there with Cindy that night and Detective Waite thinks that person is *you*."

Mia stood stock-still as the color drained from her cheeks. She could see that Landry was serious.

"Mia didn't do it," Johnny said and put his hands on her shoulders.

"I-I tried to switch off the car and open the garage door to get rid of the carbon monoxide gas," Mia said, starting to feel a rising sense of panic.

"It's looking bad for you, Mia," Landry said. "Charlie Waite has a near perfect record of getting people to implicate themselves in crimes. If you think you can outwit him, I'm here to tell you you're wrong. Now I'm going to go talk to Greg Abbott. In the meantime I think it's time you got a lawyer."

Mia could see by the stern expression in Detective Landry's eyes that he wasn't kidding. Mia was in deep trouble.

Johnny steered Mia toward the car. Sensing her distress, Tandy stuck by her side and kept trying to touch his nose to her fingertips.

"Are you okay to drive?" Sylvie said, looking at Mia warily.

"I'm fine," Mia said and slipped into the driver's seat. She gripped the steering wheel with white knuckles. Something Landry said bothered her. She mulled over his words in her mind, sifting them for clues as Johnny, Sylvie, and Tandy climbed inside the car.

"Landry said someone else was there with Cindy," Mia said.

"There must have been," Johnny said.

"He said there were muddy footprints around the body," Mia said. "That's how they knew someone was with her."

"Yeah, I heard him say that," Sylvie said.

"I saw those footprints myself," Mia said. "They were all around the body. These weird muddy prints."

"What about it?" Johnny said.

"It hasn't rained this month," Mia said.

Sylvie scrambled to check the weather app on her phone.

"Oh my gosh, it's true," she said, scrolling through the screens.

"The whole reason I'm in this mess is because I have no alibi. The evening it happened, I fell asleep with a book open. The last thing I remember before falling asleep was looking into a clear sky. The moon was full that night. No clouds."

"Then how did the mud get there?" Johnny said.

"I don't know, but I'm going to find out." Mia turned on the ignition and did a U-turn. They headed back to Swampscott.

***

Mia parked to the side of the Elmswood House, in case Detective Waite decided to drive by the front. She looked up at the old mansion. The house looked worse than she remembered, rising against the afternoon with distant scalloped clouds reflecting the sinking sun. The steeply pitched roof was even sharper at this angle, the pointed arches and front-facing gables at a jagged angle. On this side of the house, the torn wooden slates made the roof appear as if it was full of holes and the delicate verge-board trim hung in broken pieces. The salty sea breeze had lashed the house until the paint was peeling and blistered.

Mia, Sylvie, and Johnny stared, unable to take their eyes off the building. Tandy sank down in the back seat, immediately sensing the terrible energy.

"Where should we start?" Johnny said, looking at the house calmly.

"Burn it to the ground?" Sylvie said.

"Shhh, it might be listening," Johnny said. "Don't rile the thing up."

"Rile it up?" Sylvie said. "Are you serious?"

"I'm dead serious," Johnny said and winked at Mia.

Mia tried to smile, but the truth was her stomach was twisting in knots at the sight of the place.

"I think we should go around the back and try to find some evidence of how the killer trailed mud into the house," Mia said. "Maybe there's a damp patch or burst pipe or something?"

"Okay, let's go," Johnny said.

They stepped out of the car, looking up at the house. It was hard to take your eyes off the place, Mia thought as they crossed the street. It was as if the house was a dangerous animal that might suddenly move.

They started around the back, pushing past the dead vegetation and tangled branches. There was an old, broken fence that had been knocked down and they stepped over the snapped and sunken railings. As they rounded the corner, they could see the dilapidated old park. Mia felt a chill. As they reached the backyard the grass was dry and overgrown with a worn path leading to the little park. Instead of Tandy exploring the new area, he slunk by Mia's heels, head down and wary.

The back of the house came into view and Mia stopped and pointed.

"What is that?" she said.

"A storm cellar," Johnny said.

Attached to the house was a double hatchway door that should've been bolted. As they walked over to the double doors, they saw the padlock that should have held the latch was broken. Some nails were protruding on the edge of the door and caught on one was a piece of bright blue fabric.

"Can we open it and see what's down there?" Mia said.

"Hold on," Johnny said. He pulled his sleeves over his fingers. "There could be fingerprints." Carefully, he gripped the door. There was a long creaking sound as he lifted the door halfway up. Mia pulled her flashlight out of her pocket and shined the light down into the basement. She gasped.

"What's down there?" Johnny said.

"Water," she said. "The basement is flooded. Whoever left those muddy shoe prints went through the cellar."

"Before killing Cindy Moore," Sylvie said.

Suddenly, there was a rustling sound behind them.

"What are you doing here?" a low voice boomed out.

CHAPTER TWENTY SIX

Mia practically jumped out of her skin and her legs turned to rubber. She cringed, afraid to turn around. Here they were at the site of the murder trying to get inside the house. If this was Detective Charlie Waite, her life was over. Johnny lowered the cellar door carefully.

"Uh-oh," Sylvie said with the experienced air of someone who was used to being in trouble. Mia, on the other hand, let out a huff of breath as she faced the interloper.

"You almost gave me a heart attack," Mia said, both embarrassed and relieved to see Detective Landry again.

"After everything I just said to you?" Landry said. "I find you at the crime scene? What exactly are you doing here?"

"I could ask you the same thing," Mia said.

"When I saw you turn around, I decided to follow you," Landry said.

"Aren't you Salem PD, not Swampscott PD?" Mia said.

"You have a point," Landry said. "None of us should be here. Now, do you want to tell me why you came back?"

"I remembered something about the day I found the body," Mia said. "I wanted to check it out before I alerted you."

"What exactly did you remember?" Landry said.

"The day I found Cindy, she was surrounded by muddy shoe prints," Mia said. "How did they get there? I remembered that the night she was killed, the moon was full, and the sky clear. It didn't rain that night. We checked the weather and there hasn't been any rain for weeks. So how did muddy shoe prints end up all around her body?"

"You've got to admit she has a point," Johnny said.

"I'll admit it," Landry said.

"Anyway, we found something," Mia said and pointed to the piece of fabric lodged on a sharp nail.

Landry examined the fabric.

"This is from a Big Blue jacket," Landry said.

"Big Blue jacket?" Johnny said. "What does that mean?"

"The colors of Swampscott High School," Landry said. " All their football and basketball players wear windbreakers this color."

"The day Cindy gave us the house tour, she mentioned that kids had been breaking into the place," Johnny said.

"Can you hold the door up for me?" Landry said. "Leave the side with the fabric undisturbed."

Johnny walked to the hatch door and lifted it up again.

"You're going down there?" Sylvie said.

"That's the only way to understand the situation," Landry said and took a flashlight out of his pocket. He shined it down into the basement. There were steep cement steps that led down.

"Can you see the water?" Mia said.

"I sure can," Landry said and stepped down onto the stairs. When he reached the bottom step, he swept the light beam over the floor. "There's a couple of levels. Looks like a crawl space with a dirt floor, just above the main floor. The basement is flooded, maybe a pipe is leaking. There's a muddy sludge across the floor. On the far side of the basement is a staircase."

"I think that leads to the mud room," Mia said.

"Mud room?" Landry said.

"The place people took off their muddy boots and shoes," Mia said.

Landry climbed back up and helped Johnny to lower the hatch. Then he pulled out his phone and made a call.

"Agatha, could you do me a favor? Can you tell me if there have been any reports of vandalism or breaking and entering in the last month in Swampscott?" He held his hand over the phone as he waited.

"What else do you remember, Mia?" Landry said.

"Let's see. I remember Cindy's shoes were clean. That's why the shoe prints struck me as odd at the time. Do you think those footprints belong to the murderer?"

"Maybe," Landry said and turned back to his phone call. "Yes, I'm here. Who? Billy Whitehead? What's his buddy's name? Jeremy Whiner? That's an unfortunate name. Where'd they go to school? Uh-huh. Okay thanks, you've been a great help." Landry hung up the phone and his face took on a pensive expression as he considered his next move.

"Do you think it's the same kids?" Mia said.

"There's a good chance. They're both eighteen years old, graduated from Swampscott High and well known to the Swampscott PD.

They've been in trouble for joy riding, fighting, shoplifting. Nothing as serious as murder but they seem likely candidates for breaking into and entering an abandoned old house. I'd like to talk to them. Now we just have to find them. I'll check with dispatch and get addresses and—"

"Hold your horses," Sylvie said as her fingers flew over her phone's tiny keyboard. She started whistling the *Jeopardy* theme song. After a second her face lit up.

"What are you doing?" Johnny said.

"Gotcha!" Sylvie said in triumph. "Billy Whitehead and Jeremy Whiner are at the Salem Willows Arcade." She held her phone up and there was a picture of two strapping young men, their hats on sideways, posing in front of the Musical Monkeys display.

"How did you do that?" Landry said, impressed.

"They just posted on Facebook and their location is turned on." Sylvie scrolled through their streams. "Classic jocks freaking out now that they didn't get a football scholarship and their best days may be behind them."

"You'd make a good cop," Landry said and smiled, a rare sight for the detective.

"Let's face it, they're not the smartest criminals," Sylvie said and grinned.

"All right, ordinarily I'd tell you to go home and keep your noses clean, but I could use your help on this. If they see me, they might run, but if the hipster podcast celebrities chat them up, we might have a shot."

"We'd love to help," Mia said.

"I'm going to call Detective Waite and tell him about this evidence. You don't want him to catch you here, so get going."

"See you at the arcade, detective," Johnny said.

Mia, Johnny, Sylvie, and Tandy headed back to the car, circling around the backyard to avoid the front of the house. As they walked toward the abandoned playground, Tandy started to growl. Mia noticed the hackles on his neck were standing on end. Something moved deep in the dark green bushes. Tandy crouched down and barked. A bolt of fear shot through Mia. She thought she saw a shadow moving in the trees.

"Did you see that?" Mia said.

"See what?" Sylvie said, suddenly alert.

Johnny glanced at Mia, concerned.

"Let's go check it out," he said.

Mia looked up at Johnny, trembling with fear.

"I don't know if I can," Mia said. "Do you feel that? It's like the pressure in the atmosphere suddenly shifted."

Johnny took her hand. As she felt the warmth of his body heat she started to relax. "I'll be there with you, Mia. You can do this."

"Okay," she said, trying to shake off the sense of foreboding.

Mia and Johnny stepped into the abandoned park, followed by Sylvie and Tandy. There was a squeaking sound as the breeze pushed the old metal carousel in a circle, and the swings rattled and swayed back and forth. Johnny squeezed Mia's hand, trying to reassure her that she was not alone.

"Then Mia saw her. A little girl stood near the trees, almost like a shadow blending into the darkness. Mia could see the hooded cloak and, as she looked up, her solemn gray eyes. It looked like the girl she had seen in her dream.

"I see her," Mia choked out and pointed.

"I don't see anything," Johnny said.

"Me neither," Sylvie said nervously.

"Lydia?" Mia said, her voice rasping. "Is there a way I can help you?"

The ghostly little girl parted the leaves and disappeared into the bushes.

Mia ran after her, feet crunching the dried leaves.

"Lydia?" she called out. But the girl was nowhere. There was only the stillness of the old playground. *What could have happened to her?* Mia covered her mouth with her hand. She wished she could believe in ghosts, but she couldn't bring herself to abandon her rational mind, no matter how odd the phenomena she experienced. Whether or not ghosts existed remained an open problem. Maybe one day, she would solve the mystery.

"What's happening?" Johnny said, following Mia through the branches.

"She's gone now," Mia said, stepping to the spot where Lydia had disappeared. Then she pushed through the bushes, followed by Johnny, Sylvie, and Tandy. They found themselves standing on the sidewalk, just down from their car.

"What's that?" Sylvie said, pointing.

Planted on the corner of the small lot was a *For Sale* sign, but plastered across the front was the word *Sold.* At the bottom of the sign was a slogan: Halcyon Commercial Realty: Developing Dreams in Swampscott.

What could someone develop on this tiny lot? Mia wondered.

"I think Lydia is trying to tell you something," Johnny said.

"Maybe," Mia said, taking out her phone with trembling fingers. She snapped a picture of the sign. "Come on, we better get out of here before Detective Waite shows up."

CHAPTER TWENTY SEVEN

Mia pulled into one of the slanted parking spaces on Fort Avenue, facing the Salem Willows Arcade. Inside the oversized plate glass windows, the arcade was a blaze of color and spinning light. Groups of teens walked back and forth over the cosmic blue carpets with handfuls of tickets and pockets full of change, playing games. The place jangled and bleeped and hooted like a Vegas slot machine.

"I had no idea this place was here," Mia said.

"I love this place," Sylvie said. "I've been here a bunch of times. They have every game you could imagine. Drop games, app games, sports games. But I'm a connoisseur of the retro vintage games myself, Pac-Man, Galaga, Asteroids, Space Invaders, Donkey Kong, and Centipede to name a few. I'm also an official pinball wizard."

"A pinball wizard? I didn't know that was a thing," Mia said, letting Tandy out of the back seat.

"Are you kidding?" Sylvie said. "I'm ranked in the top two hundred pinball players in the world by the International Flipper Pinball Association."

"If you're such a pinball hustler, why work for *Bell, Book, and Candle*?" Johnny said and laughed.

Sylvie shrugged. "I felt sorry for you guys."

Landry pulled up in his unmarked car and rolled down his window.

"Can you find the boys and keep them busy for ten minutes?" he said.

"Leave it to me," Sylvie said. She took her phone out and showed Mia and Johnny the recently posted Facebook picture of Billy and Jeremy posing in front of the Musical Monkeys machine, with their hats on sideways.

"Charming," Mia said.

They headed into the Arcade. The sound of bleeps and bells and electronic explosions split the air. The casino-style lights were even more dramatic inside. Groups of teenagers wandered through a forest of massive electronic consoles which cast a ghoulish light across their faces. Tandy was cheerful about the whole thing. After all, the air was thick with the scent of hot dogs and popcorn.

Sylvie walked up to the ticket booth where a young man with sleepy eyes was selling tickets.

"I'll have a pizza package," Sylvie said and handed him some cash.

The boy nodded and pushed a roll of tickets and a pile of tokens through the window.

"Really? You're hungry right now?" Johnny said.

"I am always hungry," Sylvie said." Let's go."

They made their way down the carpeted aisles, searching the faces of the players, mostly boys, who were staring into their electronic tunnels and shooting at things. Up ahead were two young men wearing jeans and navy blue wind breakers with a giant "S" and the words "Big Blue" in white cursive displayed across their backs. Underneath the logo were the words "Giddy Up!"

"Billy Whitehead?" Sylvie said with one hand on her hip.

The two boys turned around and faced Sylvie.

"Who wants to know?" Billy Whitehead said.

"I heard you were good at playing games," Sylvie said.

Billy glanced down at Sylvie's pretty face and pixie-like figure.

"I'll play any game you want, babe," Billy said and nudged his buddy, Jeremy Whiner, who giggled manically. Then they both noticed Johnny Astor and Mia Bold with surprise.

"Are you the guys from *Bell, Book, and Candle*?" Jeremy said.

"That spook show?" Billy said with befuddled look on his face.

"That's right," Sylvie said. "They're the stars. I'm behind the scenes. Look, boys, we're doing a show about the haunted arcade. Management said you guys hang out here all the time and you know your way around the place. Is that true?"

Billy looked at Jeremy and puffed up his chest.

"Sure," Billy said. "What do you want to know?"

"I've heard there's a haunted game here," Sylvie said.

"A haunted game?" Billy said and laughed. "What game is that?"

"Medieval Madness," Sylvie said.

"You mean the old pinball game?" Jeremy said.

"That's the one," Sylvie said. "You catch on quick."

"Nobody plays pinball anymore," Billy said. "We play Daytona, T2, House of the Dead, and Afterburner, you know, modern games."

“Do you want to see the haunted machine or not?” Sylvie said and headed for the line of pinball machines.

She walked over to a pinball machine lit up with deep purples and reds. On the back-glass was a medieval king with a crown, holding up a sword that turned into lightning. He was standing in front of a castle in flames with dragons, ogres, and trolls all around. On the playfield was a castle and sweeping silver bridges with graphic representations of Arthurian characters.

“This is the haunted machine?” Billy said.

“That’s what we’re here to find out,” Sylvie said. “Now if you’ll start playing, Mia here will take some electromagnetic readings.” She dug in her pocket and placed two tokens in the machine. The playfield started to tremble and shake with light. Trumpets blared and a cackling voice boomed out.

Mia followed Sylvie’s lead and took out her EMF reader and scanned the machine. Billy started to play the game, making the flippers propel the silver ball toward the castle. The machine blinked and shook. He was clearly not used to pinball and was clumsy and awkward.

“Oh dear,” Mia said in a concerned voice. “I’m getting some spikes.”

“Let me see what you got,” Johnny said, playing along. He looked over Mia’s shoulder, eyebrows knit together

“Look,” Mia said.

“That looks terrible,” Johnny said. “What does *that* mean?”

“What?” Jeremy said, concerned.

“There’s a strong electromagnetic field in this area. I think we have possible ectoplasm.”

“Ecto-what? Is it dangerous?” Billy said, flicking the flippers, distracted by Johnny and Mia.

“It means a ghost, Billy,” Sylvie said.

Both Billy and Jeremy stared at her in horror as the silver ball fell back into the trough. And the *Game Over* message lit up the back glass.

“A ghost?” Billy said and glanced at Jeremy.

“What kind of haunted stuff goes on with this machine?” Jeremy asked nervously.

“That’s what we’re going to find out,” Sylvie said and put more tokens into the machine. She took the controls, pulled the lever back and propelled the ball through the shooter lane. As the silver ball arced toward her flipper, Sylvie got a crazed look on her face like Clint Eastwood in a spaghetti western. She flipped the ball up lightly so that it balanced on the lever before whacking up through one of the castle gates at the top of the playfield. The whole machine seemed to blaze and rattle as the ball landed in Merlin's pocket and rolled back. When Sylvie whacked the ball again, it shot straight through the gate and into the castle. Then the machine went crazy. The castle shook as mad laughter rose out of the cabinet. Then the castle broke apart. Lights blinked on and off.

"Holy crap!" Billy said, stepping back. "It is haunted!"

"Is it supposed to do that?" Jeremy said, looking worried.

"Billy Whitehead and Jeremy Whiner?" Detective Landry said, holding up his badge. "I need to speak to you."

Mia was surprised to see him approach the teens so aggressively. She thought he'd planned to hang back. But Landry was crafty. Who knew what he was thinking.

The boys looked at Landry, then each other. It was clear he'd rattled then and for a moment it seemed like they were deciding whether they should run.

"I wouldn't do that if I were you," Johnny said and stepped in front of their escape route. Mia had never thought of Johnny as intimidating, but he was tall and in good shape.

Billy shrugged and they followed Landry outside with Mia, Johnny, Sylvie, and Tandy trailing behind.

Once they were in the parking lot, Billy and Jeremy faced Landry. They had their arms crossed as they stared at the ground.

"It seems you two broke into the Elmswood House," Landry said.

The moment he uttered the words, the color drained from Billy's face.

"That junky old teardown?" Billy said, clearly nervous. "Who says we broke in?"

"Your jacket does," Landry said and pointed to the ripped sleeve of his Big Blue jacket. "You left a piece of it at Elmswood."

That answered Mia's question. Landry saw the tear and pretense became unnecessary. Why hadn't she noticed it?

Billy unconsciously rubbed the torn spot on his sleeve. He looked as if he was about to be sick.

"We had nothing to do with that lady dying!" Jeremy Whiner said.

"Shut up, Whiner!" Billy said.

Landry seemed to coil within himself like a deadly snake about to pounce.

"So, you know about Cindy Moore?" he said.

"Everyone in Swampscott knows about it," said Billy.

Landry leaned in closer with a menacing look on his face.

"Did you kill her?"

"Kill her? Are you nuts?" Billy's eyes darted from Landry to his buddy.

"Then what happened?" Landry said.

Billy shuffled his feet uncomfortably. Then his shoulders slumped.

"We were just going there on a dare," Billy said, looking at his feet. "We were going to break into the place. That lady chased us off a couple of times. So anyway, we were trying again when her car pulled up. She got out and started to look around, so we ran. She was alive when we left, I swear."

Mia looked at the two boys. They were nervous and confused. Billy was watching Landry as beads of sweat appeared on his forehead. Jeremy had his hands thrust deep in his pockets and couldn't meet Landry's eyes. They seemed frightened, reckless, and stupid, but not murderers.

"Did you see anyone else with Cindy Moore that night?" Landry said.

"No, she was alone, but she looked like she was meeting someone. You know, she was dressed up, checking her phone," Billy said.

"So you left. Then what happened?" Landry said.

Billy looked at Jeremy.

"We went to the beach and smoked a doobie," Jeremy said.

"So you have no alibi," Landry said.

"I guess not," said Billy.

"All right, I want you to tell Detective Waite everything you just told me," Landry said and took out his phone.

"Charlie? Landry here. There's a pair of kids you need to talk to at the Salem Willows Arcade—Billy Whitehead and Jeremy Whiner. So you do know them? Well, they were at the Elmswood House the night of Cindy's murder. That's right. Sure, I'll wait." He turned to Mia. " It'll take him fifteen minutes to get here. I'll call you once I know anything."

"Thanks, Detective," Mia said. What felt like a terrible weight lifted off her shoulders. At the very least, Detective Waite would find out more, maybe enough to take the heat off her.

***

As Mia drove back to Essex Street, she was relieved. The case felt like it was cracking. Maybe now, Detective Charlie Waite could focus on a pair of real suspects instead of her.

Sylvie was in the back seat playing with Tandy. Johnny looked over at Mia and smiled.

"Maybe this thing is over," he said.

"I hope so, but—" Mia said.

"But what?" Johnny said.

"It's kind of hard to imagine that either of those two dweebs killed Cindy Moore. "

"So you still think Mr. Fat Cat is somehow involved?"

"I think Cindy was dressed up to meet someone that night," Mia said. "Until we figure out who that was we can't be sure."

At that moment, Johnny's phone buzzed.

"This is Johnny Astor," he said and held his hand over the receiver and silently mouthing *Ollie Cooper.* "Yes, I'm listening. Isn't there any way to extend that deadline? Bummer. Okay, I'll let Mia and Sylvie know."

"What?" Sylvie said as Johnny hung up.

"Graham's been trying to talk the cable executives down. They won't budge about the deadline. If we don't turn in this episode next week, our deal is over. Right now, it could go either way. Do you have an agent, Mia?"

"What do you mean? A theatrical agent?"

"Exactly, because if the show gets picked up, you're going to need someone to represent you."

What an interesting thought, Mia said to herself.

In fact, it gave her an idea.

CHAPTER TWENTY EIGHT

Mia sat at the kitchen table, watching her phone nervously, waiting for a message from Detective Landry. Brynn had spent the night again. She was still annoyed at Jeffrey and it showed as she bustled and banged around the kitchen preparing one of Mia's favorite breakfasts, banana pancakes. Mia couldn't help being distracted as Brynn mashed overly ripe bananas and added a hint of cinnamon before pouring the batter into a sizzling pan.

A delicious smell filled the apartment as the pancakes cooked and Mia felt her stomach growl. Finally, Brynn flipped the steaming pancakes onto two plates and added a pad of melted butter and a drizzle of maple syrup to each. Then she slid the plates and two forks onto the table and took the chair opposite Mia.

"Why do you keep staring at that phone, Mimi?"

"Sorry," Mia said and took a bite. The fluffy pancakes were dense, rich, and sweet. "You know, work stuff."

Brynn picked up Rose and stroked her while taking a bite herself. Tandy lay under the table as they sipped coffee and savored their meal. Mia kept checking her phone every minute or so, trying to maintain a relaxed appearance so Brynn wouldn't figure out she was in trouble. But she was anxious about the case and the important evidence they'd found concerning Cindy Moore's murder. The fact that someone had come through the basement and left muddy footprints had led to two potential suspects being in custody. Billy Whitehead and Jeremy Whiner were not hardened criminals, but they were troublemakers. It was possible they killed Cindy by accident, and tried to cover it up.

I may have just solved the mystery, Mia thought. In fact, Detective Charlie Waite of the Swampscott PD was probably crossing her off his list of possible suspects right about now. Why hadn't Landry texted her yet?

"What is going on with you, Mimi?" Brynn said between forkfuls. "You're a million miles away!"

"I told you. Just work stuff," Mia said.

"By 'stuff' do you mean your co-host, Johnny?"

Mia looked at her sister as if she had gone mad.

"Johnny? Good grief, I already told you, nothing is going on between us,"

"Are you sure?" Brynn said, stroking Rose's silky white fur.

"Of course I'm sure!" Mia said. What she neglected to tell Brynn was that she wasn't sure how she felt about Johnny. She had never been so mixed up over a man in her life.

Brynn looked at her with calm eyes. Nothing was going to convince her that Johnny and Mia weren't brewing up some kind of chemistry.

"It's been so good seeing you, Mimi," she said, deciding to let Mia off the hook.

"I'll miss you too," Mia said and meant it. Having Brynn stay with her had been wonderful. "So, you're leaving in the late afternoon?"

"Looks like it," Brynn said.

"What are you going to do? About Jeffrey?"

"I don't know yet," she said thoughtfully. "I guess I better start packing." Brynn took one last bite of the fluffy, crispy concoction and chased it with a final gulp of coffee, smiled, and added, "I cooked. You clean." Then she picked up Rose and put her on the couch next to her suitcase. She started to carefully fold all of her coordinated pieces of clothing while the cat watched intently.

Mia stared at her messages intently. Then she checked her email. There was nothing from Landry. *What was going on with him? Charlie Waite must know everything by now.*

Mia was clearing the dishes when her phone rang with the *Dragnet* theme. Finally, Detective Landry. Awkward timing, but due to the fact he knew what was going on in Swampscott, she had to take the call.

"Hello, Clayton," Mia said in a low voice, trying to disguise from Brynn the fact she was talking to a police officer.

"Let me guess. You've got company?" Landry said, startled by her unusual familiarity.

"Exactly," Mia said, keeping an eye on Brynn as she carefully placed clothing into her roller-bag. Rose stuck close by, batting at the pile waiting to be folded with her tiny paws.

"Look, I'm calling to warn you. Billy Whitehead and Jeremy Whiner were just released from custody. Detective Waite interrogated them halfway through the night. In the end he had to let them go because once they canvassed the neighborhood, they discovered a woman saw them leaving the crime scene well before the time of death.

Then we checked that against some sodas they bought and they're in the clear."

"What about the shoe prints?" Mia whispered. "What did Detective Waite think about them? Was he able to determine anything from them?"

There was an uncomfortable silence.

"Detective Waite found the evidence inconclusive, which brings us to why I'm calling you," Landry said. Mia realized he sounded nervous.

"And why is that?" Mia said with a growing sense of dread building.

"Detective Waite is preparing a warrant for your arrest. I tried to stop him, but he wouldn't listen," Landry said in a reluctant voice. The words landed with a thud and Mia felt her head getting fuzzy.

Detective Waite was going to arrest her?

"What? Is he insane?" Mia barely choked the words out.

Brynn noticed Mia's distress. She put the sweater down that she was folding and walked back to the kitchen. She leaned against the door frame with her arms crossed in a mother hen stance.

"What in the heck is going on Mimi?" Brynn whispered.

Mia looked up at her perfect sister with her carefully chosen outfit, matching jewelry, and shiny hair. She really wished she could spare her, but there was no way to keep the situation from Brynn any longer. She just hoped the fact that she was caught up in another murder investigation wouldn't freak Brynn out too badly. Mia covered the phone and shook her head.

"I'm in trouble, Brynn," Mia whispered.

On the phone Landry's voice was heavy.

"Listen, Mia, you've got about twenty-four hours before the court approves that warrant," he said. "I'll do everything I can to stop this from happening, but I had to warn you."

"Twenty-four hours?" Mia said nervously. That wasn't much time.

"I'm afraid so," Landry said. "Unless new information turns up soon, I can't stop it."

"Thanks for the heads-up," Mia said and hung up.

"What is going on, Mimi?" Brynn said, her expression pensive and deeply concerned.

"I'm going to be arrested," Mia said.

"Arrested? What for?" Brynn's voice had gone up an octave and was verging on panic.

"Murder," Mia said, in a cold, resigned voice.

"Are you serious?" Brynn said in shock.

"I wish I could say this was a joke, but I can't," Mia said. "It's a long story but I found a body at a creepy old mansion called the Elmswood House in Swampscott. I have no alibi for the night of the murder and now Detective Charlie Waite is going to arrest me."

"You mean that real estate lady in the news?" Brynn said, horrified.

"Yes," Mia said. "I found her." Mia flashed on the horrible scene in her mind, Cindy's bright pink skin, her pristine clothes, the smeared muddy footprints. She forced the thought from her mind. Right now, she needed to reassure her sister. "I was just in the wrong place at the wrong time, Brynn. I didn't do anything wrong. I'm sure it will be OK."

Brynn's eyes narrowed. Even though Mia was trying to play it down, she realized the seriousness of the situation.

"We need to call Jeffy," Brynn said.

"No, no, absolutely not!" Mia said. "I can't let you or Jeffrey get involved in this situation."

"Listen, Mia, I know Jeffy is awful sometimes, but he's really good at his job. I promise you that this Detective Waite is going to be very sorry he picked on you. Do you have the detective's number?"

As much as Mia wanted to handle the whole thing herself, she was scared. Her whole career and future were on the line. She went to her desk, found the detective's card, and handed it to Brynn.

"Listen, Brynn, can you cover for me with the family? I think I have a lead on the murder and the best way for me to prove I didn't do it is to figure out who did," Mia said.

"Okay, do what you have to do. I'll talk to Jeffy," Brynn said. "But be careful. You take too many risks, Mimi. Sometimes I think you got that from your dad."

"I'll be careful," Mia said, brushing off the comment about her dad. Now was not the time for a conversation about Frank Bold. Instead, she hugged Brynn tightly and said, "Thanks, sis."

Brynn locked her suitcase and kissed Rose and Tandy goodbye. Before she headed out the door to join the rest of the Middletons at the hotel she turned to Mia.

"Don't worry, Mimi," Brynn said. "I'll make sure Jeffy handles this guy."

***

Once Brynn left, the apartment was incredibly quiet. Mia tried to choke back the terrible sense of fear rising up in her gut. Rose came over to touch Mia's nose before going about her kitty business.

Mia could swear Tandy looked worried.

"I'm worried too, boy," she said as she finished clearing the table and cleaning up from breakfast.

Johnny's words about getting agent representation nagged at her, but not because of her own career. The word "agent" had sparked a question. Greg Abbott said Fat Cat was a real estate nerd, always showing of his knowledge. Could he be a broker or agent of some type? She took her phone out and looked at the picture she'd taken at the abandoned playground at the Elmswood House.

So Halcyon Commercial Realty had bought a tiny strip of land, too small to build on? Why?

Mia went to her computer and searched Swampscott's property records. She was shocked to find that Halcyon had bought up *all* the strips of land around the Elmswood property.

What did they want with a bunch of inconsequential pieces of land?

Mia surfed over to the Halcyon Commercial Realty site. A pop-up began to play. An aerial drone shot of Swampscott appeared with graphic arrows showing all the properties being handled by Halcyon. There were office buildings and high-end condo projects. Apparently, the company had been acquiring property in Swampscott for years, sometimes converting single-family residential properties into condos and commercial ventures. At the end of the video, a well-dressed man appeared.

"Hi, I'm Dominic Rehm, the CEO of Halcyon, We specialize in exclusive properties for the discerning client. Call us to make your dream come true."

Mia looked at the contact page and found the company offices. She typed the address into her phone. Halcyon was located in in the middle of Swampscott.

There was only one way to test her theory. She needed to go to Halcyon and see what was going on with her own eyes. Mia forwarded the picture she'd taken of the Halcyon Commercial Realty sign with *Sold* written across it to Detective Landry.

Took this picture at Elmswood.
Halcyon's been buying up land around the house
Going to check it out!

"Come on, boy," Mia called to Tandy. From high on her cat run perch, Rose glanced down before returning to cleaning her fur.

Mia and Tandy took the back stairs and climbed into her Toyota. She didn't want to drag Sylvie or Johnny into the situation at this point. Halcyon was a long shot but it was the only clue she had. She thought of the spooky little girl who had led her to the sign. Had she really seen a ghost? Was she the ghost of Lydia Humphrey?

That puzzle would have to go on the back burner for now. Thinking about crazy phenomena she couldn't prove one way or the other would not help. Right now, she needed to keep her head straight and find out more about Halcyon Commercial Realty.

The roads were clear as she headed for Swampscott. The ride took on a strange quality, as she realized that this might be the last free day of her life. To be sent to jail for a crime she hadn't committed was an awful thought. The trees and old wooden houses rushed by and she lowered the window so Tandy could feel the breeze on his floppy ears. Who would take care of Tandy and Rose? She knew that Sylvie would step in and help her but the thought of being taken away from her new life was scary. Her new friends had been there for her before, but she hadn't understood how important they'd become in her life until Mark came to town. She really didn't want to lose them.

Mia turned down the sunny streets of Swampscott until she found Halcyon Commercial Realty. The building was tall and square and made of granite, with slabs of dark gray marble on the front. It was very ultra-modern and looked almost like a mausoleum with its featureless sharp angles. She checked her appearance in the rearview mirror, brushing her hair back away from her face and pinching her cheeks until they were rosy.

"Ready, boy?" she said, taking a deep breath.

Tandy followed her out of the car, and Mia attached his lead. They walked up the long sidewalk to the commercial building. Inside, everything was made of glass, and all the offices were on an open plan.

She walked down the hall until she found a door with Halcyon Commercial Realty embossed on the glass.

The door opened into a stark, minimalist office space with a few green trees in pots. The spacious office was empty except for a slim young woman seated at the reception desk. She was dressed in an asymmetrical, gray sheath dress. Her angular face was enhanced with airbrushed makeup and eyelash extensions. On the counter was a single orchid in a square vase.

"Can I help you?" the young woman said, displaying a thin smile. "Is that your emotional support doggie?"

"Why yes," Mia said, trying to adapt an equally dismissive air of disenchantment. "I'm here to see Dominic Rehm."

"What's your name? Do you have an appointment?" the girl said and started making a kissy face at Tandy.

"Mia Bold," she said. "I represent a production company. We're looking for studio space. I'm only in town for a day."

"All right, let me check with him," the girl said and disappeared into the back of the office, teetering on high heels.

Mia stepped over to the reception area where an assortment of high end magazines were on display. Within a moment, the receptionist returned.

"Mr. Rehm will see you now," the girl said and led Mia and Tandy into the back of the office, which overlooked an open green park. She knocked on the office door and opened it for Mia.

"Mr. Rehm? This is Mia Bold," the girl said.

"Thank you, Tina, you can take your lunch now," Dominic Rehm said and smiled. "Ms. Bold? It's a pleasure to meet you."

Mia stepped into the stark office. There was a large modern painting behind Dominic Rehm on the far wall and a 3D model of a commercial property in development on a table by the large industrial window.

Tandy lowered his head nervously and growled.

"Shhh," Mia said. "Be a good boy." Tandy obeyed his mistress and sat at her feet warily.

Dominik Rehm was tall and slender, with a high-forehead, a receding hairline and a tightly wound, angular body. He had a hungry look on his face, with narrow eyes and a straight nose with a slight bump at the top. He was clean shaven with a stiff, white collar, a slim-fitting suit, and a thin necktie fixed with a gold tie clip.

‘How can I help you?” Rehm said. “You’re with a production company? Are you looking to purchase some commercial property?”

“Why yes,” Mia said. “We’re thinking about it.”

“Well, I’d be more than happy to attend to your needs.”

“How does that work?” Mia said.

“We regularly invest in land in this area. We both convert and build commercial properties. To the highest standards I might add.”

Mia walked over to the 3D model.

“What’s this?” she said.

“A future project,” Rehm said. “We’re building some condos over by the sea front.”

A chill made its way down Mia’s spine. Dominic Rehm was flat out lying and she knew it. The makers of the 3D map had done their job accurately and in incredible detail. Mia had studied Swampscott on Google Maps enough times to recognize certain landmarks. This 3D map was not “by the sea front.” This condo project was smack dab in the middle of Elmswood Road where Connie Carol’s decrepit house now stood. So that’s why Halcyon had bought up all that property!

Dominic Rehm must be Fat Cat, Mia realized. He must have wanted to buy the Elmswood House to tear down and build the condos. Halcyon had already bought the strips of land surrounding the house. But Connie Carol wanted to sell to someone who appreciated the history of the house, not a developer who would just tear it down. A nervous flutter descended to Mia’s stomach.

Did Dominic Rehm kill Cindy Moore?

A terrible thought occurred to Mia. If Rehm was a killer and wanted that house, what was there to stop him from killing Connie Carol? Cindy told her that the older woman was all alone in the world. That meant if she died her property would be auctioned by the city. Under those conditions it would be simple for anyone, including Dominic Rehm, to sweep in and buy Elmswood House.

“We have a number of properties that might suit your needs. Do you need stage space also?” Dominic said.

“Yes, definitely. Do you have any properties in mind?” Mia said with her back toward Rehm. Carefully, she inched her phone out and texted Landry.

Dominic Rehm
Help now!

“I do have one that could be perfect,” Dominic Rehm said.

“Great, I’d love to see it,” Mia said and turned around.

Dominic Rehm was wearing black gloves and holding a 9mm Ruger handgun pointed directly at Mia’s heart.

CHAPTER TWENTY NINE

Mia stared at Dominic Rehm and the gun in terror.

"Hand me your phone," Rehm said and plucked Mia's mobile phone out of her hand. His expression had changed; gone was the fake salesman smile. Now his lips were pinched and his eyes were narrowed in rage.

Tandy snarled at the strange man and Rehm pointed the gun toward the dog. "Keep that mutt under control or I'll shoot him."

"Quiet, boy," Mia said.

Dominic Rehm read the last text she had sent Landry.

"Well, that is unfortunate. Looks like we'll need to take this party off site. Let's go." Rehm motioned toward the door. Mia turned and felt him press the barrel of the gun into her back.

"Help!" she screamed out.

But Dominic only laughed, a cold and merciless sound.

"There's no one here," he said. "I sent Tina to lunch. And knowing Tina, she's already at the mall contemplating nail polish."

"You won't get away with this," Mia said, trying not to let the fear creep into her voice.

"Oh, I think I will," Rehm said and took Mia's arm before pressing the gun into her side. "Stay close. I'd hate for this to go off."

There was no one around, just rows of sedans and SUVs. Mia tried to calculate how long it would take for Landry to arrive, but the math she came up with was bleak.

"You're making things worse for yourself," Mia said.

"Am I? That rundown heap must be your car," Rehm said. "Get inside, you're driving." He drove the gun against her rib.

"Okay, okay!" Mia said and walked toward her Toyota.

"Put the dog in the back. We're going for a ride." Rehm said.

Mia opened the door for Tandy. He looked at her as if unsure what to do. His ears were back and his backside tucked under. It broke Mia's heart knowing her loyal companion, sensing her fear, was scared too.

"Come on, boy. Up. It'll be OK," she said.

The trusting dog leapt into the back seat and Mia shut the door behind him. She desperately scanned the parking lot for another human being before sliding into the driver's seat. But everything was quiet. There were no witnesses to Mia's disappearance into this monster's world. Landry would have no way to find her, no idea where she'd gone.

Rehm got into the passenger's seat and turned to face her. He kept the gun pointed at her.

"Listen, Dominic, the cops are looking for me," Mia said. "If you let me go, they're still going to think I did it. Your word against mine."

Dominic Rehm laughed.

"After that message you sent to your buddy Landry?" Dominic said.

"He's not my buddy, he's a cop," Mia said, trying to keep her voice calm.

"Well, by the time he finds you, you'll be dead and I'll look like the victim of baseless accusations," Rehm said. "Now quit stalling and drive."

Mia turned the ignition and pulled onto the road.

"Where?" she said.

"Take Beach Avenue to Elden Street, then take a right," Rehm said.

With a chilling sense of dread, Mia knew exactly where Dominic Rehm was headed, the little yellow house near the high school—Connie Carol's apartment.

"What are you planning?" Mia said, swallowing hard.

"To kill two birds with one stone," Rehm said and cackled to himself.

Tandy growled menacingly in the back seat.

"Quiet, boy," Mia said, concerned Rehm would hurt him.

They drove along the quiet suburban streets of Swampscott. As Mia drove, she wondered if this was her last day on earth. It was an ordinary day with kids out on their bikes and people walking their dogs. Desperately, she searched for someone she could signal, a crossing guard or a cop, but the pedestrians paid no attention to her car, blissfully ignorant of the fact that the woman inside was being kidnapped at gunpoint. Mia took a right on Elden Street and headed toward the high school.

They reached Connie Carol's two-story Victorian house, the one with two front doors. Rehm looked out the window, checking the street the same way Mia was searching for someone she could signal. But the street was empty.

"Take a left up ahead on Burpee Street. See that alley? Pull in there, now!" Dominic said and jammed the gun against Mia's ribs. Once they were parked, he looked in all directions. "Now, leave the dog and get out. If you run, the dog dies."

As Mia carefully stepped out of the car, Tandy dug at the seat, frustrated.

"Shhhh," Mia said to Tandy and closed the door, leaving the window partially rolled down. Tandy looked at her with his big brown eyes. She prayed her pup would be okay as she stepped away from the car.

She looked down the street at the houses. A man was rolling his trash cans down to the street. Mia was about to shout out when she felt Rehm shove the gun into her back.

"Don't try anything. Open the gate," he said.

Mia did what he said. As soon as they stepped inside the backyard, they were out of sight of the street. Now no one could see them. They were cut off from the world. She was alone with Rehm, who was clearly psychopathic.

Mia tried not to panic. The man was a murderer and he would kill her without hesitation. She tried to think of a way to alert Connie, looking around the porch for some way to make a noise.

"I'm warning you," Rehm hissed. "Not a peep out of you." He knocked on the door.

Inside the house, Nutmeg started to bark. A high, yipping sound that was almost comical.

"Who is it?" Connie Carol's voice came from the other side of the door.

"Mrs. Carol? Can I have a word with you? It's Dominic Rehm."

"Who?" Connie said in a gruff, no-nonsense voice.

"Remember me? I'm from Halcyon Commercial Realty. We think we have an investor for your house. A nice European couple who wants to restore the property."

"You do?" Connie said and unbolted the door.

"Don't!" Mia started to call out but Dominic Rehm pistol whipped her across the jaw. The pain exploded in her head, stunning Mia and silencing her warning.

"That's right, Mrs. Carol. They want to consult with you. I think we have a solution that's going to save the property."

The moment the door opened, Dominic Rehm grabbed Mia by the collar and shoved her inside, almost knocking Connie over.

Nutmeg grabbed onto his leg with her tiny jaws and bit down fiercely, ripping his trousers and drawing blood until Rehm shook the little dog off and kicked her aside. Nutmeg yelped and ran back a few steps warily.

"What is this?" Connie Carol said, dressed in her house coat. Then she saw Mia holding her jaw with a drop of blood trailing from the side of her mouth. "What the heck! You all right there, Hollywood?"

Mia nodded, but her eyes issued a warning. Rehm was dangerous, play along.

"Both of you, into the living room," Rehm said. He was restless and starting to act more menacing as he waved the gun in the air, herding them away from the door. Nutmeg charged again and Rehm pointed the gun at the dog. "Pick up that little snapper or I will shut it up for good."

Connie Carol looked at Mia, who gently nodded to her, a warning in her eyes. The older woman swept Nutmeg up in her arms and cradled her. They all stepped into the living room, which had a Brady Bunch feel with wood paneled walls and couches in a plaid fabric with orange and avocado green tones. Connie stood near a square brick fireplace with a mantel covered in knickknacks.

"I know you," Connie said. "You tried to buy my Elmswood House."

"And you should've sold it to me," Dominic said, his body tense and his nervous system wired.

"So you're Fat Cat," Mia said. "The one who's been asking questions about the house online."

"Fat Cat is my handle in the real estate forums," Rehm said. "I've spent months trying to make this deal. Now I'll get the house anyway, only you'll be dead."

"What is he talking about?" Connie said, staring at Rehm and back at Mia, who was nursing her jaw.

"He killed Cindy Moore and he plans on murdering us too," Mia said.

"Goodness gracious, why?" Connie said.

"Because you refused to sell Elmswood to him," Mia said.

"But why kill Cindy Moore?" Connie said. "She was just the agent."

"I had no plans to kill Cindy," Rehm said. "I stopped by the house that night to reason with her, but she said the decision was out of her hands. You refused to sell to me. I pushed her a bit, I even offered her a piece of the project, but she snapped and threatened to report me to the state board and have my license stripped! She was going to destroy my career. I wasn't going to let some uppity residential broker take me down," Rehm said, his eyes so filled with rage that his face was transformed into a nightmare grimace.

"So you made her murder look like a suicide," Mia said. "Using Cindy's own car to gas her."

"That's right. And I would have gotten away with it too. But you stumbled onto the crime scene and made things more complicated. Did you think I didn't know who you were when you walked in my office, Mia Bold? Someone on the force told me about you the day you found the body. Once I realized you were a suspect in Cindy's murder, I knew you were the perfect patsy."

"Patsy?" Connie said, holding nutmeg tightly. "For what?"

"He's going to kill us and blame me for your murder," Mia said.

"Are you crazy?" Connie said. "Why?"

"To get the house, he needs you dead, Connie," Mia said, watching Rehm. "He wants to force an auction."

"An auction?" Connie said. "You mean a county property auction?"

"Let's see," Rehm said. "Mia Bold found out she was about to be arrested, so she headed to your house, Connie. She needed an alibi for the night Cindy Moore was murdered, but you refused to help. Desperate not to go to prison, she shot you, and then she shot herself. Case closed."

There was a long silence as Connie stared at him. Then she suddenly burst out laughing with a deep contagious guffaw that rang all the way through the rafters of the house.

"Oh, you really are a screw-up, aren't you?" Connie said.

Dominic Rehm looked at Connie in shocked surprise. Then the toxic glower returned, contorting his face.

"What the hell is so funny?" Rehm hissed.

"Why you are," Connie said, through fits of laughter. "I've already filed my will. This house is going to the Salem Athenaeum. I sent that information to them this morning."

“No!” Rehm said, his expression crumbling.

“Do you know why I did that?” Connie said. “The ironic thing is, Mr. Rehm, it was after you tried to buy the property. That property won’t be turned into condos, not now or ever. Over my dead body.”

“That can be arranged,” Rehm said and began to shake. His eyes seemed to explode into two black pits of anger. He grabbed a couch pillow to silence the gun and put his finger on the trigger. “I’ll deal with the Athenaeum later!”

Mia stepped in front of Connie to protect her.

“Out of the way!” Dominic said in a low grumbling voice. “Or I’ll wound you first. I hear stomach wounds are an unpleasant way to die.”

Suddenly there was a screech of tires at the front of the house. A door slammed, followed by footsteps and a fist pounding on the door.

“Mia? Are you in there? Answer the door!” Detective Landry’s voice was loud and clear.

Dominic Rehm looked at the front door and panicked for a moment.

That was all it took.

Connie Carol reached down and grabbed the fireplace shovel and swung it hard, hitting Rehm on the back of the head.

Rehm dropped to the ground with a thud.

The 9mm Ruger spun across the floor and landed at the base of the fireplace.

Mia looked at the older lady, amazed. “Good shot, Connie!”

“I used to have the best batting average on the women’s softball team,” Connie said and grinned. Rehm curled into a ball, groaning and holding the back of his head.

Mia raced to the front door and opened it. Detective Landry saw she was all right and smiled in relief.

“Thank goodness,” Landry said. “It took me a while to piece it together.”

“I found the killer,” Mia said. “Meet Dominic Rehm.”

“So, he was going to kill Connie to get the house?” Landry said, stepping over to examine the man who was groaning on the floor.

Mia nodded, rubbing her sore jaw.

A police SUV pulled up behind Landry with its lights spinning but no sirens. Detective Charlie Waite climbed out of the front seat and walked slowly up the stairs. He stepped inside and scanned the scene.

“Well, well, well,” Waite said. “What have we got here. Dominic Rehm of Halcyon Commercial Realty, huh?”

"This man just confessed to killing Cindy Moore," Connie said. "He was about to kill me too when this young lady stood in front of me, ready to take a bullet. Bravest thing I ever saw."

Waite nodded his head and spoke into his radio.

"I need some EMTs at the intersection of Elden Street and Burpee Avenue. A man's been hit on the head. He's breathing fine. Looks like a goose egg to me but you can't be too careful." The detective walked over to the Ruger and carefully bagged the gun.

Dominic tried to sit up with a groan. "What happened?" he said, holding his head.

"Better stay down," Detective Waite said. "There's a pair of dangerous women here. Which one of you hit him?"

"I did," Connie said. "What're you going to do, arrest me?"

"Oh Lord no, Connie, I most certainly am not," Waite said. "Ms. Bold, can I speak to you outside for a moment?"

As they stepped onto the porch the ambulance crew arrived and hurried into the house to deal with Dominic Rehm. Landry crossed his arms, watching the scene as Detective Waite steered Mia to a quiet place on the front lawn.

"First off, I owe you an apology, Ms. Bold," Detective Waite said. "It's very clear you had nothing to do with Cindy Moore's death."

"Thank you, Detective," Mia said.

"So now that we're on the same page, I wonder if you could do me a favor?" The detective looked down at his feet rather sheepishly.

"Of course, Detective," Mia said.

"That brother-in-law of yours, Jeffrey Costa? Could you call him off? I'm in serious hot water down at city hall. He's called every official in town including the mayor. He's threatening a multimillion-dollar lawsuit. If he keeps this up, I might be out of a job by the end of the day. And now with you being innocent, it looks pretty bad for me."

"Consider it done," Mia said and smiled, but her jaw stung. "Ouch. Now, can I get a favor from you and Connie so I can save my job?"

"Sure, what?" Waite said.

"We'd like to interview you about Elmswood House. That is, if Connie gives us permission to film."

"It's the least I can do. What do you say, Connie?"

Mia and Detective Waite looked to Connie for an answer.

"No sweat off my back," Connie said. "Now where's that dog of yours? Nutmeg needs a playdate."

CHAPTER THIRTY

The noisy herd of Middletons clomped down the stairs of the Salem Inn and into the quaint lobby. Daniel Middleton was busy checking his pocket watch every five minutes for the limousine that was due to take them to the airport. Mia was still frustrated with her family, but she loved them and appreciated the effort they made to visit. She wouldn't miss seeing them off.

Daniel looked Mia up and down and nodded his reluctant approval.

"Well, this town certainly has some history," Daniel said finally. "Even if the showfolk have turned the place into a three-ring circus."

"I'm glad you enjoyed yourself, Daniel," Mia said. She was used to her stepfather's faint praise and could see right through it. This actually meant he liked the town very much.

Reynolds arrived and pushed his way through the front door, having come from his friend's house. He walked across the carpet, wheeling his suitcase behind him, and stood beside Daniel.

"Hey, Mia, good to see you," he said before turning to Daniel. "I've made shipping arrangements for all of our purchases."

"Good man," Daniel said, checking his itinerary.

"So you did find a few treasures?" Mia said sweetly.

"Perhaps. We'll know for certain when we see how they sell," Daniel said and turned his full attention to Mia. "I'm not sure about that actor boyfriend of yours, but at least he was polite. I'm impressed you landed on your feet."

Mia blushed. From Daniel that was high praise indeed.

Madison walked up to Mia, dressed nicely in her tasteful travel suit with her hair pinned back into an elegant twist.

"Well, dear, I can't say that I approve of this gypsy lifestyle you're leading," Madison said. "But your new friends seem awfully nice, so I'll try not to worry about you so much."

"Thanks, Mom. Will you also try not to interfere so much?" Mia said.

"I don't know what you're talking about," Madison said. She took a compact out of her bag and started powdering her nose.

"I'm talking about Mark," Mia said. "I know you plotted to bring him here, Mom. That was a real pain."

"I just wanted to make sure you were happy, that's all, dear," Madison said and tucked the compact away. She reached out and turned Mia's chin to have a look at the bruise along her jaw.

"How did you get that again, sweetheart?" Madison said, changing the subject deftly.

"It happened at the gym," Mia lied.

Brynn swept up beside them.

"Come on, Mom. Kickboxing class, remember?" Brynn said and winked.

"Are you sure you want to stay in Salem?" Madison said, her eyes tearing up a little.

"Yes, Mom, I am absolutely sure," Mia said and hugged her.

"Well, at least you don't look as bad as Jeffrey," Madison said. "I don't know what he's been up to without you, Brynn. Maybe you should make an appointment with a neurologist."

"I'll keep an eye on him, Mom," Brynn said and rolled her eyes.

Madison dabbed the tears away and joined Daniel, who was deep in conversation with Reynolds about the architecture of the building.

As if mentioning his name had conjured him, Jeffrey came down the steps with his suitcase bouncing behind. The hotel staff cringed when they saw him. Along with the lump on his forehead and the black eye, a new bruise had appeared, a bright red claw mark on his hand.

"How'd you get that? Mia said.

"Dunno, I might have gotten some kind of rash," Jeffrey said loudly and glared at the desk staff, who looked down at their work, trying to ignore him.

"Listen, Jeffrey," Mia said in a low voice. "I wanted to thank you for what you did for me. You helped get me out of a very difficult situation."

Jeffrey nodded and puffed up his chest.

"Let some backwater cop infringe on my sister-in-law's rights? Not going to happen. Ever!" Jeffrey said. "Next time, call me and I'll fly out, okay?"

"I will," Mia said and smiled. Maybe Jeffrey wasn't so bad after all. She'd never seen this side of him; the way he'd fiercely protected her was surprising and impressive. So, she had finally seen Jeffrey's valiant side. Her sister had always alluded to his skillful arguments. Mia noticed the pride in Brynn's expression. They were back together again, all right. All it took was Mia almost going to jail!

"Come on, Jeffy, my big, strong warrior," Brynn said and hugged him.

"Ow, babe, I think my ribs are bruised. I fell out of bed last night."

The limousine pulled up in front, and the herd of Middletons headed out to the street. Mark stepped out of the back of the limo and walked up to Mia while the driver packed each piece of luggage into the trunk.

"Hey, Mia," Mark said, with his hands stuck deep in his pockets.

"Hey, Mark," Mia said. "Have a safe trip."

She was about to turn away when Mark reached out and touched her arm.

"Listen, Mia, I know you said that Johnny Astor is your boyfriend, but are you sure that's the way you want to go? I mean, we had a good thing going."

Mia looked at Mark. She'd known him a long time, but a lot of her best memories of him were when she didn't know him very well. When they were in college together he had been charming, but once they got out into the world and started working on their dreams, he'd turned into a very different person, someone with whom she didn't have a lot in common.

"I'm sure, Mark. I've moved on and you should too. Nobody is to blame. We grew up and we grew apart. You should find someone who wants the same kind of life you do."

Mark paused, as if he was actually thinking about what she had to say.

"Okay. Thanks, Mia. Good luck," he said and climbed back into the limo.

It felt like real closure for Mia. She hoped it did for Mark too.

The herd of Middletons all piled in the limo and waved to Mia as the long black car pulled into traffic, heading for Boston and their late flight home to Pennsylvania.

At that moment, Mia's phone buzzed. It was a text from Ollie Cooper.

Mia braced herself for the bad news. She'd been so distracted with her family's visit and Cindy Moore's murder, she'd been neglecting the show. She'd also brought some negative publicity to *Bell, Book, and Candle* when rumors swirled that she might be connected to Cindy's murder. Now that she'd sent the Middletons away, finished with Mark, and cleared her name, she was ready to focus on work one hundred percent. But would Ollie and Graham forgive her? She feared there was strong possibility she might lose her job and the life she'd built for herself in Salem. But instead of the axe, Mia was amazed to see a simple text.

Bell, Book, and Candle
Episode 3: Elmswood House
Night shoot tomorrow
Call time: 6pm

EPILOGUE

Johnny and Mia stood in the abandoned playground behind the house on Elmswood. Mia held her breath, trying to be absolutely quiet. Even though it was dark and she was in the exact place where she had possibly seen a ghost, the creepy feeling that had plagued her for days seemed to be gone.

What had changed? Mia wondered. She wasn't sure, but something was different. Whatever had haunted her dreams seemed to be a warning. Now that the danger had passed, the house felt less threatening, although the mystery remained.

A breeze rustled through the leaves and the swings creaked back and forth. Jake kept the camera focused on the two stars of *Bell, Book, and Candle* while Will held up the boom mic.

"Lydia?" Johnny said. "Can you tell us why you're here?"

The ghost box Johnny carried crackled to life and an eerie voice emerged.

"*Lost,*" said a soft, sweet voice.

Johnny looked at Mia, who nodded for him to continue.

"Why are you haunting the Elmswood House?" Johnny said.

"*Home*," said the voice.

"Did you hear that?" Johnny said, turning to Mia.

"I did. It sounded like the word *home,*" Mia said. "And I have to admit I can't explain it." Mia was not just saying that for the theatrics, she had come to a crossroads in her mind. The path she had always walked was that of a skeptic. But over her last three investigations something had changed. She was no longer the skeptic she had once been. Was she "sensitive" like Johnny thought? She wasn't sure, but she knew one thing. She was more passionate than ever about understanding what ghosts were, where they came from, and why they appeared to people. But science was still her chosen tool.

The ghost box died back down to a low static and silence enveloped them.

"Cut," Graham yelled out. "That's a wrap!"

A murmur of relief rippled through the crew as Jake and Will lowered their equipment. Tandy understood the word *cut* and immediately ran up to Mia, who gave him a hug.

"You're such a good boy," she said and ruffled his ears.

"Great work," Ollie said. "I think that was your best investigation yet."

The last few hours had been grueling as Jake and Will filmed and recorded Johnny and Mia's journey through the creepy house. The EMF readings had spiked in the same places as the walk-through. They had recorded EVP for Sylvie to analyze. And by the time they reached the abandoned playground, Lydia had spoken through the ghost box. Things couldn't have gone better. But it had been a long night.

"Okay, tomorrow we have a two p.m. crew call at the office to film Detective Waite's interview and the postmortem section of the show. Looks like we'll be ready in time for the cable network," Graham said, excited. "See you at the Black Cat Inn!"

"That was brilliant stuff about Lydia," Johnny said. "The way you brought in her history, how the original house was moved. Amazing stuff."

"Thank you," Mia said, excited. She was relieved to put the Elmswood House behind her. But the most remarkable thing was the horrible feeling that had gripped her every time she walked into the house—was gone.

She breathed a sigh of relief as they stepped out of the wooded area. Across the backyard, standing by Sylvie's editing table, was Detective Charlie Waite with Connie Carol and special guest of the show Howard Adler, who beelined toward Johnny Astor to get an autograph.

As Sylvie packed up her equipment, Tandy ran over to greet Connie's little poodle, Nutmeg. The two dogs pranced on the lawn under the moon.

"Well, I gotta say, that's an interesting job you got," Connie said. "We could see and hear everything on Sylvie's computer here."

"Thanks again for letting us film," Mia said.

"Take a last look at her in this condition," Connie said, nodding toward the house. "I got a call from the Salem Atheneum. They funded my project. Starting tomorrow, a construction crew is coming. I'm overseeing the restoration of the house."

"Congratulations," Mia said and smiled.

"Lydia will be pleased," Connie said. "Oh yeah, I've got a priest coming to help the other ghosts. He's going to try and bring them to the light. Fingers crossed!"

"Well, that's all above my pay grade," Detective Waite said. "But you kept your word, Mia. You helped put a dangerous man behind bars."

"My pleasure, Detective," Mia said and smiled. She liked Charlie Waite, even if he had given her a hard time.

"Now I'll keep mine. I'll see you for that interview tomorrow," he said.

"Come on, Detective Waite," Connie said, motioning to him. "Time for you to take me and Nutmeg home. Stop by anytime for a playdate, Mia."

"I will, Connie," Mia said and whistled for Tandy.

The crew headed over to the Black Cat Inn for a drink.

Mia, Johnny, Sylvie, and Tandy rode together in Mia's car, relieved to be leaving Swampscott and the Elmswood House in the past.

"You guys have amazing chemistry on screen," Sylvie said. "I don't know what it is, but if I did, I'd bottle it and make a fortune."

Mia glanced at Johnny; there was chemistry there all right. She had no idea what to do about it, but just the mention of it made Mia's heart race.

"Do you think the cable network will like the show?" Mia said.

"If they liked the other episodes, they're going to love this one," Sylvie said.

Mia parked and they all hopped out of the car and walked over to the inn. Tandy trotted behind and Mia thought he seemed happy to put the Elmswood House in the past too.

Inside the inn, the atmosphere was lively. People were laughing. Some of the older regulars were playing darts. The inn's owners, Nelly Blythe and Billy Cranston, were behind the bar and a table had been prepared with a sign in the center that read *Bell, Book, and Candle: Cast and Crew.* Graham, Ollie, Jake, and Will were already parked at the table, as Johnny, Mia, and Sylvie joined them. Tandy ran around greeting each member of the crew as they laughed and told stories about the shoot. Mia felt more relaxed than she had for days. All the weirdness of the last past week dissolved and the future of the show looked bright as the producers talked about possible new locations and Mia's research.

Then the door swung open and Mia was startled to see Hugh Wolfe walk in. He carried a box piled high with homemade truffle potato chips. He walked around to the side of the counter and put the box down on the bar.

The moment he saw Mia, he waved. She smiled and waved back.

Hugh greeted Billy Cranston, who tasted one of his chips and grinned before shaking his hand. Then Hugh filled a basket with chips and brought it over to the *Bell, Book, and Candle* table.

Tandy's ears perked up as he saw Hugh headed his way carrying food.

"Can I buy you a round?" Hugh said.

"We'd be delighted," Ollie said.

Hugh signaled to Billy and grabbed a chair, placing it next to Mia. On the other side of her was Johnny, and Sylvie sat across from her with a "what are you going to do now?" look of humorous concern stamped on her face.

Nelly brought pitchers of ale and glasses and placed them in the center of the table. After they all had poured a drink and were chattering away, Graham lifted his glass.

"To *Bell, Book, and Candle*! The spookiest new show on cable."

To *Bell, Book, and Candle*!" They all cheered and drank the ale, which was sweet and full bodied with a light tang. Mia popped one of Hugh's delicious truffle potato chips in her mouth. The gourmet chip was garlicky and crisp with a musky aroma. The combination of flavors was heavenly.

"Did your family get off okay?" Hugh said, leaning close to Mia.

"Thankfully, yes," Mia said. "They loved Café Noir and *you*, of course."

"That dinner we had was certainly provocative," Johnny said teasingly.

"They liked *you* too," Mia said and sipped her ale nervously.

"Well, Mia, you seem to have your hands full," Sylvie said, aware of her friend's predicament. Mia nodded. The last thing she had expected was to get attention from two men she found attractive, each in their own way.

There are worse problems to have in the world, she thought and sighed.

At that moment, Mia's phone buzzed. The ringtone was unassigned so she switched her phone off, assuming it was a spam call. She would figure it out later; right now she needed the precision of a Cirque du Soleil juggler to get through the evening.

***

Mia, Tandy, and Sylvie walked up the stairs to the apartment together. Mia's head was spinning. Somehow she had managed to deftly maneuver between Hugh and Johnny so that they both seemed happy when she said goodnight.

One day she would have to make a decision about them, but tonight she was just going to enjoy the fact that two attractive men liked her.

"Well, no matter what happens, I'll be here for you," Sylvie said.

Mia threw her arms around her.

"You're the best friend I've ever had," she said and meant it.

"Me too," Sylvie said, smiling. "See you tomorrow, pal."

Sylvie headed down the hall and into her apartment.

Mia opened her door. She had to admit, she was pleasantly exhausted. Tandy darted inside and beelined for Rose. Once they touched noses, Tandy and the kitten snuggled together on the floor to play the "bat my tail" game.

Mia settled down on the couch and put her feet up.

She noticed a light blinking from the side pocket of her bag. It was her phone and the light meant she had a voicemail, which seemed odd. Usually, the spammers didn't leave messages. Mia slipped the phone out of the pocket and looked at the number.

A shock worked its way through her system.

She recognized the number. It was the same number Suzy Sharpe the reporter had traced to her real father, Frank Bold.

She pressed the playback button and listened. Then her breath caught in her throat as a familiar voice came on the line.

"Mia honey, I know you followed my trail to the Hawthorne. As instructed, Samuel Reed, the concierge, let me know you came to look for me. I know he gave you my letter. But after all these years, I thought I owed you a call. What I'm about to say is going to be difficult. Don't look for me, Mia. Please. You won't like what you find."

Mia was stunned. *Don't look for me? You won't like what you find?* How could her own father possibly have said such a thing?

With shaking hands Mia dialed the number and waited. A cold robotic voice came on the line and said, “The number you have called has been disconnected.”

Mia put the phone down and sat there. Hearing Frank’s voice again was a shock.

A tear slid down her cheek and she wiped it away. After years of dreaming her father would call her, the strange message he had left was the last thing she expected to hear.

Was Frank in some kind of trouble? Was there a way to help him?

At that moment, when everything she had hoped for seemed to be out of reach, she made a decision. Instead of feeling lost or hurt, a new sense of determination settled into her mind and strengthened her heart.

“I’m going to find you, Dad,” Mia vowed. “And whatever it is you’re hiding, whatever trouble you’re in, no matter how crazy or strange, I can handle what happens next.”

A New Series!

NOW AVAILABLE!

BEACHFRONT BAKERY: A KILLER CUPCAKE
(A Beachfront Bakery Cozy Mystery—Book 1)

"Very entertaining. I highly recommend this book to the permanent library of any reader that appreciates a very well written mystery, with some twists and an intelligent plot. You will not be disappointed. Excellent way to spend a cold weekend!"
--Books and Movie Reviews, Roberto Mattos (regarding Murder in the Manor)

BEACHFRONT BAKERY: A KILLER CUPCAKE is the debut novel in a charming and hilarious new cozy mystery series by #1 bestselling author Fiona Grace, whose bestselling Murder in the Manor (A Lacey Doyle Cozy Mystery) has nearly 200 five star reviews.

Allison Sweet, 34, a sous chef in Los Angeles, has had it up to here with demeaning customers, her demanding boss, and her failed love life. After a shocking incident, she realizes the time has come to start life fresh and follow her lifelong dream of moving to a small town and opening a bakery of her own.

When Allison spots a charming, vacant storefront on the boardwalk near Venice, she wonders if she could really start life anew. Feeling like it's a sign, and a time to take a chance in life, she goes for it.

Yet Allison did not anticipate the wild ride ahead of her: the boardwalk, filled with fun and outrageous characters, is pulsing with life, from the Italian pizzeria owners on either side of her who vie for her affection, to the fortune tellers and scheming rival bakery owner nearby. Allison yearns to just focus on her delicious new pastry recipes and keep her struggling bakery afloat—but when a murder occurs right near her shop, everything changes.

Implicated, her entire future at stake, Allison has no choice but to investigate to clear her name. As an orphaned dog wanders into her life, a devoted new sidekick with a knack for solving mysteries, she starts her search.

Will they find the killer? And can her struggling bakery survive?

A hilarious cozy mystery series, packed with twists, turns, romance, travel, food and unexpected adventure, the BEACHFRONT BAKERY series will keep you laughing and turning pages late into the night as you fall in love with an endearing new character who will capture your heart.

Books #2 (A MURDEROUS MACAROON), #3 (A PERILOUS CAKE POP), #4 (A DEADLY DANISH), #5 (A TREACHEROUS TART), and book #6 (A CALAMITOUS COOKIE) are also available!

Fiona Grace

Fiona Grace is author of the LACEY DOYLE COZY MYSTERY series, comprising nine books; of the TUSCAN VINEYARD COZY MYSTERY series, comprising seven books; of the DUBIOUS WITCH COZY MYSTERY series, comprising three books; of the BEACHFRONT BAKERY COZY MYSTERY series, comprising six books; and of the CATS AND DOGS COZY MYSTERY series, comprising nine books.

Fiona would love to hear from you, so please visit www.fionagraceauthor.com to receive free ebooks, hear the latest news, and stay in touch.

BOOKS BY FIONA GRACE

LACEY DOYLE COZY MYSTERY

MURDER IN THE MANOR (Book#1)
DEATH AND A DOG (Book #2)
CRIME IN THE CAFE (Book #3)
VEXED ON A VISIT (Book #4)
KILLED WITH A KISS (Book #5)
PERISHED BY A PAINTING (Book #6)
SILENCED BY A SPELL (Book #7)
FRAMED BY A FORGERY (Book #8)
CATASTROPHE IN A CLOISTER (Book #9)

TUSCAN VINEYARD COZY MYSTERY

AGED FOR MURDER (Book #1)
AGED FOR DEATH (Book #2)
AGED FOR MAYHEM (Book #3)
AGED FOR SEDUCTION (Book #4)
AGED FOR VENGEANCE (Book #5)
AGED FOR ACRIMONY (Book #6)
AGED FOR MALICE (Book #7)

DUBIOUS WITCH COZY MYSTERY

SKEPTIC IN SALEM: AN EPISODE OF MURDER (Book #1)
SKEPTIC IN SALEM: AN EPISODE OF CRIME (Book #2)
SKEPTIC IN SALEM: AN EPISODE OF DEATH (Book #3)

BEACHFRONT BAKERY COZY MYSTERY

BEACHFRONT BAKERY: A KILLER CUPCAKE (Book #1)
BEACHFRONT BAKERY: A MURDEROUS MACARON (Book #2)
BEACHFRONT BAKERY: A PERILOUS CAKE POP (Book #3)
BEACHFRONT BAKERY: A DEADLY DANISH (Book #4)
BEACHFRONT BAKERY: A TREACHEROUS TART (Book #5)
BEACHFRONT BAKERY: A CALAMITOUS COOKIE (Book #6)

CATS AND DOGS COZY MYSTERY

A VILLA IN SICILY: OLIVE OIL AND MURDER (Book #1)
A VILLA IN SICILY: FIGS AND A CADAVER (Book #2)

A VILLA IN SICILY: VINO AND DEATH (Book #3)
A VILLA IN SICILY: CAPERS AND CALAMITY (Book #4)
A VILLA IN SICILY: ORANGE GROVES AND VENGEANCE (Book #5)
A VILLA IN SICILY: CANNOLI AND A CASUALTY (Book #6)
A VILLA IN SICILY: SPAGHETTI AND SUSPICION (Book #7)
A VILLA IN SICILY: LEMONS AND A PREDICAMENT (Book #8)
A VILLA IN SICILY: GELATO AND A VENDETTA (Book #9)

www.ingramcontent.com/pod-product-compliance
Lightning Source LLC
Chambersburg PA
CBHW030617310726
48979CB00003B/762

* 9 7 8 1 0 9 4 3 9 0 8 4 0 *